ODIN

Copyright © 2022 Right House

All rights reserved

The characters and events portrayed in this book are fictitious. Any similarity to real persons, living or dead, is coincidental and not intended by the author.

No part of this book may be reproduced, or stored in a retrieval system, or transmitted in any form or by any means, electronic, mechanical, photocopying, recording, or otherwise, without express written permission of the publisher.

ISBN-13: 9781636960661
ISBN-10: 1636960669

Cover design by: Damonza
Printed in the United States of America

USA TODAY BESTSELLING AUTHORS

DAVID ARCHER
BLAKE BANNER

ODIN

AN ALEX MASON THRILLER

R
RIGHT HOUSE

ALEX MASON SERIES

Odin
Ice Cold Spy
Mason's Law
Assets and Liabilities

PROLOGUE

Dr. Edward Ulysses Hampton had read enough Freudian psychoanalysis to know that we never really overcome the damage they do to us when we are small. The baggage we take with us to the grave is the same baggage our parents hand us just after we are born. This was the narrative in his head as he hurried home along Sto Nino, to feed his cat. Death was on his mind. His own, that of many others.

And Felix.

The street was dark, a chaotic jumble of one, two and three-storey buildings, littered with dissonant terraces, classical balustrades and twisted wrought-iron window bars, all overgrown with palms and plantains. He kept his head down and ignored the beige walls which he had grown so deeply to hate; the beige walls that stood beside the pink walls above the blue façade of the corner shop, opposite the steel gates with their savage points. Everything, everything in Manila was dissonant chaos for Edward, and his hatred reached down into unfathomed darkness inside him. He needed to leave. He needed to escape.

His own house, brightly whitewashed, with bright green corrugated tiles, was itself set behind an iron fence tipped with sharp spearheads, and behind this there were various types of palms, plantains and a huge rubber plant, making access impossible unless you were admitted at the gate and then the door, both of which were made of steel.

Edward fitted the key into the lock and allowed himself into his front yard. As he closed the gate and locked it again, he rapidly punched the security code into the keypad beside the gate, but was unsettled to see that the screen did not light up. He would have to call the company as soon as he got in.

He climbed the three white marble steps to his white steel door and repeated the operation, pushing the door open, stepping inside, closing it hurriedly with a solid *click* and then punching in his security code. Though here too he saw the screen was dark. Still, both doors were firmly closed and it was probably merely a matter of reconnection.

The house was alarmed, but he felt safe. He chuckled to himself at the ancient joke which he had never shared with anybody.

He made his way to the kitchen, thinking, as he always did, about his parents and their betrayal. It had been over fifty years, but as he often reminded himself, one never really overcomes the damage one's parents inflict. He laid his laptop, in its briefcase, on the work surface and, taking a mug and a jar of instant coffee, he made a knowing face and nodded as he spooned. He knew he had an unresolved Oedipal complex. In his first five years he had attempted to take possession of his mother with all the power and rage of a young warrior. But his father... He gave a short laugh and reached for the sugar. His father had made no attempt to stop him. Far from it. His father had walked away, tangled in the sheets of various extramarital beds, laughing and calling over his shoulder, "She's all yours, Eddy!"

Betrayal, at every turn betrayal. For she had not been all his, he thought with an acrid twist in his mind as he stirred in the boiling water. He had been all hers, but she had belonged to every grunting Neanderthal who happened to sniff his way into their house.

And he, Edward Ulysses Hampton, had been comprehensively, emotionally crippled for the rest of his life. Loyal to a fault, with a heavy lock on every door.

"There is no time in the mind," he said aloud, and frowned, wondering where Frodo was.

He called his name in the empty, silent house. Only the light in the kitchen was on, but, as he always said, the house was alarmed but he felt perfectly safe. The joke sounded a little hollow as he went into the dark hall where the limpid light from the street filtered through the reinforced glass pane in the steel door.

"Frodo!"

Betrayal, he thought. Cats will not betray you. They are what they are. It takes a human being to betray those who love and depend on them. Betrayal was all he had ever learned from his father, and his mother. A betrayal much greater than treason. To betray your own son, your own flesh and blood.

"That's unforgivable," he said aloud. He would never betray Frodo, and Frodo would never betray him. He would never betray his country, his friends, his colleagues. Poor Marion crossed his mind. Poor Marion.

He opened the door to the bedroom and heard the small, purring meow as Frodo jumped from the bed and came trotting on small, soft feet to head-butt his calf.

"Have you been here all day, you silly cat? You had me worried, Frodo. What were you doing up here?" Frodo laced himself between his ankles and it was in that instant that Edward Ulysses Hampton noticed the dark shape half-silhouetted against the dull luminescence of the bedroom window.

"Who the hell...?"

He saw the blue and yellow flash a millisecond before he heard the soft spit. Molten lead burned into his chest. It didn't hurl him back or knock him to the floor, it just hurt a lot. He heard himself say, "Ow...!" and the shadow spat again, and then a third time.

His legs became very weak and he slowly, unsteadily hunkered down. His belly and his hands were wet. He sat on the carpet and leaned his back against the wall. He hadn't the energy left to feel alarmed, but he did feel unexpectedly very, very sad at all the wonderful things he had never done.

And then he felt nothing.

CHAPTER ONE

The dawn chorus had started. The noisy, urgent chatter of ten thousand minute, feathery creatures fluttering among the foliage of the planes and oaks that made Adams Street "leafy." It rose from a massed chatter to a glorious crescendo as the gray of the pre-dawn horizon was touched by watercolor blue. Then the world seemed to yawn and stretch, and I sat up.

I dragged on my bathing trunks, stumbled down the stairs and fell in my covered pool. I did a few lengths trying not to breathe, then stood under a cold shower for five minutes. Ten minutes with the heavy sack, a hundred press-ups, five hundred sit-ups and another cold shower and I was ready for breakfast.

This was my morning routine. It had been for as long as I was willing to remember—which was not long. In a life which is ruled by chaos it is important to have a solid routine, especially breakfast. Breakfast, my grandmother used to say, sets you up for the day. I have at times been sitting in four inches of mud, with a dozen men a hundred yards away determined to kill me, while I breakfasted on roast lizard. At those times I remember my grandmother and her advice.

Those guys thought I'd run, and they went after

me through the jungle, leaving clear tracks because they were in a hurry. So I was able to come up behind them and surprise them with two grenades and thirty .223 caliber rounds at nine hundred rounds a minute.

In the kitchen Manny Pacquiao was lying on the bread bin, observing me with ill-concealed contempt. If routine is the reason I am still alive, my cat is probably the reason I am still single.

"What the hell! Who cares, right, Manny?" I sliced two hunks of wholegrain rye from the loaf and threw them in the toaster. "Marriage is overrated anyway."

I gave him a slice of ham from the fridge and set about making half a pint of strong black coffee.

"The moment you let a woman into your house you start losing things. You reach for your shampoo. It's not there because she found a better place for it. You look for your M16, she found a better place for it. If Oedipus had paid more attention to his grandmother," I told Manny Pacquiao, waving a butter knife at him, "he'd probably still have his eyes today."

The pot gurgled. I smelt the coffee. My cell rang. I looked at the screen. Six thirty AM. The office. I answered.

"What?"

The voice on the other end was like dark chocolate that smoked and drank too much and didn't give a damn.

"Alex, baby, did I wake you? I feel like I should care."

"What do you want, Lovelock?"

"I'm on my way into the office. The old man's upset and he wants you there too."

"I'm having breakfast."

There was a rich, warm smile in her voice when

she said, "And I really *do* feel like I should care, Alex. I really do."

I scowled at Manny Pacquiao. His eyes were languidly obscene. He didn't care either.

"OK, I'm on my way."

I hung up and sat down to breakfast.

ODIN was housed on the eighteenth floor of the Commonwealth Building at 1300 Wilson Boulevard, in Arlington, Virginia. The fact that the Commonwealth Building did not have eighteen floors did not seem to be an issue for most people who, in any case, had no idea what ODIN was or what the acronym stood for. It stood for the Office of the Democratic Intelligence Network, a cooperative enterprise between the United States, the United Kingdom, Canada, Australia and New Zealand—the so-called Five Eyes.

It had started out as an intelligence sharing network, but with a substantial budget and the scope of its intelligence gathering capability, it had rapidly evolved into an agency able and willing to take on jobs others balked at.

I left my Aston Martin DBS in the underground parking garage on 17th Street, and rode the dedicated elevator to the top floor. I walked through the security scanners in the lobby and then followed the long, featureless corridor to what was generally known at ODIN as the lobby.

Here the walls were beige, the carpet was blue, there were a couple of unremarkable sofas, a palm in a pot and a water cooler. A single, small window offered a view of Freedom Park and the Rosslyn Twin Towers. Beyond them you could just glimpse the Potomac where it turns south, Theodore Roosevelt Island and the DC skyline.

There was also a door in the lobby. It was not much to look at, though under its bland, cream exterior it was in fact a two-inch-thick sheet of steel which could only be opened from within. I punched my code into the keypad beside the door, allowed a green laser to read my eye and placed my palm upon the screen. The door clicked and hissed softly, and I was admitted.

From there I followed a second passage around a dogleg and arrived at a second, similar door. This, once I had entered a second code and had my biometrics read for a second time, gave me access to the so-called Office of the Overseer, or as it was popularly known by the few who had access, Valhalla.

The antechamber to Valhalla was Lovelock's office. It had no windows, it was bulletproof and some said it was bombproof too. Her large oak desk sat beside the large red door which she guarded with her life.

She sat behind that desk now, with cool hooded eyes, a slightly mocking mouth with very full lips, and an aquiline nose that made her look like a black Egyptian goddess. She watched me enter the room and arched an elegant eyebrow at me.

"You're late."

"I've never been early in my life."

"He's not in a good mood."

"When are you going to let me take you out to dinner?"

"The day after I get divorced, which will be about the time you go to your grave." She poised her long, dark finger over the button on her desk which opened the door. "And that, Alex," she said, "is one appointment you probably will arrive at *early*. Odds on."

She winked at me and pressed the button. The big red door clicked softly open.

"At least," I said, leaning across the desk and whispering in her ear, "I won't get to dribble on my grandchildren and have attractive young women change my diapers. You, on the other hand, will suffer both." I crossed to the door and pushed in.

The office was large enough to be a small apartment, and exquisitely furnished. It was carpeted in deep, burgundy Wilton, the walls were paneled in original Tudor oak, the mahogany dresser was seventeenth-century English and the chairs beside the open fireplace were original, 1930s Chesterfields. The view from the window managed somehow to include the Potomac, the Theodore Roosevelt Memorial Bridge and the Lincoln Memorial.

The "he" to whom Lovelock had referred earlier was sitting behind a vast, nineteenth-century oak desk with a green leather blotter, watching me from beneath two eyebrows that could have doubled as an impressive handlebar moustache. He was known only as the Chief (with a capital "C"), or occasionally as Nero, because it was rumored he had once set fire to a restaurant because he was so incensed by the poor service. It was probably not true, but the point of rumors like that is, they *could* be true. And everyone who knew Nero agreed that it could, indeed, be true.

He stood six-foot-six in his stockinged feet and I estimated his weight at about four hundred and twenty pounds. Some of it was muscle. Most of it was very good food.

Right then, every ounce of him looked pissed. He growled:

"Have you ever been to the Philippines?"

"Not intentionally."

"Don't be facetious. Sit down."

I sat in a comfortable armchair opposite him and crossed one leg over the other. I folded my hands in my lap and waited. The Chief waited too, with an arched eyebrow and very little visible patience.

"Are you going to answer me, Mason, or do I have to weigh the evidence to decide whether you were telling the truth or *trying* to be funny?"

"I have never been to the Philippines, sir."

"That is," he said with great precision, turning the pages of a file that lay in front of him, "lamentable." He sighed, scanning pages with his eyes. "You are of course aware, I presume, that China is a problem."

I narrowed my eyes and raised my chin. I wondered, as I often had since being seconded to ODIN, whether the Chief said things like that deliberately. It was hard to know how to answer without being facetious. The Chief raised his eyes from the folder and scowled at me.

"I am aware," I said carefully, "that the Chinese have been aggressively expansionist for a while now, sir. Since shortly after glasnost hit the Soviet Union, and they started to liberalize their economy. More recently they have been buying up most of the Third World's infrastructure under their so-called Belt and Road Scheme. And then of course there is the question of their ambitious space program, the cyberterrorism, spying and interfering in British and American elections..."

I trailed off, satisfied I had sounded well-informed and not facetious. Silence settled on the room. The Chief said, "Have you finished?"

"For the moment, yes, sir."

His eyes returned to the file on his desk. "Most questions, Alex, can be succinctly and satisfactorily answered with a 'yes' or a 'no.' You do not need to impress me with the fact that you read the newspapers. I expect it of you. If I did not think you were adequately intelligent and well informed..." He paused to read for a few seconds, sighed and concluded. "...you would not be here."

He sat back in his large, leather chair and regarded me. "China is a problem for all the reasons you have cited, and for many more of which you are unaware. I have no doubt that there are reasons of which we are *all* unaware. And *that* is another reason why they are a problem."

He reached a plump hand across the desk and pressed a button.

"Lovelock, bring coffee." He glanced at Mason. "You'll have coffee." He looked back at his finger, still on the button. "Also, croissants, hot, unfilled. Be quick."

I said: "If memory serves, Manila is one thousand seven hundred and seventy miles from Beijing, which is roughly the distance from Manhattan to Roswell, New Mexico. Aside from that, sir, I am struggling to find any interesting connection between the Philippines and China."

Nero grunted bigly. "You waste words. Sun Tzu said, 'Therefore, the skillful leader subdues the enemy's troops without any fighting; he captures their cities without laying siege to them; he overthrows their kingdom without lengthy operations in the field.' Attack by stratagem, paragraph six. Paragraph seven: 'With his forces intact he will dispute the mastery of the Empire, and thus, without losing a man, his triumph will be complete. This is the method of attacking by stratagem.' *The Art of War*. You should read it."

"I'll put it on my list, right after *Bridget Jones's Diary*. If I may observe, sir, for a man who doesn't want to waste words, yours are taking your time in getting to the point."

The door opened and the exquisite Lovelock entered with a tray of coffee and a basket of hot croissants. According to the Chief, to add butter to well-made croissants was to gild the lily and was therefore not permitted. The unspoken threat was that if you did spread butter on your croissant, he might come and burn your house down. He shooed Lovelock away with a pudgy hand, she winked at me and left, and he distributed superb black coffee and hot croissants.

"You need to understand how the Chinese think, Alex. They are subtle, they have millennia of highly sophisticated culture behind them. It is a mystery to me that Marco Polo was Italian instead of Chinese." He stuffed a croissant in his mouth and ruminated, watching me sip my coffee. "The thing is, war between the West and China is inevitable."

I arched an eyebrow. "Seriously?"

"I never joke, Alex, so I must be serious. It is simply a matter of time. Thucydides, in his analysis of the Peloponnesian War between Athens and Sparta, observed that said war had been inevitable because an established power will always want to clip the wings of an emerging one. The United States was the natural heir to the British Empire, and inherited that imperial throne in 1947. We have ruled the Western World and most of the Third World since then. Now China is rising in power at an alarming rate, and doing so in a very aggressive manner. So we and our allies are scurrying to attempt to fence her in. But we are not doing a very good job of it."

He fell silent, chewing and thinking, with his cup halfway to his mouth. After a moment I asked:

"Do I understand that you are worried that the Chinese are going to wage war…"

The Chief shook his head impatiently. "Are already waging war, Alex. They are *already* at war with us."

I smiled and nodded, beginning to understand. "Without us knowing it." I recited: "'The skillful leader subdues the enemy's troops without fighting. He captures their cities without laying siege and he overthrows their kingdoms without battles in the field.' So, they are at war with us, but we don't know it, therefore we don't fight back. It took us eight years to respond to the Belt and Road Scheme. OK, I get it, but something must have happened, or you would have had me in here eight years ago instead of now."

The Chief nodded his huge head and said something like "Umph," because his mouth was full. He drained his cup, and as he refilled it he said, "We have been watching them. An ineffectual policy bordering on the imbecilic and the criminally negligent, but the more powerful the Pentagon becomes, the more reluctant it is to use its power unless it sees *actual physical* violence. And our secret services are so busy chasing Islamic terrorists they do not see the tiger that has just strolled into the room." He wagged a fat finger at me. "I have believed for a long time that Beijing funds Islamic terrorists in order to keep our agencies distracted while they mount a full-scale assault."

"And suspecting this assault, you have been watching Beijing."

"Naturally."

"And a good place from which to watch Beijing

without being conspicuous is Manila."

"Naturally."

"You want me to go to Manila to watch Beijing for you?"

"You see, Alex? You start well, but you get carried away with your own cleverness and then you go too far. Do you really think I have not already had someone in Manila watching Beijing for the last ten years? I have long had a cell in Manila with links in Beijing and other parts of China."

"But…?"

"That cell has disappeared."

We stared at each other for ten seconds, which is a very long time to stare at anybody, until finally I said, "When you say 'disappeared,' what precisely do you mean?"

"I mean that my handler in Manila has gone off the radar. He has not called in, he has not triggered emergency protocols, he has not been seen, and his team of four agents have all gone to ground and cannot be found, dammit! What do you *think* I mean?"

"Do we have anybody else in Manila?"

"We have a couple of officials in the police. We don't own them but they cooperate. The CIA have a field office there and they are cooperative, up to a point. But something like this is damaging to our reputation and I do not want to call on them for help unless absolutely essential." As an afterthought he added, "Mossad have a field office there too, but they are not always cooperative."

I was surprised and my eyebrows said so. "Mossad have an office in Manila?"

"I have just told you that the Chinese fund Islamic

terrorists. There is a large Muslim community in Manila. Naturally Mossad are interested in China and the Philippines. The last I know is that my handler had found a source within the embassy whom he was exploiting. He said he had acquired information of interest. The handler was due to brief me, and went off the radar. So that is all I know."

"And what do you want me to do?"

"I want you to go to Manila, find out what happened to my handler—recover his damned laptop! God alone knows what information he has on it! And find out what this information was he was due to transmit to me."

"Is that all?"

The Chief gave me the eyebrow and growled, "If you feel it's too much for you…"

"I'll need the file and all those names you have carefully avoided mentioning."

"Naturally."

"When do I leave?"

"Tomorrow midday, twelve fifteen, to be precise, with Ana United." He gazed at me and there was almost a glimmer of humor in his eye. "That is not a reference to the manner in which you will be flying, but the name of the airline, All Nippon Airlines who have gone into partnership with United."

"I love this game, sir, where I try to guess whether you are being amusing."

"You arrive at eight fifty-five in the morning local time, after a grueling twenty hours and forty minutes. You should take a book. I would suggest something by Jack Kerouac, or Allen Ginsberg. Any of the Beat Generation. They always manage to put me to sleep fairly swiftly."

"Are you still being funny, sir?"

"I don't think I have omitted anything. Lovejoy will give you all the necessary bits. You may go."

CHAPTER TWO

A week earlier and eight thousand five hundred and fifty-five miles away, on Monday, April 26th, Marion James had spoken to her mother on her cell phone. She'd been sitting on the tiny terrace of the Happy Bee Bar, on San Rafael Street, beside the Ice Shield Laundry House, where as well as washing your clothes, you could also buy clean drinking water. On the other side of a brick wall beside the bar there was a derelict factory with bamboo and palms growing rampant out of the walls, and randomly placed rusting metal drums. One of those palms tickled the back of her head as she laughed that laugh that people use to dismiss veiled recrimination.

"Of course I miss you! But I like it here, Mum. I mean, I wouldn't stay here if I didn't like it, would I?"

Stoicism fought with anxiety in her mother's voice, and lost.

"I know, darling, it's just been such a long time. You said you were coming home six months ago! Then you missed Christmas, now Easter. Are you sure everything's all right? Your father and I do miss you so much. And we're *worried!*"

Marion sagged back in her chair and fought the

lump in her throat. "I know, Mum, I miss you too..."

"Well then," her mother's voice took on a rising, plaintive tone, "if it's the money, your father and I can pay for the ticket, and once you're here..."

"No, honest, Mum, it's not the money. Really, it's like I said, it's work."

"But *surely* they can give you a couple of weeks to go home and see your family."

Marion stared down at her pale legs and feet in her blue plastic flip-flops, and ached suddenly for the mundane sanity of suburban England. She bit her lip and wiped the tears from her eyes with the back of her finger.

"You see, it's not like a normal job, Mum. It's the embassy. There are all sorts of issues of security and things."

"But surely you're not involved in that side of things, Ronny. I mean, you're not even Chinese!"

She smiled at the old nickname. "No," she said with a small, wet laugh. "No, of course I'm not, but they have to work to schedules and things like that, and if they say you have to work, well you can't very well say no."

Her mother was quiet and they sat in silence together, though they were six thousand seven hundred miles apart. Finally her mother said, "I'm your mother, sweetheart. Are you sure you're telling me everything?"

Marion screwed up her face and bit hard on her finger. She fought to control her breathing, took a deep, shaking breath and said, "'Course I am, Mum."

"Then why are you crying your eyes out, Ronny? Look, if you're in trouble, if there's any problem, your dad and I are here to help. Why don't you just tell me...?"

"Honest, Mum. There is no problem." She forced

herself to sound cheerful. "It's just, you know what it's like in a new job. You get stuck with all the jobs nobody else wants to do, all the overtime nobody wants. Long term it will be great for my CV, though, Mum. I mean, the Chinese embassy! I could get a great job when I get home, with that kind of experience." Her mother sighed. Marion said quickly, "Look, I'd better go. I've got to get back to work. I'll call you later, or tomorrow."

"Talk to them at work, will you, darling? You must have a supervisor or something. Tell him your family needs to see you."

"I will, Mum, I promise. I love you."

"Love you too, Ronny. Stay safe, darling."

She hung up, and there was suddenly an enormous, all-encompassing silence. Inside the bar two women were screaming like laughing parrots, then a two-stroke motorbike with the silencer removed passed, setting the birds in the trees to flight. Four skinny kids in shorts forgot their blue ball and started hitting and kicking each other, shouting in Tagalog. But none of it encroached on the enormous silence that hung around Marion after her mother's voice fell silent.

She sat then for a few minutes staring at the two plastic grocery bags which sat on the floor beside her chair. If she was careful they would see her to the end of the week, but she was going to have trouble making the rent for May.

She took her cell from her pocket and stared at the screen. It showed nothing new, offered no hope. She went to the address book and found Ed. He had told her never to phone him, but he was leaving her no option, and she watched her finger, as though it were somebody else's, hover over his number, then press call. It rang six times and she was about to hang up when his voice came on the line.

"I thought I had told you never to call me."

"Ed, I can't go on like this. I've just been talking to my mum—"

"Please! Spare me! This is *not* the way we conduct business. Do you realize how risky this is?"

"No, Ed, you have to listen to me."

"Stop using my name! Are you insane?"

"I have hardly any food for the week, and I am not going to make the rent. You *said* you were going to pay me!"

"Marion! Stop immediately!"

Her voice became shrill. "So what am I supposed to do? How am I supposed to eat? Where am I supposed to live?"

"*Shut up!*" She fell silent. "It's your own fault," he went on, "for getting yourself into this situation in the first place."

"I know, Ed, but I *can't* go on the streets here. I'd be dead within the week. My mum is already talking about coming out here to take me home. You *have* to help me."

"All right. We have to get off the line. Look, we'll meet. Tuesday, meet me at eleven thirty at the National Museum, in Gallery One, you know it? Religious art of the seventeenth to the nineteenth century. When you see me, act as though you don't know me. Stop and admire one of the saints. If we are clear I will happen to stop beside you and we will discuss the statue or the painting. Is that understood?"

"Do you think you can help me?"

"Yes, but you must absolutely not phone me again.

You have no idea how dangerous it is."

"All right, I won't, but you mustn't abandon me."

He hung up and she was left with that pervasive, penetrating silence again.

She finished her Coke and was aware that her hands were trembling slightly. She was close to panic, but told herself Ed would come through. He would sort things out. He would not leave her out on a limb. He would see to it she was OK. Apart from anything else, he needed her. He needed her memory.

She rose and walked the three hundred yards up San Rafael and along Santa Ana to San Joaquin, with the knot of anxiety twisting in her gut and making her feel sick. She turned left and walked with short steps toward the children's clinic, and the abundance of trees that partially obscured the crumbling apartment block opposite her apartment. With every step she felt more as though she were entering a prison. Everywhere she looked she saw white-painted iron bars: on windows, on doors, on terraces and balconies. Every house she passed, it seemed to her that the door was made of painted, peeling steel.

The scrape and slap of her rubber flip-flops was suddenly loud in her ears, like a panicking, failing heart. A gang of boys in shorts stopped their game of street football to watch her pass. She was acutely aware of how she stood out because of her very pale skin and her blonde hair. She passed the vegetable-stall-cum-grocery-store-cum-chow-house which occupied the corner of the street under a vast, dirty Coca-Cola parasol. The parasol was supplemented by a filthy awning made of bits of plastic tacked to an improvised wooden frame. Beneath it, in its shadow, the women doing their shopping paused in their screeching conversation to watch her. A man with a beer belly and an Argentina soccer shirt slouched out of the chow house holding a bottle of beer, to watch her fit her key to her iron door and go inside.

She ran up the uncarpeted wooden stairs, unlocked the white door to her apartment, slammed it closed behind her and ran to the kitchen, where she threw her groceries on the small, folding Formica table, dropped onto the Formica chair beside it and burst into convulsive tears. She didn't cover her face. Her hands clenched into small, pink fists in her lap and she stared at the stack of dirty plates in the sink, at the flies that walked over them with insolent impunity, at the accumulated grime on her windowpanes, and she moaned and wailed as she hadn't since she was six years old. But now there was no mummy and daddy to hold her and tell her everything was going to be all right. There was no mummy and daddy now because now she couldn't tell them what was wrong. She could not tell them what was wrong because it was not going to be all right.

She couldn't tell anybody, except Ed.

She rocked gently back and forth, her bottom lip curled in over her teeth and her face sodden with tears, repeating over and over, "*Oh, God, what am I going to do? Oh God help me, what am I going to do?*"

What she did, eventually, was to retreat to her bedroom, curl up under the covers and withdraw into sleep. She slept for almost twelve hours and rose at midnight to put a partially defrosted pizza into the oven. When it was done she took it back to bed, and went back to sleep until seven in the morning. Then she rose, made an effort to shower and make herself look almost respectable, and went to work at the Chinese Embassy.

There her supervisor, a man with a badly cut blue

suit and cruel eyes, shouted at her and told her she looked like a tramp. She could not work at the Chinese Embassy looking like a tramp, so she had better buy herself some new clothes before tomorrow. To which she nodded, kept silent and got on with her work.

On three occasions her supervisor came to the door of her small office and looked in. Each time Marion pretended not to notice him and concentrated on her computer screen. Eventually he went away.

The week ground by. She made a point of cleaning her apartment, laundering and pressing her blue suit and trimming her hair. Steadily the food in her refrigerator became more depleted. The hope that Tuesday might bring some kind of help sustained her, and as the weekend drew nearer her despair began to turn, if not to optimism, at least to cautious courage. Ed would help her out, she told herself, because if he didn't she could cause him a lot of trouble, and he knew that. What she didn't know was whether she would have the courage to confront him and challenge him. On the other hand, what courage alone could not achieve, perhaps despair could.

On Monday she asked her supervisor for Tuesday off. He shouted at her, called her a lazy slut and threatened to sack her, but instead gave her the day off, telling her that she would have to work overtime without pay until the eight hours were made up.

She returned home where she ate boiled white rice and wept, until she fell on the bed and covered herself in her blanket to sink into miserable sleep.

She awoke in a panic at seven AM, with the roaring of small motorbikes outside, the constant shouting of Filipinos all talking at once and the screaming laughter of the women. She sat up, with hot, writhing anxiety in her belly, and ran to the bathroom where she tried to vomit but couldn't because her stomach was empty.

She brushed her teeth, showered and dressed and looked at the clock. It was only eight twenty. Still three hours to go. She had no money to get a pousse-pousse, let alone a taxi, so she would have to walk. She figured it would be at least four miles, a good hour and a half. She might as well start now.

She left her apartment, made her way to Boni Avenue and turned north along the grimy street with its messy tangle of crisscrossed overhead cables, leaning telegraph poles and broken sidewalks. She had grown in the last year to hate the city, and so, as she walked, she saw only what she hated: the buildings which were old, but not venerable or ancient, their unpainted walls made grimy with pollution, uncared for, the graffiti, the jumbled signs placed anywhere and anyhow, the noisy, dirty traffic that respected neither pedestrians nor road signs. All of it filled her with anger, frustration and hatred. And as she walked she prayed to a god in whom she did not believe, that Ed would be able to help her today.

And if he did—she slipped into a walking daydream—if he did she would pay off what she owed and immediately phone her mother and accept her offer of a ticket home. Maybe they could send her a few hundred pounds extra and she could buy some new clothes, get her hair done, maybe spend her last night in a decent hotel, have a proper bath and sleep in a decent bed with crisp, clean sheets.

She smiled as she saw herself coming out of arrivals at Heathrow, with her mother and her father waiting to receive her, waving at her. Maybe Bobby, her brother, would come too, since it had been so long and she had been so far away. They would put her in her old room until she could get a job and find a place of her own. They would fall into their old routine, up early, helping Mum in the kitchen, Sunday dinner...

She told herself she would never speak to them about what had happened, but in her mind's eye she saw herself having breakfast with her mother, and everything spilling out, her mother hugging her, and she sobbing and begging for forgiveness.

At New Panaderos she turned left, and noted absently to herself that the whole of Manila was like one vast industrial estate. She walked south now, toward the Lambing Bridge that spanned the Pasig River. A white Toyota passed in the opposite direction, going too fast, swerving from lane to lane. She scowled at it, cursing Filipino drivers.

She found herself unexpectedly remembering that night by the bay, having drinks in a seedy nightclub on Adriatico Street. She could see in her mind every feature of its interior. She had been bored and wanting to go home, thinking already back then of giving up on her eastern adventure and returning to London.

Her close friends back then had been Matt and Susan. Every detail of what they were wearing was as fresh in her mind as though she were looking at them now. Everything they did that night, every place they had been, was vivid and vibrant. She shook her head as she walked. They had all been drunk, laughing, dancing, and then the young American had approached her.

She hadn't been dancing. He'd asked her why. She could hear his voice clearly in her head. Was she OK? He held out his hand. His name was Don. He didn't like this kind of noisy place either, he'd said. He'd come with friends, but it wasn't his scene. If he'd wanted this kind of stuff he would have stayed in Los Angeles, right? Right.

He had been standing till then, but now he sat.

"Hey," he'd said, with a big, friendly, handsome smile, "do you want to see some real Filipino nightlife?"

She had cocked an eyebrow at him and laughed. "I'm not sure that I do."

He had laughed too. "No, it's not what you think. They get together in these kind of seedy bars, they drink beer and they play Filipino Mahjong. The game is great, you really get into it, they are crazy about it. And hey! At least you can hear yourself think. We can have a couple of beers and a game, and then I will drive you home like a perfect gentleman. Scout's honor."

He had said that. Scout's honor. She remembered every word of it.

He had seemed so likeable and so credible she had agreed.

Without realizing it she had reached General Luna Street. She turned in and walked down, past the Cathedral of Praise toward the museum complex. She was early, as she had expected to be, so she made her way to the small garden opposite the museum that backed onto the golf course, found a bench and sat. Her legs ached from the long walk, but she was barely aware of it.

Her thoughts went back to that night. She had often wondered, if she had said no to Don that night, where would she be now? Back home in London, probably; maybe married, with a mortgage, thinking about having kids.

But all of that, all that hope, potential, possibilities for happiness—all of it—everything—had been wiped from her life, obliterated, because of one game of Mahjong.

CHAPTER THREE

At that very moment, four and a half miles away as the crow flies, when it flies slightly east of southeast, Bao Liu, or as the Chinese would have it, Liu Bao, was seated in a small room on Katipunan Avenue, staring at the screen of a laptop computer. The software was not anything he was familiar with, and that was his first problem, because before he could even start to think about hacking into it, he needed to know what the operating system was, and how it worked.

It seemed, at first, to be based on Apple technology, but as soon as he started probing it, all sorts of defensive systems arose that had nothing to do with Apple. In fact it was like nothing he had ever seen before.

That worried him, not just because it would make his job that much more difficult, but because his supervisor had made it clear to him that this job was about as important as any job could ever be. He had sat in the chair beside his desk and observed him with steady, expressionless eyes.

"You are enjoying your work here, attached to the embassy, Bao? Working also at the new faculty, so young! Not many men as young as you get these opportunities."

"Yes, Mr. Wang. I am very happy here, and very

grateful."

"You understand that we are giving you challenging work, to help you improve yourself."

"Yes, Mr. Wang, I am very grateful."

Mr. Wang had nodded, then added, "This work is not just important for you. It is important for *Zhōng Guó*," a wraith of a smile touched his thin lips and barely creased the corners of his eyes, "*Tián Cháo*, our Heavenly Kingdom, Bao. Do you understand that?"

Boa nodded. "Yes, Mr. Wang."

The smile faded from Mr. Wang's face. "It could have far-reaching consequences for your family, your mother, your father, and for your girlfriend. You are planning to marry in December, am I right?"

Wang gave the subtle, implied threat a few seconds to register, then offered Bao a smile that drained the blood from his face.

"Do this job well, Bao, and you can offer your girlfriend and your family a happy, prosperous future. You are at a fork in the road of your life, Bao. Solve this problem, and many, many doors will open for you. Fail..." Mr. Wang had shaken his head. Failure, he seemed to suggest, was something he did not want to talk about.

But it seemed to Bao that all doors were not open, but closed to him. Because without knowing the operating system, how could he possibly hope to get inside?

His head throbbed and his eyes ached. Yet, there was perhaps some hope. If this was not truly a different operating system, but simply different software grafted on to an Apple system, like a parasite program running within the operating system and modifying it without replacing it, then perhaps...

He sat forward, with hot fear and anxiety fueling his brain, and began to type.

***

Just five miles south and east, Jay Hoffstadder sat in his modern, minimalist office overlooking the parking lot of the Law Department. Beyond it he could see the roofs of Romulo Hall through the dense foliage of the trees. He stared and he wondered about plans. He wondered why Ed had not contacted him as he was supposed to. How long should he wait? It was totally out of character, and Ed was always in character. That fact added considerably to his unease. In the two years and more that he had worked with Ed, Ed had never once been late.

So was it time to trigger the plan?

Joseph Heller had said, "Nothing ever works as planned." He had not been wrong. The very act of initiating a plan seeds it with chaos and alters it before it has even started.

"What then," he asked aloud, "is the point of a plan?"

He became aware that he had been tapping his fingers to the tune of "Breathe" from Pink Floyd's *Dark Side of the Moon*. "All you touch and all you see, is all your life will ever be."

The point of a plan was to let you know where you're going, and fool you into believing you know how you are going to get there.

His buzzer snapped him out of his reverie and he lifted his internal phone. It was his secretary.

"Yes, May."

"You have Inspector Gerardo Baccay here to see

you, Dr. Hoffstadder." He felt the burn in his gut, but hid it and said, "Send him in, please."

The door opened and a slim man in a badly cut, shiny gray suit stepped in. Jay stood and smiled, extending his hand.

"Gerry, good to see you. How are things?"

The inspector took the proffered hand and shook it once without enthusiasm. His English was good, with little accent.

"I've been better, Jay. How are Gloria and the kids?" He recited it as a formula and sat without being asked.

"Good, they're good. What can I do for you, Gerry?"

The inspector's eyes strayed to the window and his fingers drummed an unconscious tattoo on the arm of his chair.

"You know Dr. Edward Hampton." The intonation was not interrogative.

Jay had known the question was likely, but even so he was not prepared for it. To cover his anxiety he smiled and said, "You have time for coffee?"

The inspector smiled at the window, then turned to Jay. The smile said he knew he had shaken him. "Yes," he said, "that would be nice."

He watched Jay press the intercom. "May, bring us some coffee, would you?"

"Right away, Dr. Hoffstadder."

Inspector Gerardo Baccay continued to watch Jay, waiting. Jay frowned and smiled simultaneously. "Uh, Edward Hampton, Ed, yeah, sure. Why?"

"When was the last time you saw him?"

Jay scratched his ear. "I'm not exactly sure. He's not exactly the most sociable member of the expat community. Must have been about a month ago? I seem to remember he was at an event at the Department of International Trade. That's his field, isn't it?" Inspector Gerardo Baccay didn't answer. He just watched Jay with a trace of a smile in his eyes. Jay frowned. "If you tell me what this is about, maybe I can help you."

Baccay's eyes shifted to the edge of Jay's desk. He reached out and touched it gently, as though he wasn't absolutely sure it was real.

"Dr. Hampton is what we call a person of interest."

Hoffstadder laughed, then seeing it was not well received, became serious. "*Ed?* Seriously?"

There was a trace of irritation in Inspector Baccay's eyes now.

"You would be surprised, Jay, at the people we find interesting. Academics and diplomatic staff are among the people we find most interesting. They always seem to be doing things that are not exactly related to their declared jobs. Dr. Hampton fell into both of those categories."

Jay nodded. "Yes, I know he was attached to the US Embassy as an advisor on trade. What surprised me was that you should find him of interest. I can hardly think of anyone less interesting!"

The inspector ignored the comment. "As a person of interest we have been watching him. And in the last thirty-six hours he has disappeared."

Hoffstadder sat forward. "Disappeared?"

"Yes, Jay, disappeared."

Jay took a deep breath and slowly raised his shoulders. "I wish I could help you, Gerry, but as I say, I had very little contact with Ed. It was more of a nodding acquaintance than anything else."

The door opened and May came in with a tray of coffee, cream and sugar. She set it down, smiled at the inspector and left. Jay poured and the silence grew heavy and uncomfortable. As he handed Baccay his cup, Jay said: "Gerry, what's on your mind? We've known each other a few years now, and I'd have to be blind not to see that something's troubling you." He took a sip of his own coffee and held the policeman's eye. As he set down his cup he went on. "I've told you Ed and I were acquaintances, and the last time I saw him was," he paused, "I guess it was about six weeks ago. If the precise date is important I can get May to check when that conference was."

Inspector Gerardo continued to watch his face, like he was watching a scene playing out on a TV screen. "We know when the conference was, Jay."

Jay shook his head. "No," he said, and raised the index finger of his right hand. "No, I tell a lie—"

Baccay raised an eyebrow. "A lie?"

"It's a manner of speech, an expression. I did see Ed more recently. It must have been a week or ten days ago. He called and asked if we could meet for a chat in a bar somewhere." He frowned as though in thought. "The Skyro, I think it was called, on Kalayaan Avenue."

"What did he want?"

Jay laughed. "Money! He knew I was close with Professor Carlo Pangalangan, the dean of the Law Faculty, and wanted me to pull strings to get him an honorary chair at the faculty. I told him I couldn't do that. I had a Scotch, he had a sparkling water, and we went our separate ways."

Inspector Baccay nodded a few times, then sighed and sat forward with his elbows on his knees, staring down at the floor.

"Let me tell you what's on my mind, Jay."

"Sure. If I can help you know I will."

Baccay raised his eyes to meet Jay's and he smiled. "What's on my mind is, why are you lying to me?"

Jay scowled. "Take it easy, Gerry."

"Where is Dr. Hampton?"

"I have no idea."

"You are going to attract a lot of unwelcome attention, Jay. You don't want that."

"I'll be damned, Gerry! Are you threatening me?"

"I am not threatening you, Jay. I am warning you as a friend."

Jay took a deep breath and sat back in his chair. He prayed that he had timed it right. He let out the air as a sigh and closed his eyes.

"OK, Gerry. I'll come clean with you. It's no secret that the war on drugs in the Philippines is pretty heavy. We have unarmed women being shot dead in the streets, kids being bundled into back alleys by cops and killed, local officials being shot in jail without a trial. Regardless of the rights and wrongs of it, to a middle-class American academic, it's pretty heavy stuff."

Inspector Baccay shook his head. "So what?"

"Ed has," Jay shrugged and spread his hands, "emotional issues. And the only way he can sleep most nights, so he told me, is if he is stoned. He needs his cannabis and he wanted to know if I could get it for him. I told him no way. I was not going to put my family at risk to get him dope. I told him to go see a doctor."

"You are telling me Dr. Hampton was trafficking drugs?"

"No, Gerry! I am telling you he had trouble sleeping if he couldn't smoke a joint!"

Inspector Gerardo Baccay put his hands on his knees and stood.

"My advice to you, Jay, as a friend, is to be very careful whom you associate with in the next few weeks. We will be watching."

He left without finishing his coffee, and without a farewell. The non-linguistic communication was clear. He could not depend on Inspector Gerardo Baccay's friendship to get him out of hot water, if he was careless enough to get into it.

The thought triggered a discharge of adrenaline into his belly and he reached for his telephone. His secretary's voice said, "Yes, Dr. Hoffstadder?"

"May, get me my wife, will you?"

"Right away, Dr. Hoffstadder."

He hung up and leaned back in his huge leather chair. The sky above the foliage above Romulo Hall seemed oddly motionless. It reminded him of the one time he had taken acid, in college in New York. Then he had also had that sense of utter stillness and timelessness, that time was a chemically induced illusion that masked an infinity of other realities, coexisting with this one. This time it was growing terror that some of those other realities might suddenly become unmasked. Realities like getting thrown into a Filipino jail.

The phone startled him and he sat forward to pick up the receiver.

"I have your wife on line one, Dr. Hoffstadder."

"Thank you, May." He pressed line one. "Hey, honey."

"Jay, everything OK?"

"Sure, can't a besotted husband call his wife from time to time to tell her he loves her?"

She was silent a moment, then, "I can think of several of my coffee morning friends who would tell me to be highly suspicious right now, and if you bring me flowers tonight I should divorce you."

"That's cynical, expat American wives for you. You know what I have a fancy for, Gloria?"

He used her name deliberately, to draw her attention to the fact that he was being serious. They had had the conversation—or as she referred to it The Conversation, with capitals—years ago, when he had told her about the dual nature of his job. He reminded her about it from time to time so she wouldn't rest on her laurels. Now he noticed from her voice that she had caught the signal.

"What do you have a fancy for, Jay?"

He injected a warmth he did not feel into his voice. "You remember that cute restaurant we discovered a few months ago on Bacoor Bay?"

"Sure, yeah, the food was great. You want to go there again? It's a fair old drive."

He could hear the strain in her voice. She knew what he was telling her.

"Half an hour, no more. You fancy going there at the weekend? Maybe we could stay over, come back Sunday night."

"Yeah, I'll tell the kids. They'll be excited."

He gave a warm chuckle which he did not feel and asked, "What's for dinner?"

This was her cue to confirm that she had understood. "Oh," she said, "um, I was thinking of roasting a chicken, and making an apple pie."

"My favorite," he said and laughed, a hollow shell of a laugh. "You're a doll, honey. I love you. You know that, right?"

"Of course."

"You tell those cynical coffee wives to go to hell. Me and you, baby."

Her voice was barely audible. "Me and you..."

"See you tonight, kiddo."

"See you tonight," she replied, though they both knew they wouldn't.

Gloria hung up and the first thing she did was to go to the settings in her cell and switch off the global positioning service. Then she ran up the stairs to her husband's study. She opened his stationery cupboard, removed the wooden panel and revealed the safe. She quickly turned the dials with trembling fingers and, on the second attempt, pulled open the heavy steel door. Inside there were three passports, one for her, one each for the kids, in the names of Julia Henson and Mark and Elizabeth Henson. They had chosen Mark and Elizabeth because those were their children's first names, and there would be no need to inform the children of what had happened, or tell them they had to use different names.

There was also a white leather handbag containing five thousand dollars in cash, a black Visa and a driving permit. She snatched them all out, took ten minutes to book three passages on the next flight to LAX, printed the boarding passes and slipped them in the white leather purse. Then she ran down the stairs.

She took nothing from the house but her car keys. She went to the parking garage and climbed behind the wheel of her BMW. There she sat with her eyes closed, breathing slowly and counting backwards from ten to one and zero. Then she pressed the remote control to open the garage door and gently eased out.

She drove south on Katipunan Avenue as far as the intersection with Aurora Boulevard. All the way she recited to herself the mantra of the instructions her husband had given her. Above all, stay calm and act as though nothing had happened. Take the car and park it at the Metrobank, then walk the three blacks to Harvard, one hundred and fifty yards up Harvard, on the left was Aries Rent-a-Car. She would not immediately recognize it as a car rental business.

She came to the intersection with 15th Avenue, did a U-turn and drove up to the parking lot outside the Metrobank. She parked and locked her car, and walked back to the pedestrian crossing on 15th Avenue. There she crossed among the chaos of the traffic and hurried past the 7-Eleven to Harvard. The men at the *traysikel* rank on the corner watched her, smoking. A couple called out to her with ill-concealed insolence, "Taxi *traysikel!* You want *traysikel*? American? American?"

She ignored them. She hurried past the Rapture Café and walked quickly down Harvard past bare concrete walls, buildings with peeling yellow paint and the ubiquitous empty lots overgrown with plantain and rubber plants. Farther on was the chaotic superabundance of pavement shops, parasols and signs upon signs, against every surface and in every color under the sun: "no parking," "for sale," "Vote Ramon Lucena," "chow here," "beware electric cables." And the store owners and their families sitting on doorsteps and on plastic chairs, always in Bermudas and flip-flops.

It was not something she had seen a lot of in the years she had been in Manila. She and her friends had tended to remain in their expat world, consorting mainly with English speakers, academics and diplomats, which, she thought thankfully, had been a little piece of California in Manila.

The car rental shop, as Jay had warned her, was not immediately apparent. It was in a yard, through a rusting iron door in a raw, concrete wall. At some point in history somebody had painted the door undercoat orange. Now the orange undercoat was peeling off, exposing the orange rust underneath. Over the door there was a hand-painted sign that said "Cars."

Inside she spoke to a man with thin, nicotine-stained lips who, when she mentioned her husband's name, took a hundred dollars cash from her for a Volkswagen Golf. He told her where to park it when she was done, and told her he would collect it the next day from the airport parking lot.

From there she drove, with increasing anxiety, back up Aurora Boulevard through the swarming, claustrophobic traffic. At the intersection with Katipunan Avenue she crossed under the bridge and past the psychedelic, Sergeant Pepper Jeepney depot before accelerating up the ramp onto the avenue. She knew she was going too fast and forced herself to slow down and match the traffic until she arrived at the kids' school. There she turned into the parking lot, found a space out of sight of the school office and sat quietly panicking for thirty seconds, trying to get her trembling hands and her breath under control.

Finally she climbed out of the car and walked briskly inside. Helen, the head, was in the office talking to

Judith, the secretary. They both looked up and smiled as she came in. Helen spoke.

"Gloria, hi. What can we do for you?"

Gloria laughed and shook her head. "Helen, I am *so* sorry. I *completely* forgot the kids had a dental appointment today with Dr. Hirsch. And you know how busy he is. If I have to postpone there is no knowing when he'll be able to see them again. I hate to do it, but I am going to have to pull them out of class. I'll bring the note in tomorrow morning."

"Oh, sure. I know the feeling. That guy is gold dust. Judith, do you mind getting Gloria's kids for her?"

"Of course."

Judith slipped out from behind her desk and hurried off to get the kids. Helen said something like, "We should do lunch sometime, it's been too long."

And Gloria, grateful that for a few minutes at least she could pretend everything was as normal, smiled and said, "You should come over, with Hank. We'll have dinner. Jay has been dying to try out his new barbeque. We can dump the kids in the pool, get Hank and Jay talking about power tools and you and I can relax over some gin and tonics!"

They both laughed and a couple of minutes later Mark, who was ten and Elizabeth, who was eight going on forty, appeared carrying their bags and holding Judith's hands.

"Mommy," it was Elizabeth, "how come you didn't tell us we were going to see Dr. Hirsch?"

"Because grown-ups don't tell their little babies everything. Now, come along, hurry up or we'll be late."

She led the kids out, waving goodbye, and they

threaded their way through the cars in the lot to the white Golf. There, Elizabeth complained that this was not their car. Her mother told her that Daddy had got it especially for them to go on an adventure.

They climbed in back and belted up, and Gloria drove out of the lot and headed for the airport.

CHAPTER FOUR

I picked up a Toyota Fortuner from Avis at Ninoy Aquino Airport and made the half-hour drive through Manila to the Grand Hyatt on 8th Avenue. The drive was an education and reminded me of that line of Tom Waits' in "Waltzing Matilda": "Everything's broken and no one speaks English, and I'm down on my knees tonight." The fact that English was the official language, alongside Tagalog, didn't seem to matter much. Just as the fact that this was reputed to be one of the most dynamic economies in the East didn't seem to affect the abject poverty evident in the sprawling shantytowns, the broken sidewalks and the neglected infrastructure of the city.

I booked into the Grand Hyatt, where everyone spoke English and nothing was either neglected, abject or broken, and had my cases taken up to my room. With the bellhop suitably rewarded, I stripped and stood for twenty minutes under a hot shower, occasionally switching to cold. After that I changed into a fresh linen suit, ordered a pot of strong, black coffee and some breakfast, and sat on my terrace, going through the file again, committing facts to memory.

It seemed the last person to set eyes on ODIN's man

in Manila was a cop by the name of Daniel Alcantara, who was part of a team run by Inspector Gerardo Baccay. According to the file, Baccay was about as bent as a used car salesman running for president. I made a mental note that Baccay would be a good place to start.

Apparently, Superintendent James Canosa was a friend of ODIN's and was willing to arrange any interviews I needed. I picked up the phone and called him. His secretary put me through.

"Mr. Mason," he said, as though my name was amusing to him. "I was not expecting your call till tomorrow. It is a long flight from Washington. Most people need a good sleep after they get here."

"Never on the company dime, Superintendent. No time to waste."

"Very admirable. Tell me, how can I help you?"

"As you know, we are concerned about the disappearance of an American citizen..."

"Yes," he said, with that amusement evident in his voice once again. "We are fully aware of your concern, Mr. Mason."

"Good. So I would be very interested in speaking to Inspector Gerardo Baccay, and also Officer Daniel Alcantara. Can you arrange that for me?"

"Of course, Mr. Mason. I will have Inspector Baccay call you within the next hour. Alcantara is one of his boys, so he will arrange that."

We chatted for a bit about weather and gold and he told me I had to see him before I left for a barbeque. I said I'd do that.

Baccay's call came not in the next hour but in the next fifteen minutes, as room service was delivering my coffee and croissants to my room. I gave the kid ten bucks and answered the phone as he left and closed the door.

"Mr. Mason, this is Inspector Baccay. How can I help you? You were a friend of Dr. Hampton's?"

"Inspector." I sat and took a second to pour myself a demitasse of very strong black brew. "Thank you for getting back to me. I'm sure you'll appreciate that this is not a subject I am keen to discuss on the telephone. I wonder if we could meet somewhere. I'm sure it won't be a waste of your time, Inspector."

It was as smooth as silk drawers, and the smile was evident in his voice when he replied.

"I am sure it will be advantageous to us both, Mr. Mason. How about the Uptown Mall on 11th Avenue at twelve o'clock noon? The Burgers and Beer restaurant is very good."

"It sounds irresistible. I'll be there."

I finished reading the file over my late breakfast, collected my car and drove the five hundred yards to the Uptown Mall. There were no shanties in this part of town, and most of the sidewalks seemed to be pretty much intact. In fact, everything seemed to be made of shiny glass and steel. Maybe this was where the dynamic Eastern market was.

I left the Toyota in the subterranean parking garage and rode the escalators to the second floor. After a short walkabout I found a fast-food restaurant that had been designed to look like a Wild West saloon, with big red plastic letters above swing doors that read "Burgers and Beer," and beneath that, "Food and Drink the American Way." I could just see Jefferson, smiling peacefully in his grave, content in the knowledge that his vision had become a reality.

I was a little early, so I found a table by the plate-glass window and ordered a beer, the American way. The pretty waitress brought it to me and I asked her if she knew Inspector Baccay.

She nodded. "Oh yes, he coming here a lot. He like to meet his friends here."

"When he comes in, tell him Mr. Mason is here."

She nodded and went away. For the next fifteen minutes I played a guessing game through the window, seeing if I could spot the cop. When he finally showed up in a double-breasted shiny gray suit that hung like it was one size too big, I had no doubt I had spotted him. He pushed through the swing doors and I was pretty sure that in his mind he could hear Ennio Morricone whistling. The pretty waitress caught his eyes and pointed to me. He turned and walked over on crisp little feet. I stood.

"Inspector, it's good of you to see me."

He smiled with thin lips and expressionless eyes. "You know in Philippines we like to cooperate with the USA whenever possible, even if we then ask you to pay for that cooperation."

I smiled at his oblique reference to the Visiting Forces Agreement and nodded as we shook hands and sat.

"Believe me, I am sensitive to the fact that everything has an administrative cost which has to be met." I held his eye and added, "And I am happy to meet it."

"That always makes things much easier. You know, a lot of Filipinos worry that if the United States abandons us, the Chinese will move in and take over. There they sit," he said, gesturing vaguely toward the west, "at the Whitsun Reef. All we want is to get on with life, nobody telling us what to do."

"Politicians make messes, Inspector Baccay; people like you and me clean them up."

"Let us hope so, Mr. Mason. So, how can I help you?"

"Our friend, Dr. Hampton, seems to have disappeared. And I am here to try and find him."

The pretty waitress toddled up and put a cup of coffee in front of him. He didn't acknowledge her, but reached out and touched the saucer with the tip of his finger. "Your friend, Dr. Hampton, is a spy."

I allowed my face to turn to stone. "That," I said, "is the kind of talk that discourages friends from helping with the administrative costs of operations that can end up becoming very expensive, Inspector Baccay. Let us be clear, Dr. Hampton was a consultant on international trade and international law, who specialized in Chinese affairs and consulted for the US government—on China. He was not a spy."

He chuckled at his coffee cup. "Forgive me, Mr. Mason. I stand corrected. So, maybe the Chinese got tired of him consulting so much about them. The Chinese can get pretty aggressive when they think they can get away with it."

I sipped my coffee. "Are we in the land of speculation here, or do you have facts that might have an administrative cost attached to them?"

"I have some facts, Mr. Mason. Do not be so quick to throw away your money, or to judge the Filipino police. I actually believe we should cooperate with the Americans. I am not crazy about the idea of replacing you with the Chinese."

"OK, now I stand corrected."

"We'll talk about administrative costs later. Right

now I can tell you that we were watching Dr. Hampton because our Chinese friends had asked somebody on the top floor to keep an eye on him."

"Any idea who?"

"Oh." He shrugged, pulled down the corners of his mouth and shook his head. "Probably the director general, but I think on instructions from the president's office. The Chinese Embassy had become aware that Dr. Hampton was watching them and they did not like it. So they asked the police to keep an eye on him on their behalf, and report on his movements."

"And so you put Officer David Alcantara on him."

"Among others, yes."

"To what extent were they aware of the nature of the job?"

"Not at all. They were told to report all movements, and that was it."

"So when did you first realize that he was missing?"

He pulled a pack of Camels from his pocket, shook one free and lit up with a green, plastic disposable lighter. He tucked his paraphernalia back in his pocket and sucked hard, drawing in his cheeks. When he withdrew the cigarette, he took a deep breath before letting out the smoke in small puffs as he spoke.

"Alcantara was on duty. It wasn't a difficult job. Dr. Hampton is a man of habit. Out of his house at eight in the morning. Work in the morning, then the American Embassy, then home in the evening. Like a clock. But two weeks ago he became erratic. It started when he arranged to meet Dr. Hoffstadder at a bar called the Skyro."

The name tickled the edges of my memory. "Dr.

Hoffstadder?"

"Professor of International Law at the University of the Philippines."

I nodded. He was in the file, one of the known members of the cell Dr. Hampton had recruited. Baccay was talking again.

"He arranged to meet him at the Skyro, on Kalayaan Avenue near the Quezon Memorial Circle."

"Was that unusual?"

He made an ugly face and shrugged. "No, Dr. Hoffstadder like to pretend they hardly knew each other. But the fact is they would meet more or less regularly either by chance at some university event, or discretely in town. On this occasion they met for maybe half an hour and Dr. Hoffstadder left a little before Dr. Hampton. But Hampton did not go home. That was very unusual. He went *back* to the embassy. He then went to a number of hotels, where he stayed about fifteen minutes in each—the Hilton, the Grand and the Continental. After that he went to a restaurant—"

"He was trying to shake his tail."

"Maybe."

"What kind of restaurant?"

The question seemed to surprise Baccay. He stared at me for a moment, then repeated, "What kind of restaurant? The kind of restaurant he usually went to: cheap, Filipino, not fancy like the restaurants they have at the Grand Hyatt."

"Where? What's the restaurant called?"

"It's a dive in Project Six, Quezon City. The street is called Road One. The restaurant is Starving Sam."

"Great name."

"Yeah."

"So he had dinner in there. Did your man go in too?"

"No, his instructions were to wait outside."

"So we are assuming he had dinner in there, but we don't really know what happened."

Baccay shook his head. "We don't know anything, because that was the last we know of him. As far as we know, it's the last anybody saw of him."

"So he left through the kitchen..."

He interrupted me. "Not necessarily. The toilets are in the backyard there. We assume he went to the toilet, then down a back alley and onto Road Two. We questioned the kitchen staff, of course, but they know nothing, saw nothing, heard nothing, say nothing."

I gave a soft grunt. "What about his house?"

He shrugged. "What about it?"

"Have you looked there?"

"No. In the first place we have no evidence that a crime was committed, so we have no grounds for a search warrant. We can't just go marching into somebody's house because we don't see them for thirty-six hours, especially if they are an American citizen, and especially in these diplomatically sensitive times."

"You mean the Chinese said they didn't want you snooping in the house?"

He shrugged. "The Chinese said nothing. We need a reason to go into somebody's house," he repeated. "Especially an American attached to the embassy."

"Fair enough. How about me, can I snoop in the house?"

"I told you, in these diplomatically sensitive times,

we try not to meddle in the affairs of Americans, unless they are trafficking drugs. Then we just shoot them. But if you are a close friend of Dr. Hampton, and he told you you can go in and out his house when you please, we are not going to make a fuss. Just don't walk out with two kilos of heroin under your arm."

"I doubt Hampton was into drugs."

"That's not what Dr. Hoffstadder told me. According to him, Hampton used cannabis regularly. Could not sleep without it."

"You believe him?"

He sniffed and stared out the window for a while. Then he shook his head. "No." He turned and engaged my eyes again. "No, he upset the Chinese and either had to leave Manila in a hurry, or they neutralized him." He sat forward. "My opinion, he had a friend waiting on Road Two, he bribed the staff of Starving Sam to say nothing, went out to the toilet in the yard, down the narrow alley and out to Road Two. There he climbed in a car and disappeared. If he was killed, it had to be in the restaurant, and there was no possibility of that. So he escaped because he was scared of the Chinese."

"Can I talk to Alcantara? Sometimes there is some small detail that means nothing to them, but might mean something to me."

He shook his head. "No, Alcantara is on indefinite leave in the far north of the country. He cannot be reached. Right now he thinks Dr. Hampton was suspected of trafficking drugs. If you talk to him, he will know this is international espionage."

I sighed, telling myself if Alcantara didn't know that already, I wasn't surprised Hampton got away from him so easily. I said:

"OK, well, we'll start with a visit to his house. See what I find. Then we'll take it from there."

He nodded, staring out the window again. It was clear from his lack of expression, and the fact that he failed to move, stand up or shake my hand, that he still had something to say. I waited. Eventually he sighed deeply.

"Philippines has one big advantage. That big advantage is also big problem." I continued to wait and he went on. "Our position. We are the gateway to the Pacific, like Japan. Big difference with Japan is we had no Hiroshima, no Nagasaki. When you Americans took us from Spain, there were no atomic bombs. When the Second World War came, we already belonged to you. No need to crush us into submission. So we were never really destroyed. Japan died at Hiroshima, and was reborn in the American image. But Philippines, we remain part Spanish, part Indo-Chinese. So today, we are not so much a staunch ally of America," he gave a short, dry, humorless laugh, "we are more a battlefield, where America and China fight their battles."

"What are you trying to tell me, Inspector Baccay?"

"I am not going to stop you from investigating Dr. Hampton's disappearance. In fact, unless you pull big diplomatic strings, I am going to do my best not to see you again. But I don't know what the Chinese are going to do. And I will be honest with you, Mr. Mason, I have no control over what the Chinese are going to do. Like I said, this is a battlefield. Manila is in chaos. You are gunning for the Chinese. The Chinese are gunning for you. You both want to control the Philippines, and what are we doing? Shooting women and kids who sell marijuana." He shook his head. "Don't ask me for help. The best help I can give you is to stay out of your way, and that is what I am going to do."

I watched him stand. He paused a moment leaning on the back of his chair. "No administrative charge today, Mr. Mason. Tell your boss. No administrative charge today."

The way he said it, it was clear that was not a good thing. The Philippines were no longer for sale. He pushed out through the saloon bar doors into the shopping mall, that small piece of Manila that was still America.

CHAPTER FIVE

I sat a while turning over what Baccay had said to me. The warning was clear. The Chinese influence over the Philippines was growing stronger, and the will in the Duterte government to resist that influence was not strong. I was on my own, and our strongest ally in the Pacific was off hunting junkies.

I paid up and strolled out into the crowded mall, wondering what the hell Hampton had been doing that night, running around Manila like a son of a bitch searching for his father. Maybe he knew the cops were tailing him, but I figured he knew the Chinese were on his tail too, and he was trying to lose them. I wondered what my next step should be.

My starting point had to be that Edward Hampton was either dead or alive. If he was dead, he had been eliminated by the Chinese and the chances were the body had been disposed of where it would never be found. If he was alive, then he had fled and would make some effort to either make contact or leave a message to indicate where he had gone.

I decided that either way my best move right then was to visit Hampton's house and go over it with a fine-toothed comb to see if he had left any kind of message.

After that a visit to Dr. Hoffstadder at the University of the Philippines might be in order.

I also had the CIA field office I could talk to, but I didn't see how they could be of much help right then and decided to put that visit on hold.

But like the man said, nothing ever works as planned.

I took the escalator down to the parking garage and walked across the dark, grimy cavern listening to my steps echo in the shadows. It was as I was approaching my vehicle that I became aware of a second set of echoing footsteps tangled in with mine. I listened with care as I walked and noted they were getting closer. As I drew level with the Toyota I patted my pockets conspicuously and turned, as though to return to the mall.

He was about eight feet from me and stood at an intimidating six-six, with shoulders you'd have to make special arrangements for. He was in an expensive sky-blue suit and had expensive-looking shades perched on the top of his crew cut. He had Chinese features, a lipless mouth and a cruel smile.

"Mr. Mason?"

His voice echoed in the shadows. I traded him an affable smile for his cruel one and asked, "And you are...?"

"That's not important."

"To whom? To you? To me it's quite important right now."

"Oh," he nodded, still smiling, "then you can call me Ren."

"Ren?"

He nodded and repeated with emphasis, "Ren."

"That means person in Chinese, right?"

"I am a person. Please, Mr. Mason, I must ask you some questions."

"OK, Ren, you can ask me some questions."

"You are here to investigate Dr. Hampton's disappearance?"

"You just told me your name is Person, and you expect me to be cooperative and answer a question like that?"

He stared at me a moment without answering, reading my face, then nodded. "You should go home. It is very dangerous for you to stay here investigating these things."

"Right. Well, thanks for the advice, Person, I'll be sure to go and pass it on to Joe at the White House. Was there anything else?"

He blinked and gave a small frown. "You will be very foolish not to take my warning seriously, Mr. Mason."

I shrugged. "I might be more inclined to take you seriously if I knew who you were. But a seven-foot guy comes up to me in a parking garage and tells me his name is Person? Well, that sounds like the start of a joke. So I am not inclined to take you very seriously, no."

"Oh, OK." He gave another nod. "Soon you will find out good and proper who I am, Mr. Mason."

"Great, I look forward to it, Person."

I climbed in the truck, backed out and drove out of the garage. All the way I could see the giant standing there in the shadows, immobile, watching me. "Good and proper" was an Anglicism used mainly by Cockneys. I wondered absently if he was from Hong Kong.

As I emerged onto 11th Avenue, instead of heading

north and west toward Boni Avenue and the Maysilo Circus to have a look at Hampton's place, I did a few large figures of eight around the Fort Bonifacio area, where the Uptown Mall was. I was changing my plan and called the local CIA contact. It rang twice and a pretty, Valley voice answered.

"American Embassy Overseas Enquiries, how may I help you?"

"Overseas Department of International Novelties here, I have a Code one-i. I wonder if you could give me some guidance."

"I'll put you through to our local desk. Hold the line, please."

There was a pause long enough for a short conversation and then a man came on the line. He had the kind of voice you'd expect your slightly left wing, friendly high school teacher to have. I figured it was even chances he had a blond beard and an affable smile. Gone were the days of dark suits and Wayfarer sunglasses. The CIA was not what it used to be.

"I've been expecting your call. Before we get chatting, you want to give me a reference number?"

I recited the alphanumeric code and knew that voice recognition software was analyzing what I was saying as I spoke. After a moment the voice spoke again.

"That's just fine, we are on a secure line, my name is Julian for the purposes of this conversation. You don't need to give me your name. Will this take more than a minute?"

"I don't think so. Six foot six, Chinese, possibly Hong Kong, built like a tank and speaks English fluently, but with slightly incorrect use of British slang."

"He approached you?"

"Yeah, warned me off. Told me to leave the investigation."

"Sounds like Zimo Chew. He's a dangerous dude. Hit man for the Chinese Ministry of State Security. He works for a sub-department known as *Táotài bù*, it literally means the 'Elimination Department.' We know he arrived in Manila about a week ago. Did he say anything else?"

"Yup. He told me I would soon, and I quote, find out 'good and proper' who he was. He knew my name and in my experience it is not good when a six foot six Chinese hit man who is built like a tank knows your name. That is something I would definitely put into the 'not great' category."

His voice said he had smiled, but he didn't laugh. "You're here to look for Dr. Hampton, right?"

"Yeah."

"We've been told to stand by on this one."

"You have something for me?"

"Where are you now?"

"Fort Bonifacio, on my way to Hampton's house."

"So you're like fifteen minutes away. Why don't you drop in, say hi and have some coffee?"

"You'd recommend that?"

"Well, you know, like I say, we've been told to stay out of this one, but we always keep an eye on things. That's what we're here for. It might be helpful to you."

"OK, thanks, Julian."

I approached past the National Museum, along Padre Burgos Avenue, and made a right onto Roxas Boulevard, a block away from the US Embassy. The Embassy of the United States in Manila is like a fortress. Since just after World War II it was the "government behind the government" in the Philippines. It is still one of the State Department's largest posts and employs some three hundred Americans as well as about a thousand Filipinos. The grounds are a full five hundred yards across and two hundred yards deep, and house the new Embassy Annex, the US Chancery and a half dozen other buildings that have no precise designation. It's like a small town right on the bay, within the harbor, and even has a discrete quay where officials and their luggage can be embarked or disembarked, or ferried out to waiting ships should the need arise.

I pulled up at the big double gates in the fifteen-foot white walls and a Marine approached me. I showed him my ODIN badge. He saluted and told me Mr. Hoffmann would see me in the Chancery Building. A moment later the big gates rolled back and I rolled into the embassy complex. I left my car in the parking lot to the right of the gates and strolled across the gardens to the Chancery. As I climbed the steps to the doors a man emerged to meet me. He was in a blue and white striped shirt and blue jeans. He had a blond beard, thinning blond hair and an easy smile. He held out his elbow.

"Captain Mason, Paul Hoffmann. Please, call me Paul. And forgive all the cloak and dagger stuff. Sometimes it's necessary." He laughed and slapped me on the shoulder. "Look who I'm telling! How are you?"

I returned the slap more gently. "I'm good. Alex, please. Trying to get a handle on what happened to Hampton. You guys have anything?"

He turned and I fell into step beside him. He led me across an empty, echoing lobby toward a bank of elevators. As we walked he spoke.

"The truth is, Alex, we've been interested in Dr. Hampton for some time. We were acquainted, of course." He gave a small, amiable laugh. "He was not a nice guy, not exactly approachable, but we bumped into each other occasionally."

"Was? Is he dead?"

We stopped at the elevator and he pressed the button. "I honestly don't know. It's entirely possible, particularly in view of what you have just told me about Zimo. The Philippines has always been a dangerous place. It is particularly dangerous now. President Duterte has created a very volatile environment. He is fostering anti-American feeling and he has the Chinese champing at the bit. They would sell their collective grandmothers to control the Philippines." He laughed, creasing his eyes at the corners. "And that's a lot of grandmothers!" He sighed, shook his head at his own wit and went on more seriously. "We believe Dr. Hampton was pushing hard to see what he could learn about Chinese plans for the Philippines. We got the feeling he had a sense of urgency about it. He was playing a very dangerous game."

We stepped into the elevator, the doors hissed closed and we rode up one floor. There we emerged into a short passage that led to only two doors. Ours was at the end and opened after a scanner on the wall had had a look at his thumb. He pushed the door open and gestured me in.

It was a bright, corner office overlooking gardens and the Bay of Manila. It was furnished in a minimalist, functional style that evoked Scandinavia without evoking IKEA. He dropped into a white leather chair behind a blond, oak desk and gestured me to a smaller white leather chair on my side.

"I imagine you've spoken to the local cops." I nodded and he acknowledged it with a nod of his own. "Ed, Dr. Hampton, wasn't real fond of Filipinos. He didn't like Manila and he didn't like the South Pacific. I often asked him why he was here if he hated it so much, and he usually replied that somebody in Washington had wanted to punish him." He shrugged and spread his hands. "Who knows? The point is, the Filipino establishment grew to dislike him—the feeling was completely reciprocal—but on the other hand they didn't know what to make of him. The truth is he understood the Filipino culture quite well, and the Chinese too, but they had no idea what to make of him. He was rude, patronizing, disheveled-looking, and very unsociable. He was also deeply disrespectful of their customs and beliefs. In the end I think they just decided he was crazy and pretty much ignored him. If it was a deliberate cover, it was a very effective one—until now."

"You're not suggesting they killed him because they thought he was rude?"

He gave a laugh that said the idea wasn't so farfetched and gave his head a little tilt and a twist.

"I wouldn't put it past a Filipino. They'd kill for far less. That's true of the Chinese too, though they are a lot more subtle about it. But no, I don't think he was killed for that. I don't even know that he *was* killed. I'm just saying that he was not real popular among the Filipino and Chinese communities."

"You keep mentioning the Chinese. I'm getting that the Chinese are a big deal here right now."

"You could say that. There is a dynamic right now between Beijing and Duterte which is driving a lot of change. Some people believe that if it were not for the pro-American elements in the government, the Philippines would by now be essentially a Chinese protectorate. To many Filipinos the USA is a waning power and China is the rising, Asian star, and they want to hitch their cart to that star."

I grunted. "So what do you think made Hampton disappear?"

"You guys at ODIN probably know a lot more than we do, but if you want my reading, being here on the ground, I think he either got really scared and ran, or the Chinese took him out."

"Based on what?"

He sighed and stared out at the bay, where the sunlight was making transitory gems of the small waves.

"Based on," he shook his head, "I hate to say it, but it is a gut feeling, that steady accumulation of small things that individually are nothing, but cumulatively are like pointillism. They make a whole picture." He shrugged. "I can't tell you exactly what it was, but in the last couple of weeks or three, he was different. He had always had that air of hopelessness about him—what's that line of Pink Floyd's, hanging on in quiet desperation? That was Ed. That was always Ed, hanging on in quiet desperation. But in the last couple of weeks or three, something had changed. He was more assertive, more aggressive, more buoyant. It was like something had happened."

"And you think whatever that was..."

He interrupted. "*Think* is too strong. It's more a feeling I have from having seen him around, bumped into him a few times. You get to know a person. And suddenly he was cheerful, smiling, bossy. And whatever it was that made him that way, either it made him run and start a new life, or it killed him."

"You know who his contacts were here? His cell?"

He raised his eyebrows. "Seriously? You don't know?"

I offered him a low-fat smile. "I know what he told us. But I don't need to tell you that it's not real smart to trust disappearing people."

He gave a snort of a chuckle and reached in a drawer. He pulled out a folder and extracted from it a slip of paper. He slid it across the desk to me.

"I had a feeling you might ask for it, so I had it copied." I picked it up. It had four names on it; the last had been scrawled in by hand with three question marks after it. He went on, "These are the people we have observed him with. The list may not be exhaustive. For that matter it may be completely wrong. I doubt it, but on the other hand, we don't make a habit of spying on fellow agencies."

I raised an eyebrow at him but he ignored the implied irony and pointed at the handwritten name.

"The girl at the end, Marion James? We're not sure if she is a recruit. He kept his hand real close to his chest, I'm sure you know that, but she does not fit the typical profile of his recruits. His other contacts tend to be top academics, civil servants." He smiled. "She just seems to be a scruffy kid who came here on a gap year and got stuck. We haven't looked into her."

"How long before he disappeared did they make contact?"

"As far as we could make out, about three weeks."

"Where is she now?"

He shrugged. "We were going to bring her in and talk to her, but we got the word to back off because ODIN were sending their own man. If she's smart she's going about her business like nothing has happened."

"You got an address for her?" He gave me the address on San Joaquin and I frowned, trying to visualize it. "Isn't that around the corner from Hampton's place?"

"Pretty much, about a three-minute walk."

"That was stupid. That's not the kind of mistake a man like Hampton would make."

"Like I said, she was not the typical profile of his recruits. Maybe she was just a whore! I don't know."

We'd talked some more for another fifteen minutes, and then I left with promises to meet again and have coffee before I went home.

***

I had two questions on my mind as I drove out of the embassy gates. The first was, what had Marion James given or told Dr. Hampton that had made him disappear —or got him killed?

And second, how had the Chinese Embassy found out I was here so fast that they were able to send a hit man to warn me off? ODIN security was about as tight as you could get without employing androids instead of humans, so I figured the leak probably came from Baccay and his superiors: ODIN had called Superintendent James Canosa to tell him I was coming and to provide me with assistance, and Canosa had hung up and called the Chinese Embassy. Inspector Baccay had intimated as much. I thought about it as I pulled out onto Roxas Boulevard and studied my rearview mirror.

But even as I looked I decided there was no point in closing the stable door if the dragon had already bolted.

They knew I was here, and they knew why. So there was no purpose to be served now in hiding the fact. I turned north and west onto Qurino Avenue and headed for Pedro Gil Street and the Lambingan Bridge.

It was as I was coming off the bridge and into New Panaderos Street, negotiating the chaotic traffic, among the vast plethora of signs, placards and advertisements which seemed to characterize Manila, that I realized I had, in fact, picked up a tail. I smiled and changed lanes a few times, dodging and crawling among the motorized, enclosed *traysikels*, motorbikes and psychedelic Jeepneys. But wherever I went, the Mercedes tail stayed with me, keeping a few cars back, but making no real effort to conceal his presence. I noted also it had diplomatic plates.

They were confident, sure of their growing power in the Philippines.

I figured just because he was making it easy for me, it didn't mean I had to reciprocate. So I cut across the outside lane, causing several bikes and cars to screech to a halt, and accelerated into a street glorying in the name Right Reverend G Aglipay. I burned rubber all the way down to Boni Avenue watching the Merc in my mirror, trying to keep up. At Santo Rosario I fishtailed into a right-angled turn and plowed across the traffic, did another fishtail into Santo Nino and stopped dead in the middle of the road with my hazard lights on.

This was Dr. Hampton's street. The Merc, I could now make out it was an AMG Roadster, came up behind me, paused, swung smoothly past me and continued on down the road. When he'd gone I started to move again and cruised past the big green and white house on my right, keeping one eye on my rearview. I pulled in fifty yards past the house, killed the engine and waited.

The Merc appeared ahead of me, about seventy yards away, turning in off Santa Ana. It came to a halt thirty or forty feet away, directly in front of me. I sighed and climbed out of the Toyota, then walked the ten paces to where they were parked. Through the tinted windshield I could see that they were Oriental. They remained staring straight ahead without acknowledging I was there. I tapped on the driver's side window. It slid down and the driver looked up at me with a face which was a little less expressive than unpainted concrete.

I leaned on the window and smiled. He looked down at my hands. I said:

"You guys are following me."

He looked up at my face and slightly narrowed his eyes. He followed this emotional outpouring by doing nothing. I said:

"I want you to stop following me."

Still nothing. I sighed one more time and reached in my inside pocket. That got a reaction of alarm as they both reached for their pieces. I held up both hands and said, "Relax, I'm going to show you my ID."

They remained with their hands halfway to their holsters while I pulled my passport and showed it to them. I said, "See? I am a US citizen, going about my business, and you should not be following me."

They were frowning at the passport like I was crazy. I closed it and kept talking as I put it back. "I am aware that the Philippines is a democracy only in name, but still, guys..."

Now they were staring at my face like I was crazy. I slipped the passport in my pocket, said, "Give a guy a break," and pulled the prototype Maxim 9S from under my arm. It was smaller, slimmer and more manageable than the old Maxim 9. They had slightly less than a second to shift from frowning like I was crazy to gaping like I was crazy. The Maxim went *phut! Phut!* And it was all over.

I opened the door, raised the window and took the key from the driver's pocket. I closed the door again, pressed the lock button and the lights flashed and beeped. Then I walked back toward Hampton's house. The diplomatic plates on the Merc would ensure the car was not investigated for the next few hours at least.

CHAPTER SIX

At eleven-twenty Marion rose from the bench and made her way to the museum. She found her way to Gallery One, the section for religious art of the seventeenth to nineteenth centuries, and tried to look around as inconspicuously as she could.

He had said that when she saw him she was to do nothing but act as though she did not know him. Well, he was not there, and there was no sign of him in the adjoining rooms. He had told her to stop and admire one of the saints and if the coast was clear he would stop beside her and they would discuss the work of art she was looking at.

She wandered around the adjoining rooms for half an hour, returning every five minutes or so to Gallery One, bur there was no sign of Ed, and she was aware that she was starting to become conspicuous. So at eleven forty-five, with a growing sense of panic, she made her way through the galleries and out of the museum, into the crowded glare of the midday sun.

For a long time she just stood on the sidewalk, unaware of the vast, magnificent building behind her, aware only of the wild panic thrashing inside her chest, and the despair like a hole in her mind through which sanity was starting to drain away. One thought filled her mind, one thought dominated all others: she had to get away. She had to get away from Manila and the Philippines, and only Ed could help her do that. Ed was her only way out. Ed was her doorway to freedom.

He had told her never to phone him and never to go to his house. But she knew where he lived, and if he didn't want her to go there, then he should have shown up at the museum. Despair began to turn to indignation, and then cold rage.

She began to walk, oblivious to the aching in her feet and in her legs. She retraced her steps along General Luna and Pedro Gil, among the hated, ever present tacky signs, banners, placards and posters, under the eternal mess of overhead power cables, like black spider webs across the sky. She walked through the swarms of people in shorts and flip-flops; and as she walked the hatred grew, the violent rage inside her grew deeper and blacker.

She came at last to her house at San Joaquin, but walked past it, unable to face the prospect of going back inside with her nightmare hanging over her. She kept going and turned into Santo Nino and continued until she came to the green and white house. There she found the gate pulled to, but unlocked. She reached to push it open, hesitated a second with her heart pounding, then thrust forward.

Inside the small yard she stood at the front door and saw that here too the door was pulled to, but unlocked. Again she pushed, but more gingerly. The door swung open. She stepped into a small hallway and noticed that the alarm on the wall was off. There were no lights on and the screen was dead. She pushed the door closed and called out softly, "Ed...?" aware of the irony of wanting to be heard but keeping your voice down so as not to be.

She went into the living room, noted all the books cramming every inch of shelf space, noted the TV table beside the sofa, the shambles of newspapers and magazines piled on the coffee table. There was nobody here, nothing here, she told herself and went into the kitchen. There was a mug on the side with instant coffee and sugar in it. Both jars stood beside the mug. She felt the kettle. It was cold.

Back in the hall she found the stairs to the upper floor and climbed them. They were tiled concrete and therefore did not creak as you climbed. But each footfall sounded like a drumbeat in her ears. She reached the landing and saw his bedroom door ajar.

And she noticed the smell. She had never smelled death before, but some primal race memory, some hardwired ancient instinct told her that this was what she was smelling right here, right now: real, organic death.

Compelled by the need to know, she moved forward and placed her fingertips upon the door. She pushed softly and felt the dead cold trickle through her skin. Her stomach lurched and her fingers went to her lips as the room rocked.

He was sitting inches from the door, slightly to her left. His knees were bent and his large belly and his crotch were thick with drying, coagulating blood, as was the carpet where he was seated, with his back against the wall

A sudden dread overwhelmed her. What if the killer was still there? She turned and stared at the landing, and at the steps that led down to the lower floor. And what of his records, his computer? If he had been killed by the Chinese, they would surely search the house, and if they did they would find out about her.

She ran. She ran along the landing, pushing open each door, finding only his study, an empty bedroom and a bathroom. She ignored the empty bedroom and scoured the study and the bathroom, tipping out drawers and cupboards, spilling shampoo, conditioner, soap, documents, toothpaste, correspondence and toothbrush into the sink, bathtub and over the floor. She went through the medicine cabinet, sweeping the contents onto the floor. She found nothing, not knowing what she was looking for.

She clattered down the stairs and went through the living room and the kitchen, again tipping the contents of drawers onto the floor, weeping as over and again she found nothing. The desperation and the hopelessness of her task took hold of her.

She ran from the living room back to the kitchen and grabbed a kitchen knife. She slashed and tore at cushions, ripped open the upholstery of the chairs and the sofa. Back in the kitchen she threw the cutlery on the floor, pulled the pots and pans from the cupboards, wiping her tearful eyes and her running nose with the back of her wrist as she went.

Two and two made four. If they had killed Ed, and if they had found whatever information he had, then they would come looking for her and they would kill her too. She sat on the kitchen floor and tried to center her mind. She must escape from Manila. She must get out of the Philippines, but they would have every point of exit on high alert for anyone named in his records. And she knew beyond a shadow of a doubt that she was named in his records. He was too fastidious, too persnickety, far too precise and meticulous. Surely he must have had a computer, or a little black book, something.

And equally as surely, his killer must have found it, because it was not here.

She knew what the Filipino police were like. She knew what they would do to a girl like her in prison. If, that was, she was lucky enough to get arrested by the Filipino police and tried. Far more likely, they would hand her over to the Chinese, who would torture her for information and then hand her back to the Filipinos, who would label her a drug trafficker, take her to some back alley in Six Forty-Nine, or Addition Hills, and shoot her dead. She thought of her mother and her father, sitting in their cozy living room in Surrey, watching the news, seeing their daughter, shot dead as a drug dealer. She began to weep in violent, noisy spasms of grief.

She stared at the knife lying beside her on the floor. Its handle looked long and black, the blade long, slim and cold. She heard the ugly, wet noise of her sobbing slowly subside. She wiped her face on her sleeve, then went around the house trying to remember what she had touched, and wiping her prints off. Then she climbed the stairs again to the small room Ed had used as his office. The floor was strewn with papers, paperclips, paperweights and files.

She went through them again, carefully this time, until she found what she had been looking for, his passport, which had been in a drawer she had dumped on the floor, and a Manila envelope she had discarded earlier in despair. She had discarded it before because she had not bothered to look at it. What she had been looking for was information, and the plain envelope, at a glance, offered her none.

But now, with her mind chilled by the certainty of

death, she recalled that the envelope had contained something. She recalled the pressure on her fingers and the flash of a scrawl on the front.

She picked it up and saw, as she examined it, that the scrawl she had seen before and ignored was in fact her name written across the front. This was the envelope—the money—he had been going to give her that very day at the museum, but they had killed him before he could deliver.

She looked inside. There was ten thousand dollars in cash. Nothing else. She had hoped for more, had needed more, desperately, and she needed documents, but now this would have to do.

She went then to his bedroom and found a shirt, which was much too big for her, and a Panama hat. She pulled the shirt on over her own blouse, rolled up the sleeves and stuffed the tails into her jeans, trying to make it as inconspicuous as possible. She put the hat on her head, though it too was a couple of sizes too big, and with her sunglasses on, even if somebody suspected she was trying to hide her identity, she figured the important thing was that she would not be recognizable.

She hurried downstairs, opened the door, stepped out into the small front yard and closed the door behind her. Then she stepped out onto Santo Nino. A quick glance told her the street was pretty much empty. Some distance away there was a man leaning into a Mercedes. She noted the diplomatic plates, crossed the road to the far side, put her head down and started walking fast away from the Mercedes, toward Maysilo Circus. Once, as she reached the corner of the street, she turned back to look and saw the man in the cream suit pushing into Ed's front yard.

She made the corner and ran. She ran down San

Francisco, tearing off her hat and her borrowed shirt as she went. She dumped them behind the orange, steel door of a car wash and kept running until she spotted a Jeepney. She flagged it down, not knowing or caring where it was headed.

    She paid the driver, then found a space to sit and fell into deep thought. Now panic vied with a kind of raw excitement. If she could pull it off, if she could disappear, convince them she was dead. But how? She had to think through each step with great care, but she was too excited, too afraid. She needed to go somewhere and be quiet, somewhere peaceful where she could calm down and think through the steps she needed to take.

    At first her mind turned to parks, gardens, even hotels. But then an image came to her. A coastal town, a remote fishing village where she had gone with friends a couple of years earlier. They had spent a couple of weeks there and it had been paradise. No tourists, kind villagers who had looked after them, fresh vegetables, fruit and fish every day. She smiled at the memory. She reached for the name and, as always, it came to her crystal clear.

    Nayon ng Pangingisda. It was a long way, on the southernmost extreme of the island of Mindanao, six or seven hundred miles away as the crow flies. But it could be done. When they had gone before they had rented a car and taken the ferry. She could not rent a car now, but she could take the coach. It would take a couple of days, maybe a little more, but it would be the last place they would think of looking for her.

    And once there?

    The first green shoots of a plan began to spring out of her dark unconscious. She wanted to go north, back to England, but what if she went south? How could she do that?

She saw suddenly that they were crossing the Pasig River toward the Makati business district. With a stab of excitement she told the driver to let her off at Makati Avenue and there, among the well-tended gardens, the clean streets and the tall towers of steel and glass, she hailed a cab and told the driver to take her to the Philtranco Pasay Bus Terminal on Aurora Boulevard.

Five minutes later she paid off the cabby with a ten-dollar bill and ran into the terminal building. Among the white tiled floors, the plastic benches and fast-food stands she found a currency exchange machine, changed five hundred bucks and joined the line for the ticket windows. In front of her were a young Filipino couple, a middle-aged woman and then a big man who spoke through the window with an American accent. He asked for a ticket to Mabalacat and she felt a sense of relief that he would not be on the coach with her. Mabalacat was in the north.

Two policemen walked by and paused to look at the line, one person at a time. It seemed to her they looked at her a little longer than at the rest, and for one terrifying second she thought they were going to talk to her. But they muttered something to each other and moved on.

The American turned and walked away from the ticket booth toward the coaches, and she averted her face so he would not see her or remember her if he was later shown photographs.

A moment after that she was at the window herself. The attendant, a sour-faced woman with glasses, jerked her chin at her. "Where?"

She would remember her. She suddenly felt that as a certainty, but decided it did not matter.

"Nayon ng Pangingisda," she said, "on Mindanao. When is the next bus?"

The woman gave her the ticket and took the money. "Next on at two twenty."

She looked at her watch. She had a little less than an hour to buy some basics like toothpaste and a toothbrush, a rucksack and a change of clothes and underwear, but first she needed to eat something.

She stepped out onto the Pan Philippine Highway and ran across the road toward the Metro Point Mall on the corner of Taft Avenue, three hundred yards down the road. As she ran she heard a bike misfire behind her and stopped at the partition in the middle of the road to look back. She saw people running and screaming in all directions, and she saw a vaguely familiar-looking man lying facedown on the sidewalk.

Hot, sick nausea turned her stomach. She vaulted the central reservation and made for the shopping mall at a sprint. Behind her the man lay, seeing the concrete before his eyes in minute detail. He was aware his life was fading, and he longed to see his children and his wife before he died. He wondered if sheer willpower might make that happen. The last thing he ever heard was the rattle of his own breath, and then there was nothing.

CHAPTER SEVEN

Jay Hoffstadder hung up from talking to his wife and immediately went to settings on his phone and disabled the GPS. Then he stood and crossed his office to an oak cabinet that stood against the far wall. He hunkered down to open it and revealed the blued steel door of a safe. He spun the dials six times, this way and that, and pulled open the door.

From inside he removed a sports bag which he opened to check the contents. A pair of jeans, Timberland boots, a sweatshirt with the Harvard logo on the front, a pair of heavy, dark sunglasses and a Red Sox baseball cap. There was also a passport and a driver's license in the name of John Jones, an attorney from Washington, DC. There was a wallet, too, with a credit card and enough cash to get him to the States.

At the bottom of the bag was a tablet also registered in the name of John Jones. From it he booked a flight for the following day from Clark International Airport to Dubai with Emirates. Clark was between Angeles and Mabalacat on the Luzon Expressway.

His intention was to book a rail ticket north as far as Baguio, and jump the train at Mabalacat City. For some reason he had assumed that by the time this became necessary, the Philippines would already have a functioning railway system. No such rail system yet existed. So much for plans.

His options were now to take some form of public transport as far as Santa Maria or Guiguinto in the north of the city, and then hire a driver to take him the rest of the way, or to play tourist and get a bus to Clark.

Time was not of the essence, exactly, but he didn't have enough to waste, either, so he opted for the latter.

He stepped out of his office with his bag and paused at May's desk.

"What have I got for this afternoon, May?"

She consulted her diary. "*Terra Nullius and the Jurisdiction of the ICJ*, at four o'clock."

"Four o'clock? He pretended to think. "OK, I'll be back by then, but if there is no sign of me by three thirty, have Greg Newman stand in. He's up to speed. But I'm pretty sure I'll be back."

May tilted her head as she did when she thought Dr. Hoffstadder was misbehaving.

"Problem?" she said.

"The kids have the dentist, and Elizabeth hates it. She won't go in unless Daddy is with her."

May smiled. "Of course not. She's gotta have her daddy."

He left and as he trotted down the stairs he wondered if she'd believed him. He thought she probably had. He and Gloria had become a fixture in Filipino society and were liked and well respected. But sometimes it was so hard to tell what went on behind those smiles. Even though he thought she probably did, he had to assume she did not. He had to assume she was reporting back to somebody. It was probably a huge injustice to a woman who was likely a loyal, decent employee. But that was the ugly nature of the game. To be safe, he had to assume she was a spy.

He climbed into his dark blue Audi and nosed out of the gate, but instead of doing the obvious and turning right and south, he turned left and north, headed toward Congressional Avenue and Quezon City. There, at the Tangdang Sora Flyover, he turned left onto the Don Mariano Marcos Avenue, southbound, toward the Quezon City Circle, but he came off the avenue at McDonald's and started a series of elaborate, convoluted circles and figures of eight that took him through what should have been pleasant, middle-class suburbs but were instead overcrowded, shambolic acres of rusting corrugated roofs, lots invaded and overgrown with palms and banana trees, vines and rubber plants; and the eternal, ubiquitous overhead cables that always managed somehow to darken the sky.

All the while he had one eye on his rearview mirror, seeking for that car or that license plate that was seen once too often. Either he was not being followed, which he doubted, he had shaken his tail, or his tails were very good and taking a lot of trouble not to be seen.

He came to Project 6 and drove past the Starving Sam restaurant. It was a place he knew Ed had frequented, and he felt a twist of inarticulate anxiety in his belly.

Finally he took Quezon Avenue and España Boulevard in a straight run and turned into the Isetann shopping mall's underground parking garage. He went down to the bottom level, keeping his eye on his mirror all the way, plunging deeper and deeper, with the squeal of his tires echoing through the cavernous bowels of the building, waiting for the twin headlamps to show behind him. They didn't and he felt a burning of hope in his belly.

He climbed out into the gloom, locked the car and ran for the elevators. Up in the mall, in the bright glare of the neon lights and the cream-tiled floors, he dropped his keys into a trash can and went directly to the public toilets. There he changed his clothes: pulled on the jeans and the sweatshirt, the Timberland boots, the baseball cap and the dark glasses. From the side pocket of the sports bag he extracted an actor's stick-on moustache and stuck it to his upper lip. Then he folded up the sports bag, opened the cistern behind the lavatory bowl and pressed the bag in and replaced the lid.

Finally he slipped out and, trying to affect an ambling shuffle—a manner of walking he despised—he went through the mall and out to the sidewalk, where the sun was brilliant, the sidewalks were teeming, the dense traffic was honking and the smell of hot asphalt and carbon monoxide was rich in the air.

He hailed a cab and as he climbed in the back he said, "The Philtranco Pasay Bus Terminal, please."

The driver smiled too much and was too chatty, but Hoffstadder decided to go with the flow and relaxed back in the seat, smiling.

"Going somewhere nice?"

"Yeah, been a couple of days in Manila, now I want to see the north of the island, you know? Baguio, Laoag City, I heard Ballesteros and Aparri are cool."

The driver agreed enthusiastically, he had a cousin up there, or it might have been a brother-in-law. Hoffstadder kept his eyes on the traffic behind, but still saw nothing and began to wonder if he was going to get away with it. He had had a fatalistic feeling from the start that if this day ever came, he had to ensure that Gloria and the kids should get away, though he had resigned himself that he wouldn't. The people he was up against were just too good and too ruthless.

He paid off the cabby, who cheerfully wished him good fortune, and made his way into the echoing, white-tiled coach station. He joined the line for the tickets and wondered where Gloria was at that moment. He prayed that she was thirty-five thousand feet up in the air, headed for home.

He was aware of people joining the line behind him and fought the impulse to look back, but a voice, quiet, somehow almost reptilian, spoke at his shoulder: "Dr. Hoffstadder."

It was peremptory, authoritative, and his reaction was instinctive. He jumped and turned and stared into a face that was smiling at him. The smile was not a happy one, or pleasantly surprised. The smile was cruel to the point of being evil. The owner of the smile was tall, maybe six-six or more, Chinese, dressed in a well-cut sky-blue suit. After a second Hoffstadder said, "I'm sorry, you startled me. I'm afraid you have me confused with somebody else. My name is Jones." He added a self-deprecating laugh. "And I am not a doctor."

The Chinese man smiled some more and shook his head. "No need to apologize, Mr. Jones. I am sorry I scared you."

A window had become free and he approached it. He spoke quietly to the bespectacled woman at the desk, having to repeat twice what he wanted. The woman's glasses flashed angrily. "Speak louder, please!"

"One way to Mabalacat."

She gave him the ticket and he paid. When he

turned to leave he saw with relief that the tall Chinese had left. He absently noticed a shabby foreign girl who had been just behind him in the line and made his way outside.

The traffic was noisy and the day was hot; he had some time to kill and was thinking about finding some food and a cold beer. He didn't fancy the fast-food joint on the corner, but knew there was a mall on the far side of the road, about two minutes' walk south. He headed for the covered walkway that spanned the avenue thirty paces away, and noticed that the girl he'd seen in the line, behind him, was attempting to cross the same avenue by dodging through the traffic. There was a central reservation she would have to vault. It was a dangerous game for younger people. He hoped she made it without getting run down.

He turned and started to walk, and at that moment he heard a shout behind him, "*Dr. Hoffstadder! Dr. Hoffstadder!*"

This time he was ready and he did not react, but kept walking. Then he heard the loud, flat crack, then another, and then the screams. He turned.

A small group of people near the body scrambled, shouting and screaming, but most skirted the scene with indifference and went about their business, either unaware or uninterested.

The tall, broad Chinese holstered his weapon, walked up to the prone figure and rolled him on his back. It was not Hoffstadder. It was protocol, so he removed his cell from his pocket, took a photograph and sent it back to the office for confirmation. But this man, though he had a passing resemblance to the heavy, swarthy Hoffstadder, was Filipino.

However—Zimo scratched his chin—given the fact that he was not Hoffstadder, his reaction when Zimo had called out Dr. Hoffstadder's name was surprising. On the face of it, it was hard to explain. Zimo thought back, replaying the scene in his mind: He had heard the shout, "*Dr. Hoffstadder!*" and he had turned, startled, even shocked, and he had stared, scanning the crowd, searching for the caller.

Zimo searched the dead man's pockets, aware that the police would soon show up, but not caring much. He found, in the breast pocket, a US passport and driver's license in the name of John Cardenas. In the opposite pocket he found a wallet containing ten thousand dollars. Standard urban escape pack. Change identity and head for the nearest moderately safe international airport, by the most inconspicuous means possible.

He thought back to the short list he had been provided with. This man must be Juan Carmona, one of the four people Baccay had recently observed associating with Edward Hampton. He had done precisely what Zimo had expected Hoffstadder to do: change his identity and take a bus north to Clark International.

He smiled the way a gecko might smile at a fly. Perhaps in any other city, in any other country, it might have been easier to get away. But in Manila they were being funneled into his hands. The rail system in the Philippines was virtually nonexistent, which confined long-range travel within the island of Luzon to either car, plane or coach. Movement by plane was out of the question—they were far too easy to watch. Cars—especially hired cars—were moving death traps. License plates made them easy to identify, roadblocks made them easy to intercept, and they were not even bulletproof.

So the only realistic option was the bus, and Zimo was confident that sooner or later all four of them would pass either through this coach station, or another. It didn't matter which, he had them all covered.

He slipped a small sachet of cocaine into the corpse's pocket and stood as his cell rang.

"Yes?"

"This is Mr. Wang. The man you killed was Juan Carmona, employed at the Department of Foreign Affairs. He was number three on the list. He had several meetings with Hampton. What about Hoffstadder?"

"I haven't seen him yet. A couple of lookalikes, nothing more."

"What about the girl?"

"I have told you already, I need more information on the girl. You probably haven't noticed, Mr. Wang, but this town is full of girls. You need to talk to Baccay again and get more details. There was a girl waiting to buy a ticket, but she was a tourist and traveling south. Our woman is a resident and will be traveling north."

Wang ignored the implied slur on his sexuality. It was the kind of insolence you expected from agents of the MSS, or *Guanbu*, particularly the department known as *Táotài bù*, who made a profession out of killing. He asked, "And Marcos?"

"No sign of him yet. He will be lying low for a while, but I will find him. What about the laptop?"

"We have our best man on it. He is suitably motivated. He will crack it soon."

Zimo grunted. "Soon may not be soon enough."

From the covered walkway that spanned the avenue, Hoffstadder stood and watched the scene. He watched the two patrol cars arrive, followed by an ambulance and a crime scene van. He saw Inspector Gerardo Baccay approach the tall Chinese guy in the sky-blue suit, and he saw the latter dismiss the forensic team. There was nothing he wanted them to learn there. He knew who the killer was. He knew already who had means, motive and opportunity.

He watched Zimo hunker down and reach inside Juan Carmona's pocket. He saw Baccay hunker down beside him and receive something in his hand. Hoffstadder didn't need to see it to know what it was. It was dope, most probably heroin or cocaine, planted to justify the killing.

First Ed, now Juan.

He felt somebody tugging at his arm and turned. Gradually he became aware, among the jostling stream of humanity that swarmed in both directions through the grimy walkway, that this terrible, filthy place was a home. It was a home to a family of Filipinos who sat and slept on the floor, among cloth tenders where they laid out the wares they sold—sandals, sneakers, socks, sunglasses, hair bands—he stared uncomprehending into the face of a young Filipino and noticed absently that he had four teeth missing. The Filipino was telling him, "We got nice sock for hiking. You walk lots you need good sock."

But Ed was dead, and now so was Juan Carmona. How many more, he wondered, of those he'd never met? All of them? The whole cell? Was he the only one left?

On the parapet across the walkway the man's wife or mother or aunt or sister was lying sleeping, inches from death but apparently unconcerned. Seated against the same wall was a man in rust-colored shorts and a yellow vest, and beside him a skinny child sitting on the filthy floor, eating a scrap of bread. They all watched him with curiosity, but an absence of interest.

"I'm sorry," he said, as though they might care, "I have to go home," and then, absurdly, "My wife is expecting me."

He ran away from the family who lived in the covered walkway and slept inches from death, pushed and shouldered his way through the streaming torrent of humanity, down the steps to the street, and ran.

CHAPTER EIGHT

I turned away from the Merc and made my way back down Nino toward Edward Hampton's green and white house. There was an oddly dressed young woman on the far side of the street in a Panama hat and a shirt that were both several sizes too big for her. She looked strange and for a moment I was about to cross the road and talk to her, but I was keen to see the house so I let it pass.

I found the gate closed but unlocked. As I pushed it open some instinct or intuition told me I was going to find Dr. Edward Ulysses Hampton dead. From what I had heard and read about the man, he was not the type to leave his gate open.

I frowned as I climbed the stairs and reached the door. The door was closed. The gate was open but the door was closed. I wasn't sure what it meant, but I knew it meant something. It was an inconsistency, and inconsistencies could tell you a lot. Like the fact that there might well be fingerprints on the door handle, prints belonging to the person who closed the door.

The image of the girl in the big hat and the shirt came into my mind, but it was too late now to go after her. I pulled my Swiss Army knife from my pocket, selected the awl and then removed the toothpick. I slipped the awl into the lock and fiddled around with the toothpick till I heard the click, then gently pushed the door open.

Inside I noted that the alarm was dead. There didn't seem to be any damage to it, so I figured his killer had disabled it from outside, or remotely. I pushed the door closed again and stood listening to the house. It was silent. Very still.

But one small sound scratched at the back of my hearing. It was coming from the back of the house, I figured it was coming from the kitchen and moved down the hall. I stopped dead as I went through the door. It was like a gang of bikers on speed had played a rugby match in there. All the cutlery had been strewn on the floor and half the drawers had been dropped on top of it. The contents of the cupboards had followed. There were two burst bags of flour, sugar, salt, tins of tomatoes, various vegetables.

I picked my way across to the kitchen door which led out onto a backyard which was in fact more of a garden, overgrown with tall grass, rubber trees and various types of palms.

There was a cat, small, smoky gray, sitting on the doorstep looking up at me.

"I guess you're hungry, huh?"

I fished through the mess till I found his bowls, filled one with water and the other with dry biscuits, then set them down outside.

The kitchen had little to tell me other than that somebody who was out of control had been looking for something there. Without a forensic team, there wasn't much hope of finding out who.

So I made my way to the living room. Here there

was more of the same, only more so. The furniture had been ripped to shreds, all the upholstery had been disemboweled, every drawer and every cupboard had been opened and emptied.

There was one small, bald patch where whoever had done this had sat to tear open the chairs and the sofa, and all the cushions, and right beside it was a kitchen knife with a large, silver blade and a black handle. I hunkered down to look at it. It was a Sabatier. I took a handkerchief from my pocket and picked up the knife by the blade, then took it to the kitchen in search of a plastic bag.

I found a grocery bag and carefully wrapped the knife in it. Then returned to the living room for another look. It kept nagging at my mind that the only thing I could reconstruct from what I was seeing was an attack of rage or panic. But whose, or motivated by what, was impossible to say.

I climbed the stairs, pretty sure of what I was going to find up there, and I was not wrong. It was impossible to miss—aside from the fact that the door was open, there was the smell, sickly sweet and slightly cloying.

He had been shot in the chest at fairly close range, though not point-blank. There was no singeing on his shirt. By the position of the body I figured he had been between the shooter and the door, so the shooter came in first. He'd waited till Ed was out, disabled the alarm, then went upstairs to wait for him. It made me wonder why Ed hadn't noticed the alarm was disabled. He was cautious, with huge attention to detail.

Whatever the reason, he had climbed the stairs and walked into the bedroom. And the killer had hit him from across the room. I hunkered down beside him. There were already flies on the wound, and the blood was caked and dry. That didn't tell you much. Time of death is pretty much impossible to establish at the best of times. It did tell me that the three shots were tightly grouped. The shooter wasn't shaking. He was cool and focused. Not a man, or a woman, for that matter, who was about to tear a house apart searching for something. Besides—I stood and sighed—if the killer had been that desperate to find something in the house, he would have shot Ed in the knee, not in the chest.

The killer had not ransacked the house. He had found what he came looking for, Ed. If he'd wanted something else he would have asked before killing him.

I stood staring at the wardrobe. The bedroom was the only room that had not been ransacked—further evidence of panic—but the wardrobe was open and the shirts had been disturbed. One of the hangers, bare, had hooked inside one of the shirts, as though something had been yanked from it in a hurry, and it had swung back at an angle. Something like a shirt three sizes too large for a small woman.

I cursed myself quietly for ignoring my own instincts and moved down the landing to his office. It too had been ransacked, like the rest of the house. I went to the chair and sat, observing the room and making movies in my head.

The killer had arrived, disabled the alarm, maybe reconnected it when he was inside. Then he had gone upstairs to the bedroom and waited for Ed to arrive. Ed had duly arrived and proceeded to the kitchen, put away his groceries and then come upstairs to the bedroom. On going inside he had been shot, three times, in the chest and collapsed into a sitting position against the wall.

The killer had then left, disabling the alarm again

to avoid triggering it when he left. Had he taken anything with him? Possibly. Later, in fact just a little while ago, a woman had come looking for Ed. She had wanted something from him, but she had found the doors open and him dead. She had gone frantic searching for whatever it was she needed. Had she found it? Impossible to know, but the frantic nature of the search suggested she hadn't —so maybe the killer took it with him.

My working theory: what she was looking for was some kind of a list, a list of the members of Ed's cell, a list on which she figured. And the evidence suggested that Zimo Chew, the dangerous dude, had taken that list with him.

Maybe.

As I was thinking I was allowing my eyes to travel across the room, picking things out at random. Now they found a Manila envelope with a name scrawled on it. The name was Marion. I stood and went to pick it up, with great care, using a handkerchief. Not many people realize it, but paper is one of the best surfaces for extracting fingerprints. And my gut told me that Marion had just left a fine pair when she collected whatever it was Ed had wanted to give her before he was killed. My money was on a false ID and a few grand in US dollars. The urban survival kit.

This kid was no pro, or she would not have panicked and she would not have left the envelope behind. The fact that she did told me more than the simple fact that she was an amateur and scared out of her mind. It told me also that she believed she was on a hit list—or if she wasn't already, she would be soon. Ed had not been tortured or interrogated. So either they had the information they wanted, or they had his "little black book"—or the laptop computer which was so conspicuously absent from the house—and she was in it.

So, if I was going to find out what Ed had done to incur the wrath of the dragon, I needed to find Marion before the dragon did.

I took my two bits of evidence back to the kitchen and found a second plastic bag for the envelope. I bundled them together in a third bag and left the house very quietly. I made my way to the Toyota, set my phone in its nest, dropped the evidence on the seat beside me and called Paul Hoffmann at the embassy.

"Alex, how can I help you?"

I fired up the truck and moved away from the house. "I thought you'd like to know I just went to visit an old friend."

There was a moment's silence. "Really? Was he at home?"

"Well, I guess that depends on your views regarding the nature of the human soul. Let's just say he was physically present, but otherwise very absent."

I was trying to talk without using buzzwords.

"Well, I guess that comes as no great surprise."

"Right. What did come as a surprise was the state of the house. A real mess. Everything upside down. Very unlike him, wouldn't you say?"

"Completely. You think he was burgled?"

I turned onto Boni Avenue, taking it real easy while I thought.

"We should meet. I picked up a couple of things that might be of interest to a..." I thought for a moment and came up with, "A forensic archeologist, let's say. There is an ancient cutting tool and I am sure the palm prints would be fascinating to anyone interested in the, um, the end of the Edwardian age."

"Do you have children, Alex?"

"No, children tend to point and scream when they see me. Why?"

"Fathers tend to develop awful punning when they try to make their young kids laugh." I chuckled. He added, "We're on a secure line. You can speak plainly."

"Point taken. OK, so, Ed was shot. He's at his house now. Looks like a professional execution. There was a knife on the living-room floor, and there was an envelope on the office floor. I think the prints on those would be very useful."

"You think they belong to his killer?"

"No, I'm pretty sure they don't. But they belong to somebody I need to find before the Chinese do."

"OK, we can do that. You willing to share?"

"I'll scratch your back if you scratch mine."

"That's good news. Drop the stuff at the embassy and I'll get our team on it straight away."

"You have access to Five Eyes databases, right?"

"Of course. Just identify yourself and drop it off at the gate. There'll be a lieutenant there waiting."

"OK, Paul, I owe you. Listen, one more thing."

"Sure."

"It might be an idea to get a cleanup team in there before the cops or the Chinese do."

Sure, we can see to that."

"Also, there's a cat who needs rescuing."

"I'll take him home for the kids."

So I swung by Roxas Boulevard, gave my parcel to a Marine lieutenant at the gate, received a receipt and took it back to my hotel with me. By the time I got up to my room it was late afternoon and I was in need of a shower, a couple of stiff martinis and a slab of singed meat. So I stepped in the shower for fifteen minutes, shaved, smacked painful aftershave on my face (the kind men use) and pulled on a Savile Row evening suit, tied a not-quite-perfect silk bow and headed for the Peak Grill, where, I had been told by the concierge, they would have everything I wanted. He didn't say it, but his eyes suggested I might find a little more than I was bargaining for.

He wasn't wrong. Five-star hotel concierges are very rarely wrong.

When I arrived, the sun was just losing its grip on things and casting a burnt, rusty glow behind the steel and glass towers of the city, igniting the windows with apocalyptic fire and dirty red smoke. I leaned on the bar and told the barman I needed a Vesper Martini.

He was a big Australian in a burgundy waistcoat and he smiled at the reference.

"You know that's impossible, sir. They just don't make the ingredients anymore. But I can get as near as dammit."

"Give it a try, just make sure you don't stir it."

He laughed. "Like I'd dare!"

While he mixed the ingredients over crushed ice and shook them, I put together the ingredients of the day in my mind and wondered what kind of cocktail they made. I had very few facts. Edward Hampton had been shot at comparatively close quarters by somebody whose hand didn't shake. Somebody had torn his house apart. Somebody had left a knife on the living-room floor. Somebody had taken the contents of an envelope addressed to Marion.

On the other hand, as Heisenberg and his pals in Denmark were always trying to make Einstein and Schrödinger understand, you cannot divide the observer from what he observes. They are part of one and the same thing. So there were more facts than those. There was the fact that Zimo Chew, aka Ren the Person, had taken the trouble to warn me to leave Manila and not to investigate Hampton's disappearance. There was the associated fact that Zimo Chew was known to work for the *Táotài bù* section of the Ministry of State Security, as a hired assassin.

So far as those facts went, they suggested that Marion had stumbled on information that was of extreme value and had passed it to Hampton, making herself in the process a prime target. Perhaps she had been careless and had got found out. As a consequence Hanson was killed and she had run. That was speculation, though.

As far as the rest of Hanson's cell was concerned, I still had to talk to Hoffstadder, Juan Carmona, who worked for the Philippine Office of Foreign Affairs, and Dr. Felix Marcos, head of the new department of Viral Cybernetics at the University of the Philippines. It was a fair guess that, unless their positions were very secure, they would all have gone to ground by now too.

The Ozzie kid had finished mixing the drink and poured it into a glass for me. "Shaken, not stirred," he said, gilding the lily.

I took it and sipped, and sensed a sinuous yet soft presence beside me. I turned to look and saw an exquisite woman in a red velvet cocktail dress climbing onto a stool beside me. She had eyes the color of sinfully dark chocolate, hair as black as sin pulled up into a bun, tanned skin which was taut over a completely immoral neck, and shoulders and curves that were to chastity what bacon is to vegetarians.

    She used full red lips and very white teeth to fog my mind with a smile. "Sparkling water," she told the bartender with a vaguely East Coast accent that didn't quite fit anywhere. Then she said to me, "Mind if I join you?"

CHAPTER NINE

I took another sip of my martini and set it down carefully on the bar.

"Is this the bit where I say, 'Not at all,' and you pull off your wig and take out your teeth?"

She gave a small frown which failed to wrinkle her brow. "Sorry, I don't follow."

I leaned one elbow on the bar and returned the frown. "I apologize. I was being facetious. That's probably something you never do."

"Not if I can avoid it. It's frowned upon at finishing school."

"Perhaps they should have sent me to finishing school. My name is Mason, Alex Mason."

There was more humor in her eyes than her lips. "If we were allowed to I'd take your hand."

"What would you do with it when you had it?"

She arched an elegant eyebrow. "Why, shake it and say, 'How do you do?' of course. My name is Aila."

"Aila?"

"Captain, Captain Aila Gallin."

"Captain..." It wasn't exactly a question, but it begged an answer.

"IDF Infantry, then field intelligence."

I nodded. "And now Mossad."

Her smile was a little warmer this time. "Not exactly worthy of Holmes. I think Dr. Watson might have got that one."

"So I guess you didn't join me because of my chiseled good looks and my debonair air of savoir-faire."

She managed to hood her eyes, raise an eyebrow and produce a lopsided smile all at the same time. "That's a lot of air," she said, "and most of it's hot. You want to get a table?"

I nodded. "Sure."

We carried our drinks over to a quiet table with a vast, sweeping view of Manila sinking into a smoggy darkness perforated by a million tiny dots of light.

Gallin coiled herself into a gray upholstered chair and I sat opposite, trying to visualize her delivering a straight lead and a side kick, with camouflage paint on her face. It wasn't easy. Before I could say anything she went straight to the point.

"Let's not waste time, Mason. Let me tell you why I am here."

"What, no small talk? You don't want to talk about the weather? I believe New York is lovely this time of year."

She remained expressionless until I had finished, then said, "Done?"

I shrugged and spread my hands. "Shoot."

"I don't have to tell you that the United States is our closest ally."

"Agreed."

"But even with close allies you don't always share everything." She gestured at me. "You yourself, in your conversations with the Agency, are not sharing everything, nor are they being fully open with you, and you're not even allies—you're the same country."

"What's your point?"

"My point is that Mossad and ODIN have not always had the most cooperative relationship—"

"Odin? Isn't he some Norse god or something?"

She sighed and pulled her cell from her purse. "Odin One Eye," she said as she dialed. "The god of war and magic."

She didn't hold the cell to her ear, but stared down at it. After a moment she said, "Good evening, Nero, how are you? Alex would like a word with you."

She handed over the phone and there was the Chief's fat face filling the screen. He had a linen napkin hanging from his shirt collar and he was eating oysters. I didn't say anything.

"Good evening, Alex. This is Captain Aila Gallin. Be cooperative. I have spoken to her superiors and we have a shared interest."

"*Bon appétit.*"

"*Faut-il toujours être facétieux?* Stop wasting time and talk to Captain Gallin."

"What did he say?" she asked, but I knew she had heard.

"He asked if I always had to be so damned facetious."

Her face was about as expressive as white noise. "That is a subject I am afraid I am not interested in. Can we get down to business now?"

"Go ahead. You came to see me. How can I help you?"

"We need to find Dr. Edward Ulysses Hampton, and we understand you are looking for him too."

"Is that so? And why do you need to find Ed?"

"How does that concern you?"

"That," I picked up my drink and smiled at her, "is exactly what I am asking you." She remained expressionless. Presumably she was thinking. I sipped and said, "It seems to me you want us to cooperate with you, just so long as you don't have to cooperate with us."

"That's not it."

"What is 'it,' then?" She hesitated and I snapped, "Cut the crap, Gallin, I know as much about you as you know about me. We're both under orders and our orders are to cooperate, but I'll be damned if I am going do all the cooperating while you flash your big brown eyes at me and tell me how interesting you are. This works both ways or it doesn't work at all."

She arched an eyebrow. "You're not always facetious, then."

"Right now you're the one being facetious and wasting time. What is Mossad's interest in Dr. Hampton?"

"OK, a couple of years ago the Chinese government started investing discretely in the University of the Philippines. It started with small amounts by anonymous donors. Then modest amounts to fund cooperative research into fairly uncontroversial subjects. Fairly soon the steady trickle of Chinese money had grown and become something the university pretty much depended on, and the Chinese had become donors the university, and the government, were loath to upset or offend."

I picked the olive out of my martini and put it in my mouth. "Don't tell me, that's when the real investment started."

"Correct. It was an offer they could not refuse. A whole new department for a whole new area of research."

I raised a finger and frowned. "The Department of Viral Cybernetics, headed by Dr. Felix Marcos."

"Very good, Dr. Watson."

I made a face of dubiousness. "The Chinese have been leading the way in cyber warfare and computer viruses for a long time. The fact they have opened up a faculty specializing in that, here in the Philippines, is not of itself remarkable. It allows them to tap into Western talent in a way they could not back in China."

"You asked me a question. Are you going to let me finish my answer or are you going to try to answer it yourself?"

"Are you a vegan?"

She frowned. "Good god, no!"

"Good, let's eat." I signaled the waiter and he brought over two menus and I told him to bring two martinis. When he'd gone she went on.

"We were very interested in the new university department, not least because there are a lot of Muslims in the Philippines who might well end up studying at that college. They could well end up being enemies of Israel, too." She paused. "And of the United States."

"I get that. So you kept an eye on Dr. Felix Marcos and found that he had occasional, discrete contact with Hampton."

"You're doing it again."

"Sorry, but am I right?"

"We noticed Marcos and Hampton were in bed together, but we also noticed something else. The department seemed to be about forty percent richer than it ought to be."

"What does that mean?"

"It means that China committed X amount of money to the department and the Philippine government committed Y amount—perhaps ten percent of the total budget, but the two together only made up about sixty percent of the department's actual annual expenditure. So forty percent of the money they spent was coming from where?"

"Loans?"

"Obviously that was the first thing we thought of, and it was not loans. So our forensic accountants started to dig and we found that the money was coming from—"

"The Middle East, Saudi, accounts associated with jihadist organizations."

She gave her head a little shake. "You know, that's not impressive if you leave it to the very last minute, when the answer has already become obvious."

She graced the comment with a small smile.

"It's a bad habit, I know. But let me indulge it just a little more. You are concerned that China and Al-Qaeda, and/or other jihadist groups may be collaborating on a cyber-terror attack, which may be being developed here at the University of the Philippines."

"It's not an unreasonable concern."

"It's not an unreasonable concern at all. But does Dr. Felix Marcos have any ties with Islam or anti-American groups?"

She shook her head. "No, but whom does he have working under him?"

I echoed her head-shaking. "I don't know."

"But I do. Of his six project leaders, three are Muslims, two from Saudi and one from Egypt. The other three are Chinese. All six were selected by the Chinese. Felix Marcos had no say in the matter at all."

"Sounds like he could be an interesting man to talk to."

She nodded. "He could be. Let's just hope he's not dead by tomorrow, like Juan Carmona." She smiled and picked up the menu. "Are you going to tell me where, when and how he was killed?"

I blinked at her a moment. "No. I am going to choose a steak."

She spoke to the menu. "I'm sharing and being cooperative, right? Carmona was shot outside the Philtranco Pasay Bus Terminal shortly after midday. It's not clear whether he was trying to board a bus or if he just happened to be there for some other reason. The police say he was there to do a drug deal. They claim he had cocaine on him, he tried to resist arrest and he was shot. They'll keep it muddled for a while and hope it blows over."

"You're saying he was assassinated by the Chinese?"

"We don't know, do we? But he was one of four people known to associate with Hampton, and probably constituted part of his cell. Am I right?"

"You're right. He worked for the Department of Foreign Affairs. It's speculation, but maybe he had knowledge of an arrangement with China."

She shrugged. "Possibly, but like you say, right now it's speculation."

"You got this from Inspector Baccay?"

"He is the universal source. He has made himself invaluable to the West and to the Chinese. We all know we can't trust him one hundred percent, but we also know eighty to ninety percent of what he tells us checks out."

"So that leaves Felix Marcos, at the Viral Cybernetics Faculty, Dr. Jay Hoffstadder at the International Law Department and, possibly, Marion James, scruffy foreign dropout."

She glanced at me over her menu. "And Edward Hampton."

I grunted and picked up my menu. After a moment she said, "I am a great believer in getting to the point, Mason. You know you want a sirloin steak, singed on the outside and raw on the inside. You are not particularly bothered what it comes with, beside the robust Burgundy, but you'd like something from the sea first to open your appetite; perhaps some prawns—or oysters."

I stared at her a moment and couldn't avoid growling, "Oysters."

She smiled but didn't share it. "Now, let me see, Burgundy with the steak, that would be a *Nuits St. George, Henri Gouges*, a good, solid Burgundy. 2008 was a good year for that region, and though you don't want to drink a *premier cru* too soon—certainly not before five years—neither do you want to leave it too long. Thirteen to fifteen years tops. I would imagine this one is just about ready for a good sirloin." She sighed with what sounded like pleasure and continued to scan the menu. "As to the oysters, Champagne is so overdone, isn't it? Personally I favor a delicate, ice-cold Muscadet. Here there is a *Sèvre-et-Maine sur Lie, Château L'Oiselinière de la Ramée, Chéreau-Carré.*" She said it easily, without the slightest affectation. "There was no 2017 for this particular wine, but 2018 was an excellent vintage in the Loire Valley."

The waiter arrived with our martinis and she didn't pause for breath. She told him, "We'll have a dozen oysters with a bottle of very cold *Sèvre-et-Maine sur Lie, Château L'Oiselinière de la Ramée, Chéreau-Carré*, 2018. I want the wine *too* cold, you understand?"

"Of course, madam."

"Put it in the freezer now. Then, we'll have two sirloin steaks, rare, but make sure they are well singed on the outside, incinerated, but bleeding inside. With that we'll have a *Nuits St. George, Henri Gouges*, 2008. Open it now and let it breathe."

He bowed and went away. "As my mother's therapist used to say to me, 'I hear you saying,' don't patronize me by ordering my drinks for me."

She picked up her drink and sipped it. She licked her lips with a very pink tongue and sighed softly as she set the glass down.

"I don't want to spend all night 'busting your balls,' Mason, but tell me something. When was the last time you explained why you ordered a meal?" She leaned forward and put her elbows on the table. "We are a little bit different in Israel, Mason. In Britain, the USA, women try hard to be more men than the men, more aggressive than men, more powerful and assertive than men. My theory is that they do that because there is nothing much else left to do in the modern world save fantasize, and because your society no longer has any need for men.

"But Israel is not like that. We face the threat of extinction every day when we rise to work, and every night when we go to bed. We are surrounded on three sides by people who want to extinguish us from the face of the Earth, just because we are Jewish. Women join the army in Israel, not because we have to—though we do have to—and not because we want to prove we are equal or better than men. We join the army to fight for our survival, for the survival of our families and our children. You understand?"

She waited for me to answer. I didn't so she went on.

"And, unlike British and American women, we do not go around with a hatchet in our hand trying to chop the balls off every man we meet. Because we want—and *need*—our men to be men. Real men. Not macho assholes, not gorillas, men. Fathers in peace, lions in war."

I nodded. "I understand."

She looked vaguely surprised. "Really? I don't need to fight you or break your arm?"

I smiled. "I wouldn't recommend trying, but you don't need to do it, no."

She held out her hand and we shook. The waiter saved us from an awkward silence by showing up with a platter of oysters, a frosted bottle in a bucket of ice and two frosted glasses. He poured and left us to it.

Aside from a few appreciative noises we were silent until the last oyster was gone, and the last drop of wine had been supped. Then she gave me a smile across the table, and instantly I saw her, covered in mud and dust, in camouflage fatigues, sitting with the guys, in the dirt, with a Tavor X95 in her lap. She had let me peek behind the veil.

"So," she said, "what's the issue with Dr. Edward Ulysses Hampton? Why don't you want to talk about him? Is he dead? Did they kill him?"

I nodded. "Yup."

"Bastards. I knew it would happen. You know, when you tread on Chinese toes, unless they have some use for you, they will eliminate you. They don't piss around. I told them at the office, 'He is of no use to the Chinese and he is playing a very dangerous game. They will take him out.' Did they listen?"

"Apparently not."

"They'll take them all out if we let them. Do you know who did it?"

"I can hazard a fair guess."

"Zimo Chew?"

"Now you're doing it."

She winked and grinned. "Yeah, but I'm good at it."

And she was definitely one of the guys.

CHAPTER TEN

So I told her about finding Hampton, and about the girl I'd seen hurrying away from the house in what I took to be Hampton's shirt and hat. I told her all this over coffee and twenty-year-old Bushmills whiskey because according to her the meat and the wine deserved our full attention.

"You get more of what you focus on," she'd said and shrugged. "Maybe they'll give us a second helping."

When she had completely cleaned her plate, she sat back and sighed, and gave me that grin again. She drained her glass and as she set it on the table she smacked her lips.

"Now my father would say, 'And now, body of mine, what more do you want?'" She had raised her hand and snapped her fingers and a waiter had appeared by her side as though she had invoked him using the Kabbalah.

"We are going to have two espresso coffees, two glasses of twenty-year-old single malt Bushmills, but you are going to put them in cognac glasses with no ice. You will also bring a selection of cheeses, mainly blue."

I had commented, "You're used to giving orders." And she had replied, "Yup, so tell me about Dr. Hampton," and that was when I had told her about finding him and seeing the girl I assumed to be Marion, during which narrative the coffee, the whiskey and the cheese had arrived.

She sat swirling her whiskey and occasionally sniffing it. "It's like a fine brandy," she commented.

"So, in my opinion, with Hampton dead, Marion seems to have become central to this."

She nodded. "Because she is the one who actually, physically provided Hampton with whatever it was that got him killed." I gave a single nod and sipped. "Otherwise we have Hoffstadder and Marcos."

"Both of whom we must talk to in the morning. Felix could be of special interest."

"We? I'm happy to share…"

She shook her head and reached in her purse. She pulled out a folded piece of paper and passed it across the table to me. I opened it out and saw it was an agreement between ODIN and Mossad, signed illegibly by the Chief, agreeing that we would cooperate in every way with their agent.

"You an' me, pal. Like Bing Crosby and Bob Hope, Starsky and Hutch, Mulder and Scully."

"Mason and Gallin doesn't have quite the same ring to it."

"We'll make it work. Where you go, I go. Believe me, you won't regret it. I can be pretty useful."

I sighed. "I don't doubt it, but I warn you I am not a great team player."

"Real carnivores rarely are, but you'll get used to me. Who was that? Was it Dirty Harry? They tried to force a partner on him, and all his previous partners had got killed, and he growls, 'I always work alone.' Then it turns out, to cap it all, his new partner is a dame!"

She laughed and I noticed her eyes were warm and moist. The booze was going to her head and I figured she didn't often drink.

"I don't mind working with a partner. I'm just not very good at it. So what's the plan for tomorrow?"

"I'll join you for breakfast eight sharp, then we go in my car to visit Dr. Hoffstadder. Then at lunchtime we ambush Felix Marcos. He usually goes home for lunch. We catch him there, at home."

"Sounds OK. Why your car?"

"Because I've seen your car. It looks like robots died of boredom putting it together. Can you imagine how hard it is to bore a robot? Your car could do that. I have a Corvette C8, four hundred ninety-five horses, one hundred ninety-five miles per hour, and get this, naught to sixty in two-point-eight seconds. That is an efficient use of torque. Your face goes like puddles when a helicopter is landing. Did you ever see that? It goes kind of flat, with ripples wobbling at the side. Your cheeks can't keep up with your face. It's one mean mother of a car."

"Corvette C8. Are you the same woman who joined me at the bar? You seem different somehow. Listen, we'd better make a—"

"I look the part, but I find it hard to keep up the act. You have an Aston Martin DBS."

"I do."

"I read your file."

"Shall we…?"

I went to stand but she still had that warm, mischievous smile on her face.

"What?" she said. "Dance? Promenade? Adjourn?" Her face became suddenly sad. "Take a rain check?"

"How about get some rest for tomorrow?" I stood and she sat looking up at me.

"Smart and sensible. My mother would have disapproved of you. 'He'll kill your creative spirit!' she would have said. 'Find a nice boy who will drink himself to death just to write one poem about truth.'"

Our eyes locked for a long moment. Then I said firmly, "Gallin, we should go. We have an early start tomorrow."

She seemed not to hear me. "My mother gave me a lot of advice." She gurgled a laugh. "And I mean *a lot!* 'Never have sex on a first date unless you're sober.' That was one of hers. And then, 'Never have sex with a guy who doesn't get you drunk on a first date. He's too good to be true.'"

I repressed a sigh. "Clever. I see what she was doing there."

"You do? I don't. Also, 'Make love not sex.' She was a hippie. Berkeley '68."

"A Jewish hippie?"

"No. There were some, but she wasn't one of them. She was some kind of WASP converted to Hinduism or yoga or something. Christians are always searching for something that is more Christian than Christianity. Then she met my father and fell in love. It was easy to fall in love with my father. He was a mensch. Kind, strong, loyal, faithful…" She trailed off.

She drummed a sad tattoo on the table. I wanted to ask. I wanted to know. But I knew it would be a mistake: too much too soon. Maybe after the job was finished. I held out my hand.

"I am going to take you home, and look forward to

seeing you at breakfast bright and early tomorrow."

"I can take a hint. You're right. Let's go."

She rose and, with perfect composure, linked her arm through mine and we walked to the elevators. There I pressed the call button and the doors hissed open. And as I reached for the lobby button she gently smacked my wrist, shook her head and made that negative "tut, tut, tut" some women make. Then she pressed the sixth floor. My floor, and gave me a smoldering smile from under her eyebrows.

I started to say, "Gallin, this is not...," but she grinned and punched my shoulder. "Don't flatter yourself, handsome. I'm booked in at the same hotel, same floor. When I hook a fish, Mason, I don't throw it back. I cook it and eat it."

The elevator stopped and we stepped out. She pointed to my door fifteen paces away. "That's you," she said. Then pointed to the door in the far wall slightly to our right. "This is me. And I will see *you* when glorious morning gilds the streams with heavenly alchemy."

I watched her step inside and close the door, then stood for a while wondering what the hell had just happened. Finally I walked the fifteen paces to my room, had a long cold shower and went to bed.

* * *

At seven thirty she was knocking on my door. Fortunately I was showered and dressed. I opened and stepped out, closing the door behind me.

"What kept you?"

She made a noise that sounded like, "Tshah!" and followed me to the elevators. I noticed she had very black sunglasses on her head.

"You don't drink a lot, do you?"

"I keep in shape. I have a seventh Dan in Tae Kwon Do. Naturally I have a black belt, third Dan in Krav Maga and I hold an instructor's degree in Jeet Kune Do."

The elevator arrived and the doors opened. "So you're pretty tough, but you can't hold your liquor. It happens a lot."

"Yeah, well holding my liquor is not something I ever aspired to. Besides, did you know that the healthier you are, the faster you get drunk?"

"Yup. Let's get coffee. And you need protein. Best cure for a hangover is protein. Bacon, sausages, eggs."

I stopped because she was turning green. She said, "Is that true?"

"I hold a tenth Dan in hangovers. Believe me."

She took my advice and after a hearty breakfast of lamb chops and fried eggs, and a pint of strong black coffee we were on our way to Rodriguez Avenue, headed north toward the University of the Philippines Law Faculty.

The Corvette was everything she'd said it was. It growled and snarled its way with extraordinary ease and elegance through the traffic, but when she hit the gas the surge of power crushed you into the seat and made your face flatten out in ripples, like she'd said.

We made it to Magsaysay Avenue in a matter of a few minutes, and I was pretty sure we had left a few traffic cops behind scratching their heads and frowning. We pulled into the leafy drive, she made a chortling noise, killed the engine and climbed out and closed the door with a soft thud. I followed.

We found the faculty office and I leaned on the desk and smiled at the secretary whose eyes said she was reserving judgment. She'd been too long around lawyers to trust anybody on face value.

"We would like to see Dr. Jay Hoffstadder, please."

Her eyebrows became politely imperious. "Have you got an appointment?"

"No, but I am sure he will see us. I represent the United States Government, and the nature of our visit is both confidential and urgent."

Her eyebrows were already pretty high, but she managed to arch the right one even higher and said, "Well, I am very sorry, but Dr. Hoffstadder is not in today. I can take a message if you like."

"No, that's OK. Can you tell me where he is? Like I said, it is a matter of real urgency."

She hesitated a moment, then, "I'm afraid I don't know where he is. He left early yesterday afternoon and he has not called in this morning. He should be in by now, but sometimes he comes in late and stays late…" She trailed off and spread her hands. "Would you like me to call him at home?"

I shook my head. "No, not at all. We'll catch him there. I'll call him on the way."

She watched us leave and I could feel her eyes on my back all the way to the car.

As we climbed in I said, "You couldn't find something a little more conspicuous? I think there might be deaf and blind people who won't know we're coming."

She fired up the beast and we slid out of the faculty drive like a rocket-propelled snake.

"You know a lot of people in the intelligence community, right?" she asked.

"Yes, and none of them has a Corvette C8."

"If we need to go anywhere incognito don't worry, we'll use your fridge on wheels. He left early yesterday and didn't come in this morning. He has maybe twenty hours on us, or he's dead."

"He has a wife and two kids."

She was quiet for a while, moving down Katipunan Avenue, past the tumbledown shacks and shantytowns that existed cheek by jowl—separated sometimes by a mere wall—with luxurious mansions that sported lawns and swimming pools. Gallin scowled out of the windshield suddenly and said, "What the hell is with all the damned power cables, and the signs. Everywhere you look there's a damn billboard, or a poster or a sign! Vote Cabrera, Eat Pad Noodles, Learn Programming and Don't Park all within six feet of each other!"

"It's the next on the right."

She accelerated from thirty to ninety in one second while overtaking bikes, rickshaws, cars, trucks and taxis, then swerved and braked into the slow lane while I peeled my face off the seat.

"I know where it is," she snapped.

The house was a big cream affair on many levels, with red, gabled roofs that were somehow vaguely Georgian, and tall windows with lots of little square panes. All of those windows were closed, and the house, with its gardens and lawns, was safely contained behind a seven-foot concrete wall with big iron spikes on top. There was a garage, but that had big ugly orange iron doors that were firmly closed. Beside them there was a keypad and a video-camera lens. Gallin prodded at it and said absently, "There's no one home. Gimme a hand up, I'll vault the wall and let you in from the inside."

"Sure." I nodded as I fit the needle and toothpick from my Swiss Army knife into the lock on the garage door. After a moment it swung inwards and I stepped through into a large, empty parking garage with room for two cars.

"Nobody's home. Close the door, would you?"

She closed the door and we stood a moment looking at the empty space. She said:

"He took his wife and his kids and he ran." She wagged a finger at me. "Now *that* is conspicuous."

"It's also out of character." I played with the lock from the carport into the kitchen and after a second or two it opened. Before I went in I pointed to the security camera half-concealed in the corner of the garage. "Let's see how true to character he is."

The kitchen was spacious, with a round, pine table in the center of the floor and big, sliding windows to the right over the sink and work surface. Through the window you could see a lawn and tall trees, cypresses and palms beside a hedge. I tried the lights. The power was on. The fridge was still humming. I said:

"If they've done a runner, it wasn't a last-minute decision. It was last second."

She nodded. "If he's a pro, it was last second, planned years in advance." I searched the ceiling above the carport door. I was hoping the CCTV camera had been put in after the house was built. It looked like it had been. The wire was discreetly tucked into the corner and painted white, but it was there.

She saw me looking and said, "It probably goes to his den."

And after staring around for a moment she added, "I don't think the kitchen has anything to tell us, except that she was teleported out of here. I think the story is upstairs."

I agreed, but still we went over the ground floor methodically. The sliding doors out to the pool were open. There was a magazine open on the couch and a pair of house shoes poking out from under it.

"Pretty much what you'd expect."

She said, "Kids were at school."

I nodded. "Figures."

We climbed the stairs and found his office. The first thing that struck you about it was the open stationery cupboard. "First sign she was panicking," I said and hunkered down in front of it.

"Safe?"

"Yup. It's empty. This was their panic protocol. He warned her, probably by telephone from the faculty. She dropped everything she was doing and grabbed the survival kit they had prepared in the safe. She went to collect the kids from school on some pretext, and they met at some kind of rendezvous." I glanced over my shoulder. "Computer off or sleeping?"

She went and sat in the big, cream leather chair behind the desk and rattled at the keyboard. "Sleeping. See? That's why panicking is a bad idea." She typed some more, grunted and sighed a couple of times and finally said, "*Three* passages to LAX yesterday early afternoon, in the names of Julia, Mark and Elizabeth Henson."

I sat on the floor and faced her. "They have two kids, Mark and Elizabeth."

She leaned her chin in her hand and watched me a moment. "So the kids don't know they're on the run. Keep their first names the same so they don't realize anything weird is going on."

"But she is Julia. At least for the duration of the flight."

"So what does he do?" she asked. "He books the flight separately? They meet at LAX?"

I closed my eyes and tried to imagine I was a solid, smart academic who was a serious, responsible patriarch who made provisions for his family. What would I do?

"No, he has jet-propelled them out of harm's way, and he will take a more roundabout route to attract the danger away from them."

We were silent for a while, then she said, "This country's transport infrastructure is shit. The railways are nonexistent. And if I was on the run in a police state with the Chinese breathing down my neck, I would not rent a car."

"Which explains why Carmona was at the coach terminal."

"We've got Clark International Airport fifty miles north of here, outside Mabalacat City. It flies mainly to the East, but it has a couple of destinations in the Middle East that could be useful if you were on the run." She rattled at the keyboard a bit more and said, "Dubai. Emirates flies out of there to Dubai."

CHAPTER ELEVEN

I got to my feet.

"So she goes straight to LAX with the kids, using false passports, while he makes his way by coach, incognito—he hopes—to Clark International, and then on home to Los Angeles via Dubai." I was pulling out my cell as I spoke. I dialed one and after a single ring Lovelock's voice said, "Office of the Director of International Navigation, how may I direct your call?"

"This is Mason, ODIN double-oh five two, I need to talk to Nero, fast."

There was a pause while the call was put through voice recognition. Finally she said, "Go ahead, caller."

Before I could speak the Chief's voice growled, "What is it?"

"Ed's dead."

"How poetic, you even made it rhyme. What else?"

I scowled at the phone. "Carmona is also dead, both murdered. You'll get the details in my report. We believe Hoffstadder is headed for Clark International at..." I stared at Gallin, she said, "Mabalacat." I said, "Just outside Mabalacat, north of Manila—"

"I know where Mabalacat is!"

"That's great. Good for you. We think he's going to

try to fly to Dubai and change there for LAX. His wife is either already in LA or on her way. You should try to pick them both up. The wife has two kids with her and is traveling as Julia Henson. The kids are Mark and Elizabeth. Go easy."

"Thank you for your humane advice. Anything else?"

"Not right now, no. Just let me know when you pick up Hoffstadder."

He grunted and hung up. She was staring at me through narrowed eyes.

"What about Marion James?"

"I don't know," I said. "Something tells me she is key to this. She went to see him just after he was killed, and she tore the house apart searching for something he was supposed to give her."

"The envelope."

"Probably. Maybe it was just cash, but she was in a panic, which means she knew something."

"She knew what was going down."

I grunted and nodded. "We need to find her, soon."

"I agree, but we should go and talk to Felix Marcos first. We need to know if he's alive, and if he is we need to take him into some kind of protective custody. Him and his family."

"How the hell do you propose to do that? We have no jurisdiction here."

She shrugged, like I was focusing on the trivial and failing to see the bigger picture. "Let's see if he's alive first. If he's not, it won't be an issue." She went to stand but flopped back in the chair, as if stopped by an afterthought. "You said she was dressed in one of his shirts

and hat?"
"Uh-huh."
"And she was walking."
"Yeah."
"That's different."
I frowned. "What do you mean?"
"Hoffstadder, his family booked on a flight to Los Angeles, with false ID and passports, Carmona, fake American passport, presumably making for the airport, but she walks away in an improvised—badly improvised—disguise after tearing his house apart. It's different."
I shrugged. "Sure. What's your point?"
"I don't know. It's different. That's all."
She rose and went to examine the rest of the house. I called Paul Hoffmann at the CIA office at the embassy.
"Mason, how can I help you?"
"I think at least two contacts of Hampton's may have attempted to leave the country via Clark International."
"Makes sense."
"Yeah, it makes sense, but I am worried for them. It looks like the Chinese have decided to wipe out what they perceive as a possible espionage cell. So far they have taken out Hampton and Juan Carmona, Felix Marcos, Jay Hoffstadder, and Marion James could either be already dead or on the hit list."
He made a noncommittal noise which said that so far this was not a Central Intelligence problem, and as far as interdepartmental cooperation was concerned, it was beyond the call of duty. I pressed on.
"There are two things you can do for me. Have someone check and see if Julia, Mark and Elizabeth Hen-

son departed Manila for LAX in the last twenty-four hours—"

"Hang on." I heard some muffled words and knew he'd issued the order. "Sorry, Mason, go on."

"And I need to know if Jay Hoffstadder and Marion James boarded flights to Dubai from Clark International, or, if not, whether they are booked on any flights to Dubai."

"OK, glad to help." Clearly I had not pushed beyond the call of duty. "By the way," he added. "Those prints you wanted?"

"You got them?"

"Yeah, they didn't show up on CODIS or any of the Five Eyes databases, but I spoke to the cops here and asked if they could let me have the prints of a number of resident British and American expats. Obviously, if they have resident's permits, they have to give their prints. I said it was part of a routine procedure and they were happy to comply. There is still, thank God, a policy of cooperation with the USA here, at least at that level. Though we have no idea how long it will last.

"So, like I was saying, I included Marion James's name on the list and received scans of all the ID cards and prints, including hers."

"That's great, but you're killing me, cut to the chase."

"Marion James handled the envelope, and she also held the knife. According to our forensic guys, her prints are consistent with her opening the envelope—thumb on the flap et cetera—and using the knife extensively, picking it up and putting it down multiple times. Apparently there are lots of prints smudged by other prints, like she grabbed it and used it over and over."

"OK, that's great, Hoffmann, thanks."

"Let's have dinner soon so you can put me up to speed."

"We'll do that. I owe you. Call me as soon as you have anything on those flights."

"You got it."

I hung up. Gallin was standing in front of me staring into my face.

"So?"

"So she handled the envelope and she used the knife repeatedly."

"But not to kill him, to tear up his house. Then when she got the contents of the envelope, what did she do? Rhetorical question, Mason. Don't answer. She put on one of his shirts and his Panama hat as a makeshift disguise, and got the hell out of there. Where did she go?"

"Is that also rhetorical?"

"No."

"Then my money is on: she went to the bus station and got a coach to Clark International."

She pulled down the corners of her mouth and gave her head a shake. "Nah," she said.

"Why not? Give me a reason."

"Because she's different. She's not doing tradecraft. She's improvising—panicking and improvising."

I thought about it. "Because she was only recently recruited and has had no training."

"So she might do the opposite of what we expect."

"And that might just save her."

She nodded. "OK. There is nothing more in this house. They are gone."

"So we close the safe, take possession of the hard

drive, remove any sign that we were here, and we go and visit Felix Marcos." I hesitated. "Something I don't understand, why didn't she wipe her hard drive? Why did she leave the information about her flight available?"

She punched me gently on the shoulder. "She started to, but I figure she was in a big hurry and a bit of a panic, and thought she and her kids would be out of the Philippines before anybody came looking. And she was right. Also, she forgot to click OK."

I nodded. "OK, I buy that. Let's go."

It was a short drive from Hoffstadder's house to the department of Viral Cybernetics on T H Pardo de Tavera Street. It was a huge, rambling, space-age building with lots of glass, steel, and ruthless straight lines in concrete. It backed onto the university's bonsai garden, and seemed to me to be equally as twisted and unnatural.

We parked in the lot in back of the new faculty, where the bonsai trees offered plenty of shade for anything smaller than a grasshopper, but nothing much for Gallin's Corvette.

The faculty office was a pentagonal room with glass walls in the center of a pentagonal, tropical garden at the heart of the faculty building. The secretary listened to us with a paralyzed smile. When I had finished telling her that we wanted to talk to Dr. Felix Marcos, the head of the faculty, she said, "Dr. Marcos is not available at present, and we are not sure when he will return. Would you like to speak to the acting head, Dr. Zhao Guang?"

Gallin was about to say something but I cut her off.

"Yes, please." As she picked up the phone I asked, "Is that Dr. Guang or Dr. Zhao? I don't want to be discourteous."

Her smile went from droid-like to frigid. "Dr. Zhao,

Zhao is his surname."

She spoke on the telephone for a minute in Chinese, then pointed out of the office across the tropical garden. "In the lobby, take the elevator to the next floor. Dr. Zhao's office in the first on left." She smiled again and managed to squeeze a worrying amount of contempt and disgust into her eyes in the process.

"Dr. Zhao is very busy man. You can keep visit very short, please."

I nodded. "I am sure we can."

We followed her instruction and, on knocking at the Head of Faculty's door, were told to "Come!" by a peremptory voice that did not sound Chinese, but American.

I opened the door and Gallin went in ahead of me.

The office was very large, and the walls immediately on the left and straight ahead as we went in were solid plate-glass. The two walls on my right were lined with books. The floor was marble and there was a bull skin in the center with a heavy, mahogany coffee table and four leather armchairs drawn up around it. Dr. Zhao was over to the left, in the corner, surrounded by plate glass, so for a moment it looked like he was floating above the very small trees outside.

He watched us enter without getting up and with no expression on his face. He had large spectacles which reflected the light and made him even more expressionless. He watched us approach the desk and, without speaking, gestured to the two chairs opposite him.

We sat.

Just when his silence was becoming uncomfortable he said, "What can I do for you?"

"We were hoping to talk to Dr. Marcos. Have you

any idea when he will return?"

His long, lipless mouth stretched into a reptilian smile. It wasn't the kind of smile you'd like to see last thing at night.

"Dr. Marcos is not available. How can I help?"

I shook my head. "I don't think you can, Dr. Zhao. You see, we need to talk to him about his acquaintance with Dr. Hampton."

I could feel Gallin's eyes burning into the side of my skull. Dr. Zhao's lenses glinted with pleasure.

"Perhaps if you tell me what it is you want to know, I can help you. I was quite close to Dr. Marcos."

"You were? You are not now?" I offered him my most winningly innocent smile.

He laughed like a creaking rocking chair, squeaking and leaning back and forth.

"Oh, we are still very close, I promise you. Just a manner of speech."

"So, Dr. Zhao, forgive my asking but, if you are still close, why can't we see him?"

The lenses flashed expressionlessness and his mouth never failed in its thin snake of a smile. He made a noise that sounded like, "Hm, hm, hm…" and then said, bizarrely, "His family are most sincerely grateful for your concern and interest. They speak always very highly of you." I frowned, wondering if we were being given the bum's rush, but he went on, "Dr. Marcos is not well. He has a sickness of the mind, anxiety, stress, overwork. So the hospital has sent him to a beautiful rest home where he can peacefully recover his health. Yes. Thank you so much for your concern."

"You've put him in a clinic?"

"For his own well-being, and we hope soon he will be back to his old self, and how we all loved to see him in the good old days."

"How long has he been in this clinic?"

"As soon as the loving and caring consortium of investors saw that Dr. Marcos was not happy, restless in soul and spirit, they immediately took steps to come to dear Dr. Marcos's immediate aid."

"But how long ago?"

He nodded like I had said something both witty and perceptive. "Immediately," he said, then added for good measure, "Right away, immediately."

I could see I had turned into a cul-de-sac, so I changed tack.

"What about his family? Have they gone with him?"

"He is supported by a devoted wife and two devoted children who pray every day for his swift return."

"Sure, I know, but *where are* his family?"

I had decided before he answered that it was a pointless exercise, but he chugged right along and answered, even though it was pointless.

"Wherever Dr. Marcos goes, his loving family hold him always in their hearts. He is very fortunate to have such a devoted family to support him in these difficult times."

I heard Gallin mutter, "*Hob rachmones!*"

I ignored her and said, "Yes, indeed. Dr. Zhao, can you tell me if Dr. Marcos is at a clinic in the Philippines or somewhere else?"

He smiled as though I had asked the very best question in the world that he had ever heard.

"Dr. Marcos has many friends…"

Gallin raised her eyes to the ceiling. "*Gevalt!*"

Dr. Zhao plowed on regardless. "The university board of directors and many friends and advisors will make sure that Dr. Marcos goes to the very best place to receive the very best help. We will of course convey to him your very kind wishes for his rapid recovery."

I smiled as emptily as he had. "We are very grateful for your time and help, Dr. Zhao."

His lenses flashed. "Please, if there is ever anything I can help you with, do not hesitate to come and see me. I will always be happy to be as helpful as I possibly can."

I stood and Gallin stood too, but as she turned to move toward the door Dr. Zhao said, "Mr. Mason, Captain Gallin, as officers you have no jurisdiction in the Philippines, and what immunity you have through links with your embassy is very limited. I advise you not to push your investigations too far. You are here to look for Dr. Hampton. You have found him. I advise you now to go home."

"Aren't you going a little beyond the scope of *your* jurisdiction, Dr. Zhao?"

The reptilian smile returned with a laugh that was more like a hiss.

"Not jurisdiction, Mr. Mason, just friendly advice. Philippines is a very dangerous country, and Manila is a very dangerous town, as your friend Dr. Hanson found out."

I nodded. "Thanks for the advice. I'll remember it."

"Good. Goodbye, Mr. Mason, goodbye, Captain Gallin."

As we exited the building Gallin stopped dead in

her tracks, her shoulders sagged, her whole body sagged with them, she covered her face with her hands and took a long deep breath, which she released as a long, ragged, "Ooooy!" I laughed and she glared at me.

"What is *wrong* with that guy?"

"Very little, I think, save the absence of a beating heart and a soul."

Her car bleeped, the lights flashed and she yanked open the door.

"So what now? His family?"

I climbed in the passenger side. "Yes, but only to confirm that they are not there."

We slammed the doors, the engine growled and we moved off. I went on, "I have a very bad feeling that Marcos and his family have been collectively terminated."

"Shit," she said it quietly, then added, "I think you're right. They are covering their tracks more than comprehensively. They are wiping out anyone who was associated with Hampton. This is more than ensuring that whatever information he got hold of goes no farther. This is making an example of him and the people who worked with him."

"I think so. And that is worrying in itself." She glanced at me, asking what I meant. "The Chinese like to be secretive and subtle. They like to get maximum results while showing a minimum of their power. They'd rather engineer a situation where the Philippines and the Americans kill each other, than move in openly assassinating people in the streets. That is out of character for them."

She turned onto C.P. Garcia Avenue and headed west toward the Pansol district where Felix Marcos had his house.

"So?"

"So that makes me nervous because it means, A, we are dealing with something of above normal importance for them—"

"And B?"

"B—" I took a deep breath and shook my head. "B, they are feeling bold. They are feeling there is no risk to them in showing their strength. Like they have already won but we don't know it yet. Like it's already too late."

She eyed me for a second or two, and we drove on in silence.

Marcos had his house halfway down Kalinga Street on the right, behind high walls and dense hedges. We parked out front and spent a couple of minutes ringing on the bell. Eventually a police patrol car rolled into the street and stopped beside the Corvette. The driver leaned out of his window and after giving me a once-over rich in barely concealed contempt, he said, "Dr. Marcos moved. Nobody home. You need to move on now please. Go, go."

I nodded. "Thanks. You have a nice day."

He gave a small laugh and said something to his pal in the passenger seat. They both laughed and he said to us, "You have nice day too," and they drove off.

I watched them leave. Gallin came up close to me and punched me gently in the chest four times with alternating fists. I looked down into her eyes and said quietly, "It now becomes utterly imperative that we find Dr. Jay Hoffstadder and Marion James. Because they are the only chance we have of finding out what the hell is going on."

"Agreed, Mason, but where do we start?"

CHAPTER TWELVE

Jay Hoffstadder ran. He ran down the steps from the covered walkway, pushed and shouldered his way through the streaming torrent of humanity, evoking angry stares and shouts; he ran west along Epifanio de los Santos, driven by an imperative need to get back home with his family and leave this whole sordid business behind him.

Panting, with a painful constriction in his chest, he came finally to the intersection with Taft Avenue. He was overwhelmed suddenly then by a sense of horror. Everywhere he looked it seemed there was chaos. Overhead the railway that ran above the street cast the street into gloom, but it was a gloom that seemed to thrive among filth, pollution and grime. A snarl of traffic that seemed to extend listless and rumbling along the length of the avenue, belching black carbon monoxide into already filthy air, inched forward while barefoot children ran and played among the vehicles, clambering onto the multicolored Jeepneys, shouting and laughing with the tourists, trapped in the logjam in the coaches and rickshaws.

Red and white plastic traffic blocks had been placed in the road to mark a motorized *traysikel* rank.

He saw young boys in the ubiquitous shorts and flip-flops, sitting on the bricks, play-fighting and laughing, while the traffic inched past them. The walls of this underground world had been painted a sickly green, and everywhere he looked there were posters, placards, pictures, billboards, randomly placed signs, all with urgent messages and smiling, laughing faces, among the din of revving engines and shouting voices.

He ran again, up a ramp and into the interior of the shopping mall.

Inside he was gripped by a strange relief. It was much like any other mall he had ever been in, in the States or in Europe, and that gave him an odd relief. The floors were made of shiny, pale beige tiles, the shop fronts were all shiny, plate glass, and along the aisles, where the people were funneled like consumer ants, all the shops were familiar, if not identical to the ones he knew.

His sudden attack of panic began to subside as he moved along with the stream. Ahead he saw a café with pine tables and red plastic chairs, set out as though on a terrace. He stepped over the red rope barrier and sat at a table. A waitress in a bright red linen apron approached him, chewing gum.

"You want?"

"Hamburger, and a cold beer."

She walked away and he saw, across the cordoned-off area that did as a terrace, the same foreign girl he had seen in the line behind him at the bus terminal. She was alone and staring at her cell. That made him think of his own GPS and that of Gloria. A moment of hot panic in his belly subsided. He had ensured that they had both practiced switching off the global positioning service, and he knew she had done it as soon as she had hung up, as had he.

He observed the girl a moment longer. He decided she looked shabby and lonely. She didn't look like she had a lot of friends. A worm of an idea wiggled in the back of his mind. They would be looking for Jay Hoffstadder, either alone or with his wife and kids. It had come damn close at the bus station, and he thanked the good lord it had been some Chinese guy from the MSS rather than Gerry Baccay. Gerry would have recognized him for sure. Which meant the disguise was good enough, but could be better if, for example, he was traveling with a companion.

The last time he had picked up a strange woman had been when he was twenty-one, and he had wound up marrying her. It was not something that came naturally to him and he was not sure he could pull it off. She'd probably tell him to go to hell.

At that moment, as though she'd heard his thoughts, she glanced up at him. She frowned for a second, he ventured half a smile and she looked away. So much for that plan.

He feigned checking his own phone and noticed that the girl had been staring at the same screen for five minutes without scrolling up or down. The waitress brought his beer and his burger and the girl glanced at him again. This time there was the trace of a smile. He smiled at her with genuine relief, leaned forward and said, "Weren't you at the bus station just now?"

She gave a goofy grin and answered with an English accent.

"Yes, you were in front of me in the queue."

"What was that that happened back there? I thought a car backfired..."

She went a little pale. "Yes, I know. I think somebody got shot. I saw someone lying in the pavement."

"That's pretty intense."

Another nervous laugh. "I know."

"Are you traveling alone?" She nodded. "That's pretty brave."

"Well, I thought I'd better see the world before I settle down. How about you? Are you an expat, traveling...?"

"Oh!" He gave a nervous laugh of his own, suddenly acutely aware of his age. "Well, I didn't do that gap year thing. I went straight from college into a law firm and spent the next twenty years in the rat race in DC. So last year I thought, what the hell! I'm going to do now what I should have done twenty years ago."

"Oh." Her eyebrows shot up. "Excellent! Good for you!"

"Say, you want a beer?" He gestured at the chair opposite his own at his table. "Save having to shout across the terrace."

"Oh!" she said again and smiled. Her cheeks colored. "Well, if you're sure I'm not intruding."

"Not at all! Nice to have some company." She stood and gathered her things and moved across. He stood to help her and they fumbled and laughed a bit as she sat and almost dropped her purse. They both said, "Oops!" at the same time and laughed some more. He said, "Trouble with traveling around the world is, sometimes you're in with a crowd and there are too many of you, and then you can spend a couple of weeks without talking to anyone who speaks your own language."

"That's true. I notice that. Sometimes you're just longing to talk to someone who speaks English."

"So, how long have you been on the road?"

Her eyes glazed slightly. "Ahh…" She suddenly laughed. "It's so long I've lost track. About six months. You?"

He'd had his story prepared for a long time and it came out easy and natural.

"A little longer than that, about nine months, and I'm on my way home now."

"Me too."

He stuck out his hand. "John Jones," and as a sudden afterthought, "but everyone calls me Jay." He grinned. "John Jones, J. J., Jay."

"Oh, yes, I see." She hesitated a moment, then, "Marion, Marion James, though most of my friends call me Mary. Please," she added, pointing at his burger, "do eat. I've already eaten."

He bit into the burger, forcing himself to appear hungry, though he could barely swallow for the anxiety in his belly. He pulled off half the beer and asked her, "So where are you headed?"

"South." She almost snapped the word. "To Mindanao. I heard there are some gorgeous fishing villages down there, peaceful, quiet, lovely people. Not like this." She looked around her with disgust.

He smiled, taken with a sudden feeling of empathy. "You're not crazy about Manila, huh?"

"I used…" She caught herself and gave a small laugh. "I used to think I would love it. But rural Philippines is one thing, Manila is another. The corruption, the cruelty and indifference of the political class, the disgusting behavior of the police…"

"I know," he felt a knot in his belly, "that guy back

there. Maybe he was into drug trafficking or something. They are pretty ruthless with that, and will shoot on sight. The cop is judge, jury and executioner."

She stared at him and something about the fear and the anxiety in her eyes drove him on. As though he recognized his own fear and anxiety in her, and by sharing his horror with her, they might find strength in each other.

"But that's not the worst thing," he said quietly. "They use that as an excuse to settle old feuds and vendettas. I saw, from the covered walkway, I was crossing over the road, I saw the cop planting something in the dead guy's pocket." He hesitated, fearing he was going too far and losing control of his tongue, but was unable to stop. "The shooter, the guy with the gun, he wasn't even Filipino." They both stared fixedly at each other. "He was Chinese."

He watched all the color drain out of her cheeks and suddenly gave a nervous laugh. "Look at us! It's worse than campfire urban legends!"

She laughed too. "I know, but I will be glad to get out of here. You get used to it, but it's a bit of a madhouse. Where are you headed?"

He shrugged. "I was going to go on up to Clark and get a flight to Dubai, then home to Washington. But I feel kind of sour now. It's not a good note to finish almost a year of traveling on."

Was that a glimmer of hope in her eyes? "No!" she said emphatically. "I can see that. Much better to end such a long trek on a happy note."

He fought the constriction in his throat with a cough and gestured at her. "Something like those villages you described in Mindanao. I've never been to Mindanao."

Her face lit up. "Oh, you should go. You'll love it. I'm going to a place right on the very southern tip. It has an extraordinarily unpronounceable name, Nayon ng Pangingisda, right on the beach, and it's so pretty!"

"Yeah, and how hard would it be to find somewhere to stay?"

"Not hard at all. The locals will rent you a room for next to nothing, and feed you with fresh fish and fruit. It's paradise."

He laughed. "Wow, you're making me really want to go. It would definitely be a happier ending to my journey than this one."

"Why don't you change the ticket? The coach leaves in about half an hour and I should be heading back. I'm sure if you talk to the driver and slip him ten dollars he'll let you on. In any case this only takes us as far as the Matnog ferry, then you can get a ticket for the rest of the journey. We go to Samar, get another coach to San Ricardo, another ferry to Surigao and then another two coaches across Mindanao to our unpronounceable destination."

"Wow, are you sure we'll be able to get back?"

She shook her head and laughed. "No! But I'm not sure we'll want to, either."

"That sounds really cool." He said it thoughtfully, with ideas playing in his mind. She smiled with real pleasure. "Are you going to tag along, then?"

"Yeah, I think I just might. But let me ask you, after a week in this village on Mindanao, what will you do then?"

Her eyes strayed. He noticed her face seemed to close up. "I'm not sure," she said, and he didn't believe her.

"I might explore some of the islands around there. It's not *that* far from Oz…"

"Right."

She gathered her things. "We'd better go. You seriously coming?"

"Yeah, if you don't feel I'm intruding."

She assured him again that he wasn't. He paid his bill and they made off out of the mall and back up Aurora Boulevard, an odd couple, twenty years between them. She scruffy, small and pale, he big, affecting to be scruffy but with an innate elegance and authority in his bearing. They were not inconspicuous, but those Filipinos who passed them didn't give them a second look, accustomed as they were to the eccentricities of travelers from the Anglo-Saxon world: boots and woolen socks, strange hats and bright pink skin were just the tip of the iceberg. The Filipinos took it all in their stride.

The coach driver accepted the extra ten bucks from Hoffstadder, issued him with a ticket as far as Matnog and told him he'd have to get another ticket for the rest of the journey once there.

They sat side by side in the cramped seats for ten minutes in a silence that could have been uncomfortable, but somehow wasn't, and it seemed to Hoffstadder that they had, in some way, reached an understanding, however temporary, of mutual support and protection. He did not know her story, but it was easy to see she was vulnerable and alone. He had no idea what she had seen in him, but it was clear to see that she was relieved to have him there. Companions, he said to himself, however temporary.

The driver, in his blue shirt with large sweat stains under his arms, clambered aboard and slid behind the wheel. A button made the doors hiss and thud closed. Then the bus shuddered and rattled and they lurched backward. An intermittent bleeping warned of their movement, but from what Hoffstadder could see, nobody was particularly concerned about it. Then they lurched forward and eased out of the station.

He smiled and pointed out the window.

"You don't see many of those in Manila these days!"

Marion looked and saw a gleaming red Corvette pulling into the coach terminal.

"It's beautiful. What is it?"

"Corvette C8, brand new. Nice car."

She stared at him curiously for a moment. "So, what awaits you when you get back?"

"To DC?" She nodded and he thought about it. It was a good question. Odin would have to help him out, but at forty-five, having pretty much lost everything he had left behind, after all these years in the Philippines, what would he do back home? He smiled at her.

"That's a good question. I'll have to go back to work, obviously, but after an experience like this you go back with a different perspective, don't you?"

She nodded, like she knew what he meant. "Yes, I suppose that's true."

"So how about you? What's waiting for you back home in England? It is England, isn't it?"

She laughed. "That obvious?" He smiled and she gazed out the window at the passing street, overloaded with traffic, people and the eternal power cables and signs. "Nothing much, really," she said. "I suppose I'll get a job, settle down..." She shrugged.

"You make it sound so appealing."

They both laughed, then fell silent, both watching the passing city. An hour rolled by. He dozed for a bit, and so did she, and when he awoke he found they were outside the city. There were less power cables now, more trees and grass, and things looked cleaner. He felt relief, sighed and smiled. Somehow he felt harder to find out here. He felt they would be OK.

After a while Marion awoke too. They exchanged comfortable small talk and the sun slowly declined toward the horizon, turning the light copper, and then taking it away completely as it sank behind the horizon. After that they both slept, she with her head on his shoulder, he with his cheek on her soft blonde hair.

CHAPTER THIRTEEN

Felix Marcos had been in the room for thirty-six hours, at least. It was impossible to be sure. They had taken away his watch and his cell phone; there were no windows in the room, no television, no radio. There was no point of reference from which to calculate the passage of time. It made every moment an infinity. And in the infinity of each passing second he lived with the uncertainty of what had happened to his wife and his children. He wept silently and cursed himself for not having made plans, for not having prepared.

Dr. Hampton had warned him and advised him. They had sat at the corner table in Starving Sam's while Dr. Hampton spooned chicken sotanghon into his loose, wet mouth. He spoke looking at the soup, slurping as he sucked it off the spoon.

"The United States Government can protect you up to a point, Dr. Marcos," he had said. "But you must understand we have no jurisdiction here, and any influence we may once have had, well…"

He had let the words trail off, then dabbed his mouth with a paper napkin. "We can pay you well, of course, but in terms of actual influence with the government, the Chinese are in the ascendant right now. You understand that."

Dr. Marcos had nodded vigorously. "It's why I am here."

Dr. Hampton had returned to his sotanghon, muttering, "Of course," between slurps. "But I must emphasize," he paused and creased his face into an abortive smile, "at the risk of being tedious, I must emphasize that the risk is high—"

"I am not scared about that."

"You should be. You have a family and if the Chinese come after you, we will not be able to help."

Dr. Marcos had frowned hard. "Are you telling me you do not want my information? This department they are setting up is designed specifically..."

"I know, Dr. Marcos, to target the United States and NATO, primarily at least, I know. And I very much want the information you can get me, but I also want you to be safe. And for that you have to make provisions, Dr. Marcos. Do you understand what I am saying?"

"Make provisions?" He had shrugged and shook his head. "How?"

Dr. Hampton had sighed, tipping the plate toward him, spooning up the last of the broth.

"You must acquire a credible American passport and driver's permit, or British or Australian, New Zealand, Canadian... One of those. And you must stash away plenty of money to cover your escape. You have to keep this all in a secure place where your wife can access it easily."

"I have no intention of fleeing in the face of the enemy."

"That's splendid, but your wife and children might

see things differently. For that matter, so might you when you discover the Chinese *Táotài bù* are coming to get you. Make provision, Dr. Marcos—the wise man always makes provision."

He had dismissed Dr. Hampton's advice as American cowardice, but he bitterly regretted not having heeded him now.

He stood and paced the room for the thousandth time. He hadn't eaten since they had come for him, but the sickness in his stomach made it impossible. The thought of food revolted him. He thought of his two daughters, wondered if they had eaten and burst into tears. He covered his face with his hands and repeated over and over, "My arrogance, my arrogance, my arrogance!"

He turned. Across the room a blank wall faced him. On the right a narrow, single bed. To the left a small table and a chair. Behind him the door and above his head a flat, glass disk from which light poured unremittingly. He rushed at the blank wall, screaming, and beat on it with his fists. The wall was unmoved. His emotions broke against it into so much foam, and like a spent wave he withdrew and sank to the floor where he sobbed like a child.

It may have been an hour later or five hours later—time had become meaningless—a key rattled in the lock and the door opened. A tall man stood framed in the doorway. He was broad, strong and athletic in a pale blue suit. His eyes were in shadow, but his smile was like a cruel razor slash.

"Your pride is broken," he said, and gestured at Dr. Marcos lying on the floor.

"Where is my family?"

The man pulled a chair from the table, spun it in one hand and sat astride it, with his arms crossed on the back.

"Whatever I tell you, Dr. Marcos, you will not know if it is the truth. If it serves me to tell you they are alive, I will tell you they are alive. If it serves me to tell you they were raped and murdered, that is what I will tell you. Both are equally possible, like Schrödinger's cat, they are both dead and alive until you look. But you will never get to look, Dr. Marcos." He laughed. "And your wife and your daughters will slowly eat their way through your stomach lining. That is their gratitude."

"You have killed them."

"No." He shook his head. His tone had changed. "You are not thinking, Dr. Marcos. How does it serve my purpose to kill your wife and your children? If I lose that bargaining chip, I lose you. I am not evil, Dr. Marcos. I do not enjoy inflicting pain. Rather, I have the soul of a reptile. I have cold blood. I feel nothing. I don't care if you and your family suffer pain. All I want from you is information."

A glimmer, a small spark, a dying ember of dark hope in his belly. He sat up. "Guarantee their safe passage to the American Embassy, and I swear to you that I will tell you everything you want to know."

The man in the blue suit smiled. "And how can I be sure that once they are in the embassy you will honor your promise?"

Dr. Marcos raised two fingers as though in the peace sign. "One, I know that if I betray you, you will never rest until you have found them and killed them." The man gave a soft grunt and Dr. Marcos went on. "I do not want just their safety, I want their peace and well-being. Two, this deal is in two parts. You give them safe passage to the American Embassy, I tell you everything you want to know, and then you release me to join them. I know there is a risk. I know that you might kill me anyway, but it is a risk I am willing to take to guarantee my family is safe."

The man's smile faded and his mouth all but disappeared. "So you admit you gave information to the Americans."

Dr. Marcos shook his head. "I have admitted nothing. What I told you was that I would tell you everything you want to know."

"Then you deny passing information to the Americans. It cannot be both."

Dr. Marcos gave an exhausted smile. "In your own words, sir, it's like Schrödinger's cat, and the only way you can get to look in the box, is when my family are at the American Embassy."

The man stood and walked to the door. There he stopped and regarded Dr. Marcos with eyes that had grown accustomed to viewing terror, agony and grief with cold equanimity. "Wisdom is good, Dr. Marcos. I recommend wisdom. Being clever will cause you problems, I guarantee that."

Dr. Marcos shook his head. "Please, do not interpret my actions as clever. All I want is the safety of my family."

The tall man left.

Five minutes later the lights dimmed. They did not go off completely, they simply dimmed. At first the change in conditions aroused abject fear in Dr. Marcos. His stomach burned and his heart beat high in his chest. But as the minutes passed and nothing happened he began to think maybe this was a reward for being cooperative. Perhaps they were allowing him to sleep. He crawled onto the bed and closed his eyes. Sleep did not come as such. His thoughts—obsessive thoughts about his daughters and about his wife—strayed into irrational sequences and short dreams, which only ended when he awoke with a spasm of terror. However, on and off, he managed to doze fitfully for perhaps a couple of hours or more.

Eventually the light came on again and the key turned in the lock again, and the tall Chinese came in with two guards pushing a TV on a trolley. They left and closed the door, and the man in the sky-blue suit reached out a hand and gave Dr. Marcos a cell phone. After a moment's examination he realized it was his own cell. He frowned at the Chinese.

"What is this?"

The Chinese man looked at his watch and after a moment nodded once, and Dr. Marcos's telephone began to ring.

"Answer it."

Dr. Marcos stared at the screen a moment, then slid the bar and said, "Hello? This is Dr. Marcos speaking."

"Dr. Marcos, this is Paul Hoffmann of the American Embassy. We have had some rather unorthodox communication with the Chinese Embassy, do you know anything about this?"

He stared hard at the Chinese. His heart was racing and he fought to control his voice.

"Yes, yes I think so, perhaps."

"Are you married, Doctor?"

"Yes, I am married and I have two children, two daughters."

"Would you mind telling me their names and their ages?"

"Of course. Sarah is my eldest, eight years old, Bell is the youngest, only five, you see we gave them American names!" He laughed and looked anxiously at the Chinese, who remained impassive. Dr. Marcos went on. "My wife is Mauie, she is thirty-two."

"Have you got photographs of your wife and daughters there, Dr. Marcos?"

He glanced a question at the Chinese, who nodded once.

"Yes, I have."

"I am going to send you a WhatsApp, Doctor, could you please reply with photographs of your wife and children?"

"What is this about?"

"When you have sent me the photographs, and we can confirm that we are talking about the same people, then I will explain what is happening, Dr. Marcos."

"Yes, all right."

His phone pinged and he saw the message was from Paul Hoffmann. He found three recent pictures of his wife and daughters and sent them to Hoffmann. A moment later Hoffman's voice came on the line again.

"That's excellent, Dr. Marcos. I can confirm that these are indeed the people that the Chinese Embassy have approached me about. Can I ask you if you feel that your wife and children are currently in mortal danger from the Philippine government?"

"Yes," he could not avoid the catch in his throat, "they most definitely are."

"I ask because the Chinese Embassy have taken the

very unusual step of making an appeal on your behalf, and on the behalf of your wife, to give your wife and daughters refugee status in the embassy. They claim you are currently the subject of persecution because of scientific knowledge you hold and that the Philippine government aims to execute you without trial. Are you willing to confirm that?"

"Yes, that is correct. Please, please give my wife and children help. Otherwise they will kill them."

He noticed a tear had run down his face to his nose and wiped it away. Hoffmann was saying:

"What about you, Doctor? What is your situation?"

He looked at the Chinese, who shrugged. Dr. Marcos swallowed hard and with pale terror inside him he said, "Right now I cannot do anything, my wife and children are the most important. Perhaps later, in a few days, I will call you."

"OK, you have my number. I believe your family are at the gates. Stay on the line please."

The tall Chinese in the pale blue suit pulled a remote control from his pocket and switched on the TV. The film was being shot from across Roxas Avenue. There was a black limousine with a Chinese flag over the front wing. After a moment an elegant, well-dressed woman with two prettily dressed little girls came and stood at the front of the limousine. They were with a gray-haired Chinese in a dark suit who bent down and spoke to the children, laughing, and pointed at the camera that was filming them. All four of them waved, then turned and walked toward the gates of the embassy.

The man in the blue suit said, "Right now there is a man in the car aiming at them with a hunting rifle. If I press the number one on my cell, he will shoot them.

What should I do?"

"Please, let them live. I will tell you everything that you want to know. I swear."

The man in the suit said, "It makes no difference, in Manila, New York, Los Angeles or Pleasantville, Wyoming, if you fail me, they will die."

"I know that."

"Good."

The Marines opened the gates and ushered the family in. The Chinese reached across and took the cell from Dr. Marcos's hands and hung up. Tears welled in Dr. Marcos's eyes.

"He said I could speak to them."

"Not today. One thing at a time. Now it is time for us to talk to Mr. Wang. He will be very interested in everything you have to tell us."

The tall man stood and opened the door. The guards came in and wheeled away the television. Dr. Marcos stood. He was shaking badly. The tall man gave his reptilian smile. "Do not be afraid, Dr. Marcos. If you are truly cooperative, you have nothing to fear."

He nodded once and turned it into a small bow. "I will, I will cooperate. You have my word. I will tell you everything you want to know."

He was led out onto a small landing and down some wooden stairs into a small hall where there were three doors, two at the front of the house and one at the back. The tall Chinese opened the door at the back and ushered Dr. Marcos into a small living room with glass doors that led out to a garden. There was a red sofa and two red armchairs. A glass coffee table had been removed to one side and a bentwood chair had been placed in the center of the room. On a lamp table beside the sofa Dr. Marcos saw a pair of pliers, a box of wooden toothpicks and a hammer.

He stopped dead and felt the big Chinese man's hands on his shoulders behind him. Dr. Marcos shook his head.

"This is not necessary. I have told you I will cooperate. I know it is the only way I will see my children again. Please, there is no need for this."

A thin, elderly man stepped in from the garden. He had the same reptilian mouth as the man in the blue suit. He smiled a cruel smile and said, "Please, Doctor, do not be alarmed. These things are just here to remind you, to keep your mind focused. We do not want to cause you pain, at least, not yet."

* * *

Eight hours earlier, and five miles away as the crow flies, Mauie Marcos, Sarah and Bell were having a typically American breakfast of cornflakes, pancakes and bacon in their spacious American kitchen. They were waiting for Dad to come home. He very rarely came home late, and almost never stayed away overnight. But last night he had telephoned his wife and told her some gentlemen from the Chinese Embassy had come to ask him for help, and he would not be home until the next day.

Mauie knew about his special work and cooperation with the US Government. She was not supposed to know, but he had told her because theirs was a relationship of deep love and trust. It always had been. She knew about the promises he had been made, about moving to California and finding a job at one of the universities in the San Francisco Bay area. She knew all about his hopes and dreams. But she didn't know that when he told her he had been asked to help some Chinese gentlemen, he was screaming at her in his mind to run.

She had listened, disappointed that he would not be home for dinner, proud that he was helping such important people, vaguely worried on some deep, intuitive level at the tone in his voice. But she dismissed it, as she had always been brought up to do, as silliness, and she left it to her man to sort it out. He would know what to do. He always did.

When she heard the doorbell she wondered why he did not use his key. She imagined he must be exhausted from working all night, and as she crossed the kitchen toward the spacious hall and the big, oak front door, she wondered if his help for the Chinese Embassy would have a positive impact on his future career. She knew they were very powerful, and could be helpful. Her mother had always said that Felix Marcos would go a long way.

But it was not Felix at the door. He was still five miles away, as the crow flies. It was a tall Chinese man in a sky-blue suit. He smiled at her and she could not help feeling it was a chilling smile, but she smiled back and asked politely, "Yes, good morning, can I help you?"

"My name is Zimo Chew. Your husband, Felix, has asked me to come. He is still detained at the embassy. He asked me to give you a message." His smile attempted to be reassuring. "Nothing important, may I come in for a moment? I won't keep you. I must be on my way."

"Of course. We were just having breakfast. May I offer you some coffee?"

He gave a small, indulgent laugh which might almost have been kindly. "No, no," he said, "it will not take that long and I do not want to detain you. But please continue with your breakfast. We were just anxious," he added, "that the children hear the message too."

They entered the kitchen and the children looked up at the tall man with curiosity. Mauie Marcos stood at her chair and looked at her children, from one to the other. "This gentleman works with Daddy," she said. "What do we say?"

They both had their mouths full and spoke in unison, "How do you do? And good morning."

He smiled down at them, and then at their mother. "Did you ever want to go to America?" he said.

There was something in his eyes now that made her go cold inside. She heard the girls shout out loud and watched them bounce in their chairs. They had often heard their father talk about moving to America. They had been taught that going to the USA was a good thing, a thing to be joyful about. Zimo Chew watched her with no expression on his face.

Unconsciously her hand went to her throat. "We have talked about it, sometimes," she said, "But never as a serious option."

He raised an eyebrow. "Oh, it is a very serious option, Mrs. Marcos. Dr. Marcos does very important work. In the USA his work would be even more important. You understand?"

"Yes, I see."

"In an hour a car will come from the Chinese Embassy. It will take you to the American Embassy. From there you will be flown, under the protection of the Americans, to the United States, and you will start a new life there."

She swallowed hard. She could feel her right leg

start to shake. "What about my husband?"

Zimo smiled. "He will join you there, of course. The embassy will arrange for a very good job for him there. It will be a dream come true for him. Won't it?"

His smile had faded on the little question tag at the end, and his face had become dangerous. She had nodded and said, "Yes, he will be very happy."

The smile returned. "All of this, China does for you and for your husband, your whole family. I hope you are grateful, Mauie."

The use of her first name was tinged with an indefinable insolence, almost a threat. A threat that carried with it both a lack of respect and an excess of intimacy.

"We are all very grateful."

"Good." Now his smile showed a row of small, even teeth. "Then you will be glad to do a favor for us in return. You understand that, if we can be sure of your help, your husband will follow very soon." He inclined his head to one side and adopted an expression that attempted to be sad. "If we are not absolutely sure, then that will delay things, and your husband will not be able to join you."

"I assure you, Mr. Chew, that my gratitude is very deep, to you and to China, and I will be very happy—honored—to help in any way I can. I promise."

"Good!" He spread his hands, echoing the broad smile on his face. "That is very good. And after all, the favor is very small. We ask only that you do what any good wife would do, take an interest in your husband's work, and the work of his colleagues. You will have a friend, she will introduce herself to you. She will look after you and you will have coffee together, and you will tell her about your husband's work, and his friends' work. And maybe she will ask you sometimes to do her a little favor. Simple, no? Not a big problem?"

She shook her head. She would have to betray her husband, spy on him, spy on his friends and his colleagues. Zimo Chew saw the horror in her eyes and smiled at the two children.

"Such beautiful young lives," he said. "Such a wonderful future for them."

"I will do everything you say, Mr. Chew."

The smile faded completely from his face. "I know," he said simply. "Pray to your god that you and your family never meet me again."

And he left.

CHAPTER FOURTEEN

My cell rang. It was Paul Hoffmann.

"Yeah. You got something for me?"

"I don't know. Why don't you tell me. First, one John Jones was booked on a flight from Clark International to Dubai yesterday afternoon. It may be nothing, but Hoffstadder's first name is Jay, his friends often called him JJ—John Jones? JJ? He never showed for the flight."

"Shit."

"Yeah. I was one of those who called him JJ."

"I'm sorry."

"Let's hope it's too soon for that. There was no Marion James, or anybody suggestive of her on the flight."

I sighed and drummed my fingers on the roof of Gallin's car.

"There's another thing, pretty bizarre."

"What?" I put the phone on speaker.

"The Chinese Embassy just asked us to take Mrs. Mauie Marcos and her kids in as refugees. They said that the Filipino government was about to kill them and her husband, Felix Marcos. They said he might come in in a couple of days."

"What the hell...?" I stared at Gallin. She was frowning hard. I said, "We are taking her in, right?"

"And Dr. Marcos too, if he can make it."

"We want him. We just tried to talk to him. They said he was in a clinic."

Hoffman shrugged with his voice. "No surprise there. I figure they are being planted."

"OK, thanks, Paul. Hang loose."

I hung up and called the office.

"Office of the Director of International Navigation, how may I direct your call?"

"Mason, ODIN double-oh five two, I need to talk to Chief."

There was the customary pause, then, "Just as a matter of curiosity, Alex, do you know what time it is in DC?"

"Time you and I went on a date?"

"I am doing double shifts."

"You must be exhausted. You need a foot massage and a martini. Can I talk to the Chief now?"

She sighed and the Chief came on the line.

"What?"

"Did you pick up the Hoffstadders?"

"Only three of them. They are in debriefing now—"

"You're debriefing the kids?"

He groaned. "They are in a beautiful mock bodega in Napa County where Gloria is gorging on gourmet food and the children are playing with child psychologists who wear leather sandals and have ginger beards and talk to their inner child. And that's just the female ones, Mason. The male ones do not produce enough testosterone to grow beards of any color!" He almost shouted the last line.

"I'm not sure whether to be reassured or not."

"Don't be! The future of democracy is in the hands

of people with freckles who shun their *toilet*"—he pronounced it the French way—"and believe that all conflict can be resolved via meaningful dialogue!"

"Freckles, huh?"

"Yes. This man has a ginger beard and an untrimmed ginger moustache, and freckles on his arms. He attempted to engage me in conversation. He told me his doctoral thesis had been a deep exploration of his relationship with his mother."

"Sir?"

"What?"

"Has Gloria Hoffstadter told you where her husband is or what his plans are?"

"No. She does not know. She assumed he would take a flight from Clark to Dubai, but they made a point of not discussing it."

"Makes sense."

"Of course it makes sense. Was there anything else? I should like to get back to sleep."

"There is one other thing. John Jones booked a ticket yesterday from Clark International to Dubai. He didn't board the flight. I need to know yesterday where else he has used that credit card."

"If you ever hang up, I shall instruct Lovelock to look into it."

"Thank you, sir. Also, the Chinese have requested asylum for Mauie Marcos and her two kids. Felix Marcos will follow shortly. They claim the Philippine government wants to kill them."

"That is very odd."

"I agree. Good night, sir."

"Good morning!"

I tried to beat him to it, but he hung up first, probably because he was using one of those old Bakelite phones and he slammed down the receiver on his bedside table. It was an image that pleased me and I held on to it. Gallin said, "What?"

I told her about Hoffstadder's wife and kids, including the scourge that was sensitive men with red beards and open-toed sandals. She gave a knowing snort. "I know the sort. You know the type? In the sack they try to be as sensitive as a woman. It's nauseating." She stared at me a moment while I stared back at her. Then she looked worried and shrugged. "I heard that."

"So, a man by the name of John Jones booked a flight yesterday from Clark International to Dubai, but never boarded the flight."

"I know. I was two feet away from you."

"Nobody who was likely to be Marion James booked or boarded a flight from Clark."

"So when you asked for other places that credit card was used, you were thinking…"

I thumped my palm gently down on the roof of the car three or four times.

"If you were running from the Philippine authorities, and the Chinese secret service, what would you do, once you discovered the coach terminal was being watched?" She drew breath to answer but I ignored her and plowed on. "I mean, it is at least possible that Marion and Hoffstadder were at or near Philtranco Pasay when Carmona was shot. It is very likely they heard about it, and even if they didn't know Carmona, even if they didn't know he was part of the cell, Hoffstadder is certainly smart enough to realize they were watching the terminal."

"Now?"

I nodded and she came and leaned next to me on the roof of the red car.

"So... We thought the only way to get out of the Philippines with a minimum risk of being seen was by bus to Clark, but obviously the Chinese were ahead of us—and them and thought the same thing, to Carmona's cost. So what is the next best alternative?"

"That was my question, only better expressed." She watched me and waited. I went on. "Hoffstadder and Carmona both seem to have gone for the same option—the one we arrived at, the same one the Chinese arrived at. But what about the inexperienced girl? The one you pointed out was so different? What about a girl who is more of a Rough Guide traveler than an Emirates to Dubai and Los Angeles girl, a girl who doesn't have much money and is in a panic? What would she do?"

Her gaze was lost up into the abundant, reckless foliage of the lot across the road and her jaw sagged slightly. After a moment she said, "Huh..."

"I think her primal instinct would be to crawl into the darkest hole she could find."

She nodded. "Uh-huh."

"So, that's a metaphor, how does that metaphor translate into reality in Manila?"

"She would not move into a dive, because she would want to get out of Manila in a hurry. She'll still go for the bus, but..."

She frowned, losing the thread of her own thoughts for a moment. I interrupted her.

"She'll go south. Her instinct will be that all the official attention will be on the international airports and the ports. So she'll try to get as far away from that as possible."

"She'll go south and try to charter a boat, or hitch a ride on a yacht."

"And son of a gun! She hit on the one thing that might work."

"If that's what she's done, how the hell do we check that out?"

"We could start with the CCTV footage from the bus terminal."

She gave a bark of a laugh. "Ha!"

I knew she was right, but short of a full-out search and rescue mission with air support, I was stumped for an answer. I thought about calling Paul Hoffmann again, but discarded the idea. They were even less likely to provide that footage to the CIA than they were to me. So I called Gerardo Baccay.

"Mr. Mason, you are still in Manila?"

"I am. I wanted to talk to you."

"We already talked. Maybe you should go back to DC."

"Yeah. Things have changed. Also, I think there were some administrative costs that got overlooked."

There was a long silence. Eventually he said, "What kind of administrative costs?"

"Pretty big ones. Look, I don't want to waste time, yours or mine. I'll make this brief and vague in case we have alien ears. Try to keep up. OK?"

"Talk."

"Some guy bought it getting on a bus. You with me?"

"Yes."

"It would be cool to see that in the movies, right?"

"I understand."

"So I figure, a busy place like that…"

"I said I understand. Those films have been collected and are hard to get hold of."

"Who has them?"

"I can't tell you that on the phone."

"So can you get them?"

"Yes, I can get them, but it's going to be expensive."

"My uncle will pay anything reasonable, but don't push it."

"Where are you?"

"Anywhere you want me to be."

"OK, Ayala Shopping Mall, on Courtyard Drive. You go to Ayala Avenue. You know it? Between San Lorenzo district and Urdaneta. You can park in the parking garage. We meet at Starbucks by the Glorietta Four Park. I'll be there in half an hour, little bit more maybe."

"That hard to get, huh?"

"You want them or not?"

"I want them."

"So be there."

He hung up and I turned to Gallin. I raised an eyebrow at her and said, "Ha! yourself."

It was a fifteen-minute drive from the Marcos residence to the Ayala Shopping Mall. On the way I stopped at a bank which made it twenty. We left the Corvette at the rather oddly named Steel Car Park and made our way on foot to the Glorietta Four Park, then crossed over to get some coffee at the Starbucks plastic emporium. It was like a set from *Star Wars*, with strange folds in the yellow ceiling, and tables that were too small for human beings.

We sat by a plate-glass window and waited for Baccay to show. Gallin was looking around like she had a hornet in her silk panties. I didn't ask her what was wrong, but she couldn't resist telling me anyway.

"It's odd, isn't it?"

"I don't know, what is 'it'?"

"No, take that look off your face. It's patronizing. Since the late Middle Ages—as long as there have been coffee shops—most of the great intellectual revolutions, the revolutions that have elevated human thought and the human condition, have started in coffee shops. Am I right or not?"

I thought about it and nodded. "Yeah, I guess you're right."

"A place to stimulate unique, individual thought. From people like Benjamin Franklin to Van Gogh through Freud and Marx to Albert Camus and Jean-Paul Sartre. Hell! Sir Isaac Newton started his work on gravity because of an argument he had in a coffee shop with Edmund Halley."

"Is this going somewhere? I mean, you're right, but what's your point?"

She gestured expansively with both hands. "Look around you. If architecture is frozen poetry, what the hell is this? Standardized, systematized thinking gone into paralysis. Welcome to the dawn of Aquarius, where every thought is an identical, hexagonal section of the Hive Mind."

"You didn't sleep well last night?"

"Don't be a smart-ass. You know I'm right. Cafés used to be unique places for unique minds, now they are standardized places for standardized minds."

I jerked my chin at the window. "Here's Baccay."

He pushed through the door, showed his badge to the barista and told her to bring him a coffee over to our table. As he approached I stood. His eyes were on Gallin. I said:

"Inspector, this is Captain Gallin, my partner."

He didn't greet her. He looked hard at me and said, "You didn't say anything about a partner."

"I didn't tell you what color underwear I have on either." I smiled sweetly. "And that's because it's none of your damned business. Now, sit down and let's cut the crap and talk business."

He scowled at Gallin, pulled out a chair and sat. I said, "I need the CCTV footage from the Philtranco Pasay Bus Terminal shooting, an hour before and an hour afterwards. Inside and outside."

"Two thousand American dollars."

I'd been expecting five but I sighed and looked at Gallin. She snorted. "You gotta be kidding! You seen them?"

He nodded. "I'm the investigating officer. But this footage is sealed, classified and to be destroyed."

"So what's on it?"

He gave me a sly smile. "Stuff you wanna see. I give you this much for free, but then you have to pay me. Chinese also have this footage, but they have not seen what I have seen, because they do not know what to look for." He pointed a finger at my face. "You know what to look for."

I looked at Gallin. We made eye contact and she gave me an almost imperceptible nod, then told Baccay, "This better be legit, Baccay."

"Or what? Chinese pull weight here, US too, but

Israel ain't shit in Manila. Don't threaten me. I know who you are, I seen your car. You big fish in USA, but you ain't nothing in Philippines."

"Hey—" He looked at me with the same insolence in his eyes. I said, "We're all friends here. In a moment I am going to hand you an envelope under the table, so just relax. Now, before I do, what about the other major terminals, the ports, airports?"

"Nothing, no incidents, no sightings. I pulled the CCTV and had teams checking it for forty-eight hours. No sign of girl or of Jay."

I frowned at him. "Jay?"

There was no expression on his face when he said it. "He was my friend, a good man."

I thought for a moment, still frowning at him. "How about the girl?"

"Marion James, I didn't know her personally, but she was just a kid, too young, too innocent to be involved in a dirty game like this."

"Do you know what it's about, Inspector? Do you know why this has flared up, what they are looking for?"

He held my eye and shook his head. "No idea." He shrugged. "I can deduce what you can deduce."

I stood and made my way across the room to the bathrooms. I found an empty cubicle and counted out two and a half grand, then put the other two and a half in my wallet.

I stood at the sinks washing my hands and Baccay came in. He stood next to me and I handed him the cash.

"I made it two and a half. I know you didn't have to do this and I know the risks. You get in any trouble or you need any help, I'll pull strings for you."

He took the money without any expression on his face, and handed me a DVD in a plastic case.

"I don't want nobody running Philippines. But especially I don't want Chinese or Russians running it. We are a small country, the size of Norway. We could have a good democracy like them. But we have two problems." He held up two fingers in the peace sign. "Corruption, and one hundred and nine million people. One hundred and three million more than Norway. With so many people, democracy is impossible, and corruption is so easy."

I nodded and we returned to our table. He left without a farewell, Gallin stood and we made our way out into the sun. After a moment she said, "He implied that Hoffstadder and Marion James were on the film, right?"

"That was what I understood. At least one of them was."

"What did he say to you in the john?"

"He told me my lipstick was too red."

"He's right, what else?"

"That with large populations democracy is difficult and corruption is easy."

"He was right about that, too."

CHAPTER FIFTEEN

We took the DVD back to my room at the hotel, ordered a couple of hamburgers and a six-pack of cold beers, and settled down to examine the footage. Baccay had helpfully scrawled onto a slip of paper what he thought were the relevant positions on the various videos.

I slipped the DVD into my laptop on the desk and pulled up a couple of chairs while Gallin stuck four of the beers in the fridge and cracked the other two. She set one in front of me and sat beside me. I pressed play.

The first video was of the ticket hall. There was a line, not very long. There were a couple of cops patrolling, moving in and out of the frame. They were obviously looking for someone, but trying to be discreet about it. A man joined the line and we both sat forward. He was not Filipino. He was big, not fat but strong. He had a baseball cap and dark glasses, and a dark moustache. He was dressed casually in walking boots, jeans and a sweatshirt.

The cops looked at him and went away. The line moved forward and a tall Chinese man in a suit approached him. I had my burger in my hands and said, "Freeze!"

She tapped the space bar and I stared closely.

"Zimo Chew," I said around a mouthful of minced beef and salad. "That's the guy who warned me off the day I arrived. He's a hit man for the *Táotài bù* of the MSS. He's the one who's eliminating them."

She hit the space bar again and we watched them exchange a few words. Then Zimo walked away. Gallin shook her head. "He didn't recognize him, but that is Hoffstadder."

She looked at me and I shrugged. I wanted to be as sure as she was, but I wasn't. "What makes you so sure?"

"It's too much of a coincidence."

"You know how many tourists there are in Manila at this time of year, travelling by bus?"

She ignored the question and instead said, "You know how many of them are lone men in their forties wearing Red Sox baseball caps?" She had a point but I ignored her and she said, "OK, so who's this?"

A scruffy young blonde had joined the line. She was a couple of places back from the guy with the baseball cap.

I pointed. "That's the girl I saw outside Hampton's house."

"You sure?"

"One hundred percent positive. That's her."

"Did they arrange to meet here?"

I shook my head. "Unlikely. That would be bad craft. Stop!"

She froze the film just as the big guy was receiving his ticket. I zoomed in. It was real grainy but I took a screenshot and sent it back to ODIN with instructions for urgent analysis. I needed to know where that guy was going.

He walked out, glanced at the girl but, though we ran it several times, there was no indication that he said anything or that she noticed him. Then the girl moved up to the window. There was a short exchange, the girl handed over money and the woman handed her a ticket. We froze it, zoomed in and sent it back to DC. Then I called. We went through the usual ritual, then Lovelock said, "We are twelve hours apart, you know? Three PM there is three AM here. So I sleep by day and stay up all night waiting for you to call."

"You're a doll. Now listen, wake up whomever you need to wake up. I have sent you two pictures of people receiving tickets. I need to know the destination on those tickets in the next hour. The shots are taken at the Philtranco Pasay Terminal. So they need to get a list of destinations from that station and make comparisons."

"Anything else?"

"Not for now."

"Ten four, over and out."

The video cut and the view was from the top of some kind of pylon or lamppost. We could see the outside of the terminal with a lot of bustle. There were people walking past in both directions, as well as people going in and out. They were moving fast and jerky.

Gallin pointed and said, "There!"

The guy she thought was Hoffstadder came out. He hesitated a moment, looking up and down the street, then headed for the covered walkway. Our eyes were on him and we missed what happened, but suddenly there were a lot of people running, clearing a space on the road by the sidewalk. I rewound and we played it again in slow motion. Hoffstadder, if that was who it was, hesitated, then turned toward the covered walkway. Gallin said,

"Look," and pointed at the screen.

Zimo was there, in the crowd, looking around, and just as Hoffstadder started to move toward the walkway, Zimo raised his hand and seemed to call out to a man in the crowd. The man stopped and turned, staring around. Very calmly and deliberately Zimo pulled a pistol from under his arm and shot the man in the chest.

The man in the baseball cap stopped and looked back, then bolted. But another movement caught my eye. We had to replay it several times before Gallin said, "There, look, look! The scruffy girl!"

We rewound again and watched as Marion James came out of the terminal, made her way to the road and, finding a lull in the traffic, dodged across to the central reservation. Just as she arrived there, Zimo called out to the man and shot him. She stared for a moment, then vaulted the reservation and crossed to the far side.

I paused the image and sat back. "Meanwhile," I said, "Hoffstadder, if that's who it is—"

"It is."

"Whatever, has crossed via the covered walkway and ended up on the same side of the street as Marion James." I scowled suddenly. "Who the hell is this Marion James?"

She fast-forwarded the video and, after a couple of minutes, he appeared, running in a reckless, crazy fashion in the same direction Marion had taken.

We spent the next three quarters of an hour drinking cold beer and watching jerky people strutting up and down the street or in and out of the bus station. Then, as boredom was turning to despair and Gallin informed me that she wanted to tear her face off, I saw them.

"That's them! They're together, coming down the

steps from the walkway. They are definitely together."

She scratched her head. "What the hell...?" She stared at me. "Why pretend they don't know each other, and then...?"

"Look, they are going in together."

"That's crazy."

We ran it another couple of times to see if there was anything else we could glean, but there was nothing. Gallin stood, went out to the terrace and stretched noisily. My cell rang.

"Yeah?"

"Lovelock, can you talk?"

"Sure."

"We're encrypted on a secure line, but I'll be brief. The lab did the best they could. The man was traveling to Clark International Airport in Mabalacat, and the closest they could get for the girl was Nayon something something Pangingi something something, which they take to be Nayon ng Pangingisda. I have no idea how you pronounce that."

"Both going to different destinations, you're sure about that?"

"That's what they said. I am not sure about anything."

"Thanks, Lovelock."

I hung up and Gallin said, "It makes sense."

"They meet by chance and he decides to go with her? That's a hell of a coincidence."

"Is it?" She shrugged. "They were at the bus station because it was the only way out of Manila, and then they were thrown together by the shock of seeing Carmona gunned down. Both of them now know that they are being hunted, but neither knows that the other knows. You follow?"

"For some reason I do. You mean they both think the other is just a tourist and will give them cover."

"That's what I meant. If Zimo hadn't shot Carmona, their plans would have proceeded as..." She made a gesture with her hand.

I said, "Planned."

"Thanks, but Carmona's death made them seek deeper cover."

"So they are both now on their way to..." I tried to read it. "Nayon ng Pangingisda."

"I thought that was like forty light years away."

"We need to lose the Corvette. We need something fast and inconspicuous."

She shook her head. "We will never catch them by road. We need a light aircraft or a chopper or something."

"Yes, that would be inconspicuous."

"Come on, Mason. Don't be a pussy. Lots of people fly light aircraft in the Philippines, because there are no trains. It's remote."

"What is your authority for that statement, Gallin?"

She shrugged. "Ask anyone. You know how to fly?"

"Of course."

"Cool."

She pulled her phone from her jacket and made a call. She spoke in Hebrew for a while to a guy with a deep voice. She glanced at me a couple of times and laughed, then said what sounded like, "*Toda, toda raba,*" and hung up.

I felt an unreasonable stab of annoyance and said,

"Were you taking a short break on the company dime to do a bit of flirting, or was that relevant to the job at hand?"

"A friend who works at the Israeli Embassy. He has a farm fifteen, twenty miles east of the city, and he has a Cessna Skyhawk at the farm."

"And he's willing to lend you his plane?"

I sounded a little incredulous and she laughed. "I told him if anything happened you'd pay, you were good for it."

"Thanks."

"It has a range of six hundred and forty nautical miles. That will get us as far as the south coast of Mindanao, and it has a cruising speed of one hundred and twenty nautical miles per hour. That's like a hundred and forty miles per hour."

"I told you I can fly. They have almost twenty-four hours head start on us. When can we get a hold of this plane?"

"He said he needed a couple of hours to fill her up and get her ready."

"OK, let's get a shower, pack an overnight bag and get going. Also, call reception, find out the itinerary of the coach they're on. We need to know where they stop so we can intercept them."

"So masterful. Makes me weak at the knees."

"Get out. Reception in half an hour."

I met her in reception twenty minutes later. She was in jeans and a sweatshirt and had a sports bag over her shoulder. She took my arm and started talking as she guided me through the door to where her Corvette had been brought up from the garage.

"OK, they have an eighteen-hour lead on us." She opened the surprisingly large trunk, dumped our two bags in and slammed it closed. She pulled open her door and kept talking as she climbed in. I followed. "Their route takes them from the Pasay Terminal to Calauag, then Naga and eventually Bulan. Total sixteen hours. So they got there two hours ago."

We slammed the doors. I said, "She wasn't going to Bulan."

"I haven't finished." The car snarled into life and we pulled out of the hotel drive. "From Bulan they then get a smaller, local bus which takes them to Matnog. That's like fifteen miles and probably takes half an hour. Call it an hour. Here they spend the night—what, eight hours?—and catch a ferry in the morning across to Allen on Samar Island. Depending on the weather that could take around two hours. At Allen they pick up another bus which takes them across Samar as far as Tacloban City. That's another five hours, more or less."

"What happens at Tacloban? Don't tell me. They get another bus which takes them to Bally-go Backward in Kerry."

"Be serious. There, they get a local bus, where you enjoy the company of chickens and goats as well as curious locals, which takes them along the coast for a hundred and twenty miles, stopping wherever requested, as far as San Ricardo. The exact time of arrival is not known, but a journey time of between five and seven hours is not unusual."

I nodded. "San Ricardo. Tell me something, simply out of curiosity, do they ever arrive at this mythical place, Nayon ng Pangingisda, in Mindanao?"

She turned from Rodriguez Avenue onto Ortigas

and began to accelerate, pressing me back into my seat.

She nodded and grinned at me. "You can see why they chose this route, right?"

I grunted, more because of the force of the acceleration than because I agreed. She went on:

"The ferry from San Ricardo to Lipata, the nearest port on Mindanao, takes one hour. And after that it's four buses, one into Surigao City, which is like five minutes away, then a coach from Surigao to Davao, which is the big city out there. That's four hours if they get the express. Change at Davao and get a further coach to General Santos, two hours if they get the express, and a final, local bus from General Santos to..."

"Nayon ng Pangingisda. I bet Ulysses didn't feel this relieved when he got back to Ithaca."

"No express here, it's the chicken and goat run again and can take anything from three to five hours, depending on cargo and detours. Gotta love country life."

"So their total journey time is...?"

"Projected fifty-one hours and five minutes. Of which they have carried out, as I said, eighteen hours. So they are now at Matnog, where they will spend the night, and catch the ferry in the morning."

"Good work."

"Gee, thanks."

"Stupid question, I know, but. Is there an airfield in Matnog?"

"Sure. Airstrip. Center of town. Used for emergency airlifts. Things like that."

I would later discover that when Gallin used that kind of staccato phrasing it meant she was lying through her teeth, but right then I was happy to nod and be impressed by her efficiency.

"Good, so Matnog is..." I checked my phone. "...a little over two hundred nautical miles away. Which gets us there an hour and forty minutes after takeoff. Agreed?"

"You bet."

"Which will be?"

"In half an hour if people stop getting in my way. ETA half past nine. There can't be many B&Bs, it's not a big tourist resort. It's a pretty remote fishing village. If we ask around nicely for our English and American friends, we'll find them tonight."

Ten minutes later we came to a road grandly named National Road, which wound its way through sleeping suburbs and villages, until we came to a large, wooden gate bordered by tall cypress trees. She stopped there and made a call on her cell. She didn't say anything but the gate swung open and we drove through.

We snaked down a winding drive toward a large house where I could not make out any lights burning. Fifty yards from the house we turned left down a beaten track and made for a field. Floodlights snapped on and I saw that more than a field it was in fact a vast lawn, and down the center of that lawn there was a black strip of tarmac. She killed the engine beside the field gate and looked at me.

"OK, cowboy, we're here."

CHAPTER SIXTEEN

Sixteen miles away and a couple of hours earlier, in an office by the banks of La Mesa Reservoir, on Katipunan Avenue, Bao Liu was speaking excitedly to Mr. Wang.

"I was terrified, Mr. Wang, because I knew how important the work was, and I thought I would not be able to do it because it was an operating system which I had never seen before. But I told myself, I must do it for *Tián Cháo*, our Heavenly Kingdom, as you said, Mr. Wang. I have not slept, *Sifu*, and I have finally been able to make a model of the operating system, and now I can get inside."

Mr. Wang regarded the young man with inexpressive eyes and a straight, lipless mouth.

"And what do you want, Liu Bao? Are you seeking praise?"

The blood drained from Bao Liu's face. "No, oh no, Mr. Wang. Not at all. I am not worthy. I am nothing but a servant of *Tián Cháo*, I meant only to inform you that I can now get inside the operating system, and I will soon be able to extract the information you want."

Mr. Wang's face shifted, as though at the flip of a switch, and he offered Bao Liu a smile that seemed to have sold its soul to the devil.

"Good, then return to work, Bao. Mr. Chew will want to visit you soon, to congratulate you. He will be very interested in your progress."

Terror hollowed out Bao's insides. He nodded and bowed a couple of times, unable to speak. He backed away, "Of course, Mr. Wang, I am always at your service."

He exited the office and ran back to his small room, where he splashed cold water on his face and forced himself to concentrate. He knew the way in now. Now he must work his way, program by program, file by file, until he found what they were looking for.

Two floors below, Zimo Chew reviewed the data—what little data there was—one more time. He knew that patience was essential, and he was capable of infinite patience when it was called for, but time was passing and the more time that passed the more his net began to dissolve and fall apart. He needed the information on the laptop: who knew? Who was in the cell? And what had been done with the copy? But the boy was too slow.

Fear would make him slower, and so would pain. Liu Bao was the best. He had been told this by the best. He was the best of the best, but he was too slow.

The data—the facts: He knew that Dr. Edward Ulysses Hampton had a cell in Manila. He knew that Dr. Jay Hoffstadder was a part of that cell, he knew that Juan Carmona was part of that cell. He had absolutely no doubts about them. Equally, he knew that Dr. Felix Marcos had been part of the cell, and he was now successfully turned. But there were others, he was equally sure of that.

The girl. Dr. Hampton had been seen with her once, perhaps a second time but it was unconfirmed. She had been described as scruffy, blonde, foreign, unremarkable. He listed the other members in his mind: the head of the International Law Department at the University of the Philippines, the head of the new Department of Viral Cybernetics, a high-ranking official at the Department of Foreign Affairs...and a scruffy, unremarkable blonde girl.

It did not seem likely, and yet.

He played again the CCTV footage that Baccay had secured for him. Every time he watched it he became more convinced he had made a mistake, and that the foreign man in the line was Hoffstadder. He dared not send it to Beijing for facial recognition analysis, not when it was there, clear as day on the video, that he had looked the man in the face and spoken to him, and failed to recognize him. But he did not need facial recognition. Logic alone dictated it was him. Logic dictated that he was the John Jones booked onto the flight for Dubai. He never boarded the plane, and he never boarded the bus.

But he did return to the terminal, with the scruffy, blonde, unremarkable girl. Who was she? Why had Dr. Hampton taken an interest in her? He had assumed at first she was a foreign whore. Hampton was known not to like Oriental women. But clearly it was not sex he sought from her. Twice he had asked Baccay who she was and twice he had told him there was no information on her. Twice he had asked Baccay what tickets she and Hoffstadder had bought. Hoffstadder had bought a ticket to Clark International, but nobody remembered the girl.

He had shrugged. "She is unremarkable. Nobody notices her."

Until he had gone to the terminal himself with two police officers and spoken to the woman at the ticket office. He had shown her the photograph and she had nodded vigorously.

"Oh yes, I remember her very well. She spoke so

quietly nobody could hear what she was saying. And she could not pronounce properly. My god, what a mess she made of it!"

"Where was she going?"

"Nayon ng Pangingisda! By bus! I thought she was mad! Go by plane! But no, she wanted to go by bus! More than fifty hours, god knows how many changes..."

And the man was with her. He would have them tonight. He would have them both tonight.

In his black bag he had a change of shirt and underwear, his toilet bag and what he thought of as his "kill kit," a suppressed 9mm, a Glock 19, a stiletto knife and a nineteenth-century shaving razor. There was also a piano wire. A surgeon's cap and a pack of latex gloves, though the luxury of working the Philippines these days was that such precautions were not necessary.

He closed the bag and his driver knocked and leaned in the door.

"The car is ready, sir, the helicopter is waiting."

He walked quickly to the car and kept his bag with him, beside him on the black leather seat. The drive was slow. At that time of the afternoon the traffic was heavy and they had to cross the center of town to get to the airport where the helicopter was waiting.

By the time they got there the sun was already low in the sky, casting copper light and long shadows.

His badge got him through security without delays and he was met at the diplomatic lounge by the pilot who led him straight away through private gates and out to the tarmac. His team of three were already onboard the AVI Copter AC 311. They greeted each other with nods, exchanged no words and within five minutes the helicopter was taking off, wheeling across the city and plunging south at close to one hundred and eighty miles per hour.

Far below them buildings soon gave way to broad, green fields. The sun spilled orange light across the horizon in the west, and the fields below them were engulfed in darkness. Zimo closed his eyes and reviewed the task at hand. It was barely a plan. They would arrive, ask where the foreigners were, kill Hoffstadder and take the woman in for questioning, then leave.

Journey time was a little over an hour and twenty minutes. In a little over three hours they would be back in Manila, job done and able to return home. If he had known, if he had been able to predict that the laptop would have such exotic software, then he would have tortured Hampton first, and none of this would have been necessary.

But it was pointless to regret the past.

The cell must be found and destroyed, but the scruffy, nondescript girl must be interrogated first, to find out why—why Hampton was interested in her. Then she would be killed like the rest.

The chopper thundered on into the night, moving south fast.

* * *

The rattling old bus had pulled into what Marion thought of as Matnog High Street in late afternoon. The bus had rattled, shuddered, banged and let out a cloud of black smoke from its exhaust, and then disgorged an improbable number of people, chickens, bags and assorted containers of fruit and vegetables.

Marion and Hoffstadder had sat, smiling at each other, and watched the colorful spectacle as it spilled from the vehicle out into the late sun. When the last person was off, they had followed. Hoffstadder had asked the driver where there was a hotel, and he had said there was just one in the town. The street had no name, but it was the one parallel to the one they were on. A two-minute walk.

"And food?"

The driver had laughed and spread his hands wide. "Everywhere! Walk down, food everywhere!"

So they had walked along the High Street. This was not the Philippines that Hoffstadder had known, and it was the Philippines that Marion had all but forgotten. To say it was vibrant was to descend into cliché, and yet it was hard to think of any other word. It was alive! Every house seemed to have some kind of market stall outside. In the street, as far as the eye could see there were motorized rickshaws in the form of motorbikes with covered sidecars, jostling with each other in all directions regardless of what side of the road they were on.

There was no asphalt here. The road was beaten earth, and the buildings were of a startling variety: Spanish colonial, washed a strange turquoise, vied with mock Chinese imperial, thatched roofs and functional boxes of concrete. It was a free-for-all architectural mayhem.

And the stalls had everything from books, batteries and socks to airbeds, flip-flops and fish and groceries.

As they walked, the air was rich with the scents of flowers, tropical plants and spices, and Hoffstadder was overcome suddenly with a sense of inexplicable happiness. He laughed for no particular reason and he was surprised that Marion looked at him and laughed too. She took his arm and squeezed it and said, "It's beautiful, isn't it?"

"It is. All these years all I have known is Manila. And here was this, all along."

They walked in silence then until the next intersection, where they turned into the parallel street and found the hotel. It was as bizarre as the High Street and seemed to have been, two hundred years earlier, the home of a wealthy Spanish colonial. The woman on reception, whom Marion took to be the owner, spoke loudly in a kind of pidgin English and laughed a lot for no particular reason.

"You wang one room two room?"

They both said, simultaneously, "Oh!" then looked at each other, laughed and drew breath to answer. He was going to say two, but she beat him to it and said, "Oh, just one!"

There was a moment of confusion while all three of them looked at each other. Marion babbled, "I mean, if that's OK, it's just cheaper but we can…"

And he babbled over her, "No, no, that's fine, absolutely, no, yeah, exactly, cheaper…"

And the woman produced two big apple cheeks and chortled and screamed something incomprehensible that sounded like, "*Aaaah, heshe nono gonna maky nookie-nookie bang bang, he nono, aaaah!*"

All of this, or something that sounded like it to Hoffstadder, she repeated three or four times as she led them up the stairs to their room. Once she had thrown open the windows and shown them where everything was, she left and Marion covered her face with her hands.

"Jay, I am so sorry! I feel like an absolute twit!"

"No! A twit? Is that a thing in England? I am sure you're not a twit. But look, it's fine. I should probably have suggested it myself. I mean, after all," he laughed, "we've been sleeping together in something much smaller than this bed all the way here, right?"

She was bright pink and staring at him as he said all this. She managed, "I suppose so," and he went on.

"Look, can I suggest something? Let's go buy some bathing costumes, have a swim, have some dinner in one of those thatched, beach diner shed things. I bet the food is amazing! Drink some wine, if we can get some, and relax. I really think we have earned it."

A strange feeling of gratitude overwhelmed her. She fought back a wave of emotion and nodded. "That sounds like a wonderful idea. Thank you for being so understanding."

"Not at all. Come on, let's go."

They left their stuff in the room and made their way down to the high street, where they found a shop that sold just about everything you might need in an average lifetime. Hoffstadder bought flip-flops, bathing trunks, a towel, cheap Wayfarer imitation shades and a T-shirt with the legend "Surfer Dream Is Wet" on it. After a moment's hesitation he also bought an orange plastic bottle of sun cream.

Marion bought a red bikini, Davidof (with one "f") sunglasses, a large towel, a wicker basket, two bottles of cold beer, two toothbrushes, toothpaste, a blue-and-white parasol and, after a moment's hesitation, an orange plastic bottle of sun cream. They met at the checkout. Marion laughed at his T-shirt and he admired her foresight. They both agreed sun cream was smart given the ozone depletion.

"Though I think you'll have to help me with my back," added Hoffstadder. "After that bus ride I am about as flexible as the IRS."

"Me too."

She smiled and they made their way down toward the beach. Hoffstadder was vaguely aware that he should be feeling guilty, but was unable to summon the feeling and found himself speaking aloud suddenly.

"It's as though we had stepped into a parallel universe." She looked at him curiously. He went on, "As though we had left that other world behind and entered a new world where we are actually different people." He shrugged and jerked his thumb over his shoulder. "For me at least, Manila, the law, all of that, it's like somebody else's life. This... This is real now. That isn't."

She nodded gently and her eyes were drawn by the vast ocean before them. Her fingers found his hand and held on. They made their way to the white sand, an odd couple: he large, carrying the basket on his shoulder, with his flip-flops flapping on his large feet, she small, scruffy, white and blonde, holding his large hand in hers.

They found a spot, dropped their stuff and set up the parasol, changed amid much laughter and riskily slipping towels, and eventually ran down to the sea where they splashed and laughed like children for half an hour before returning to the shade. There she spread abundant sun cream on his back and shoulders. And, when she was done he did the same for her after she had unfastened the top of her bikini.

CHAPTER SEVENTEEN

In the end they found a restaurant on the port opposite the ferry terminal, with waiters and tables with candles. A few other foreign couples and groups, all of whom carefully ignored each other, occupied other tables. The menu was Asian rather than strictly Filipino, and the food looked and smelled good.

They played it safe and ordered spring rolls, chicken with cashew nuts, wok-fried prawns and vegetable rice. They also risked a bottle of very cold white wine which was surprisingly good.

They ate the spring rolls in silence and, thirsty from the afternoon on the beach, with their skin still warm and salty, they finished the wine and Hoffstadder ordered another. He refilled her glass and sat back, smiling.

"Oddly enough," he said, "I haven't had this much fun since…" He paused, thinking, and shook his head. "I can't remember when."

She didn't look up. She turned an end of spring roll over in her fingers and said, "Why oddly enough?"

He frowned, suddenly alarmed. "Oh, I don't mean…" He didn't know how to finish that explanation so he started another one. "I mean, when I said oddly enough, I wasn't referring to you... Please don't take it that way."

Now she looked up and, seeing the distress in his eyes, she smiled. "I didn't take it as a personal thing, Jay. But I would like you to explain what you meant by, 'oddly enough.'"

He took a deep breath. Fortunately she did not seem to have noticed, but it wasn't the first time he'd slipped up. He was much too relaxed and feeling far too detached from the danger he was in. Now he had to talk his way out of it. He gave his head a small shake and stared out at the sea for a moment.

"I guess I spoke without thinking."

"I gathered that much."

"It's just an expression. I mean, having decided to go home, I meet you, take this unexpected detour, and..."

"Jay?"

"Yeah, please, don't make too much of this."

She gave a little laugh. "Actually, I am more interested in what you are going to make of it."

"What's that supposed to mean?"

"You told me you'd spent the last twenty years working for a law firm in Washington, DC, and nine months ago you decided to travel the world. Your exact words were, 'I went straight from college into a law firm and spent the next twenty years in the rat race in DC. So last year I thought, what the hell! I'm going to do now what I should have done twenty years ago.'"

"Wow..."

"I have a very good memory. In fact I have an eidetic memory—photographic. My point is, whichever way you look at it, according to your story, you can't have been in Manila more than a few months at most. But this afternoon, when we arrived, you said, 'All these years all I have known is Manila. And here was this, all along.' So, not only have you not been in the Philippines for a few months, you have been in Manila for a very many years."

He went to speak but she held up a finger.

"One last thing. On the way down to the beach, you said, 'It's as though we had stepped into a parallel universe, as though we had left that other world behind and entered a new world where we are actually different people. For me at least, Manila, the law, all of that, it's like somebody else's life. This… This is real now. That isn't.'"

He was quiet for a bit, then said, with very little humor on his face, "Boy, lawyers are usually careful with what they say, but with you I am going to have to watch every word like a hawk."

She gave a small snort and a lopsided smile.

"There is another alternative."

"Yeah?"

She nodded. "Sure, tell the truth."

He sagged back and sighed. "Yes, there is that. And that is usually my policy. But it is not always possible."

"Why is that?"

"Because sometimes the things we say affect more people than just ourselves."

"That is a generalization, Jay. Would you like to translate it into concrete facts?"

The waiter arrived and took away their plates, while a second replaced them with the chicken, prawns and rice. Down the road voices were raised, either in conflict or in conversation, it was not always easy to tell. He glanced over and saw two men arguing beside a car. He turned back, stared at Marion and decided he had grown fond of her. He said, "I owe you an apology."

"Jay, I don't want an apology, and I don't want you to spin me a new line. I—" She hesitated. "I like you and I trust you. I don't want you to have to lie to me."

He thought about it for a long moment, then came to a decision. "Look, Marion, I can't tell you everything, but I'll tell you what I can. I hope you believe me. I'm not sure if I'd believe it if somebody told me."

She gave a snort that sounded more sardonic than she had intended. "Try me."

"OK, that guy who got shot outside the bus terminal? I knew him. His name was Juan, Juan Carmona. We weren't close, we'd just met briefly a couple of times in the course of business."

"And you're afraid the man who killed him might want to kill you, too."

"Yes. In fact I know he intends to."

"That man was Chinese."

"Yes."

"You said you were on your way home. If you'd been flying to Washington or New York you would have flown from Ninoy Aquino airport. To get there you would have taken a Jeepney or a taxi. If you were taking the bus north, you must have been booked on a plane flying from Clark International, which means you were flying probably to Dubai, and from there to the States."

"Boy, who are you?" He asked it with a laugh, but he was frowning.

She sighed, and suddenly felt starved. She spooned rice and chicken and prawns into a big heap on her plate and started to eat. He watched her, suddenly worried. She said at last:

"Who am I? I am a girl who learns fast, whom everybody considers scruffy and stupid, but who is actually capable of putting two and two together and making four. I did all the research necessary regarding escape routes from Manila, and I know that the obvious, not-obvious way out is via Clark International and Dubai. But the Chinese man who killed your friend had also worked that out, as he obviously would."

She forked some more food into her mouth and chewed while he sat in silence, wondering what the hell was going on.

"Who am I?" she continued. "I am Marion James, exactly as I told you, the girl nobody notices, who has an eidetic memory and a serviceable brain, and works—worked—as a translator at the Chinese Embassy in Manila."

She stared him in the face. He felt the blood drain from his cheeks and his belly catch fire. "Jesus..." was all he could say.

"I am the one Ed chose because I was the one nobody would notice."

"You knew who I was from the start?"

She shook her head. "But I saw you run when you saw the shooting, and I saw your face when you arrived at the mall. The," she smiled and shrugged, "setting off around the world on a gap year in your mid-forties—it's not impossible, but it's very unlikely. Journalist or writer would have been better."

"You sound like an old hand at this."

"Not at all. Just a couple of months. But I learn quickly. I'm not as stupid as I look."

"You don't look stupid at all. Stop saying that. So how many of the..." He made an on-and-on gesture with his hand. "How many of the others do you know?"

"None. But I pieced together comments and references of Ed's, and things I read in the reports I translated and read. He told me once he usually only worked with top flight academics, but that I was going to be useful because I hid my light under a bushel."

"You're smart. You're real smart."

"Try not to sound surprised."

"I'm not, Marion. But you do that self-effacing English thing. It's like you walk around with a big sign on your forehead saying, 'I am nothing special. Please don't notice me.' But you are. You're smart."

She shrugged. "Thank you. Aren't you going to eat?"

He helped himself to some food.

"How the hell did you get into this, Marion?"

"How did you?"

He looked a little embarrassed. "Patriotism. I had settled in Manila and Ed approached me. He said the US Government needed eyes and ears in the top academic circles because we were watching the rise of the Chinese in the South Pacific. He said conversation among academics could be very revealing, but he would also put me on a list of people who got invited to diplomatic parties and events, where I could pick up little bits of information." He shrugged. "He also said it wouldn't do my career any harm if I ever decided to go home."

She drained her glass and he noticed that her eyes were shining.

"Well that certainly wasn't my case. A few months

ago I got into serious trouble and accrued a *huge* gambling debt."

His eyebrows shot up. "You're a gambler?"

"I have never gambled in my life. But I was out with friends for the night. We wound up at some club and this attractive young American came over and chatted me up, convinced me to go to a real, local place where they played Mahjong. I thought it was fun, he seemed nice, so I bit. While I was playing he disappeared, allegedly to the loo, and never reappeared. Meanwhile a very frightening Filipino with a knife told me I owed them ten thousand American dollars, and interest was starting to accrue as of right then."

"Holy shit."

"The boy was obviously a plant, because the next day Ed showed up and told me he would take care of everything as long as I did him some favors."

"How did you come to meet him?"

"He showed up on my doorstep." She sighed and looked embarrassed. "I did rather well at Oxford. I studied Chinese, and went on to do a master's in Oriental Philosophy. Somehow the word got around to Ed's department in the Pentagon. CIA, I imagine. He set me up and then recruited me."

"Son of a bitch."

"Perhaps. I think he genuinely believed what he was doing was justified, and he did try to get the money to me."

"He tried?"

"He was murdered. I found the body and ran, but he had an envelope in his study with my name on it. The money was in it."

"No papers, nothing like that?" She shook her head. He said, "So what's your plan?"

She took a deep breath. "Well, I knew the supposedly safe route would be a death trap. So I thought the best thing was to do what I always do." She laughed. "It's my 'go-to' response in all remotely dangerous situations: become invisible. So I came south. I'd spent a week in Nayon ng Pangingisda with some friends once, back in the mists of time, so I thought I'd go there and either rent or steal a boat and sail to Darwin, in Oz. It's a long way, but there are a lot of islands on the way."

"Can you sail?"

"My dad taught me when I was small."

He smiled. "Mine too. We can do it."

Her eyes clouded with fear for a moment and she frowned. "They will realize what's happened, sooner or later, and they will come after us. But it will be much harder to find us."

"I guess so."

"We must stay away from planes and taxis as far as possible. It will become very tempting."

"Agreed."

"How are you with your fists? Are you one of those indestructible quarterbacks? You're nice and big."

He laughed and shook his head. "No, I'm afraid I do all my fighting with my brain."

"Well, never mind, if the Chinese show up you can talk them to death while I kick them in the shins."

He tried to smile but failed, poked at his rice with his fork. "This is for real, isn't it?"

"Of course it is." She might have been telling him that of course he had to finish his supper. "Which is why we have to stay focused on the solutions and not dwell on the problem." He gave her an odd look and she gave him a Mary Poppins smile. "Stiff upper lip and all that."

Hoffstadder poked at his food for a while longer, then smiled sheepishly and held out his hand across the table. "Jay Hoffstadder."

She took his hand and shook it.

"Marion James, again, still."

They ate in silence for a while, he taking small bites, she fairly wolfing the food down. After a bit she waved a fork at him. "You should ask yourself, when are you likely to be dining again with a beautiful blonde on a beach on a South Sea Island? *Carpe diem*, Jay. Or rather, *carpe* chicken and cashew nuts, *carpe* prawns and *carpe vinum*."

"You're right."

She shook her head, with her mouth full, and said, "Nothing's changed, except that now we know."

"Yeah, as long as we were pretending, I could pretend it wasn't real. Now this has brought it back to me. It's made it kind of real again."

She grinned. "Does that mean you want your own room now and you're going to stop holding my hand?"

"I'm married, Marion. I have two kids. I feel kind of a heel, but it really was like a different life, a different reality."

"I don't want to know. We have enough to deal with without bringing that kind of thing into it." She waited a moment, staring at a prawn. "Personally I am feeling the need for somebody big and strong I can hold on to—metaphorically and actually physically. If you are no longer him, then I'll have to buy a teddy from the market."

"You're remarkable," he said.

She gave a soft belch and put her fingers to her lips. "Excuse me. Thank you."

"Shall I get the check?"

She shook her head. "I intend to live the next few days as though they were my last. They may well be. So I am going to have a large Baileys with ice, and I strongly recommend you have the best whisky they have."

An hour later they strolled through the crowded High Street, still bustling, with all the houses and shops still open to the crowds, with her arm linked through his. Far out to the north a red light winked rhythmically in the sky as it grew steadily brighter.

They climbed the stairs to the bedroom, went inside and locked the door with an old-fashioned key, and Marion sat on the bed.

"The ferry leaves at seven thirty tomorrow morning. We have to be up and breakfasting by six."

He nodded. "Got it. You bought toothbrushes and toothpaste?"

"In the basket. I don't know about you, but my back is burning." They stared at each other, he in the bathroom doorway, she still seated on the bed. "Probably a good idea to put some more cream on," she added.

"Marion, I am not a cheat. I love..."

"Don't!" She shook her head. "That's another life. This is a different, parallel reality." Her face contracted with pain and tears welled in her eyes. "You don't have to if you don't want to."

He didn't move, didn't answer for a while. Then he said, softly, "But I do."

And as they clung to each other, neither of them heard the engine's roar above them.

CHAPTER EIGHTEEN

He snored, and for a while that kept her awake. But she didn't mind, because the feeling of being held was so good and so welcome, and eventually she slipped into an uneasy demiworld of sexual pleasure and peaceful satisfaction on the one hand, and fear and insecurity on the other: dreams of warmth and kisses that descended eventually into nightmares of violence and cruelty.

She awoke suddenly. Moonlight was streaming in through the open window, casting a silver-blue glow on the floor and on the wall, pushing inky black shadows into the corners. She sat and picked up her plastic bottle of water and drank from it, watching the sparkling path of light that lay across the still waters.

She only really noticed the noise the second time she heard it. Then she looked sharply at the handle of the bedroom door and felt a hot jolt of terror as she saw it turn.

* * *

We had flown in silence, keeping low to avoid radar and air traffic controllers, and after an hour and a half Gallin had pointed to a cluster of lights ahead and said, "That's it, that's Matnog."

"This is probably a stupid question, but shouldn't you be talking to the control tower by now?"

She pulled down the corners of her mouth, shook her head and then shrugged. "Nah," she said, "it's not that kind of airfield."

I nodded like what she'd said was somehow normal. "Right, not that kind of airfield."

We were coming in low over the treetops, and the roofs of houses started to flash by beneath us. I saw roads, cars and oval gaping faces staring up at us. I remember thinking, "Oh, dear God," or perhaps I said it, as it dawned on me that she was going to land the Cessna on the Matnog, Filipino version of the village green: a roughly triangular stretch of public parkland, about three hundred yards across at its widest point, and some four hundred yards long, bordered by houses and cottages on all sides.

We skimmed over the last set of rooftops and I heard myself say, "You're out of your mind!"

We hit the grass and bounced, sailed for a few yards and hit the ground again. The brakes engaged and I felt myself flung forward as we lurched along the uneven grassy surface of the park. We slowed, the engine went to idle and we taxied gently for a while toward the cover of some trees. There the plane stopped and she killed the engine. A group of children came running through the darkness from the brightly lit streets a hundred yards away.

"Inconspicuous, subtle, woman of the shadows. These are all terms I will never associate with you."

"Where are we?" she asked bitterly.

"Matnog!"

"So shut up and let's get going."

"What is that?" I pointed through the windshield at a large, dark shadow that was sitting near a row of trees maybe a hundred yards away.

"That is a Chinese AVI Copter AC 311. You'd better pray we are not too late."

A small multitude watched us climb down from the plane, smiling and greeting us. We smiled back and I asked the nearest adult, "Hotel, please?"

They all started talking and shouting at the same time, pointing across the park. One woman was louder than the rest.

"You go downdown pig stweet!" She said it several times, stabbing with her whole hand at where she wanted us to go. "You go bake shop, in fwont pig yarrow how. Bake shop! Bake shop! Pig yarrow how! You go in down. My sista hotel. Onry hotel in Matnog. You no go odda hotel. My sista hotel onry hotel. OK!"

We managed to disengage ourselves and crossed the expanse of grass toward the brightly lit road, followed by a small band of people whose curiosity had not been sated by simply seeing us climb from the Cessna. This bunch wanted the whole show. They wanted to know how the story ended.

We came eventually to a broad, busy road which looked like the entrance to the town. Here our followers stopped and watched us curiously to see what we would do next. Gallin asked me, "You reckon this is a pig stweet?"

"I'd say it was a stweet, and as stweets go it's a pretty pig one. So now we have to go that way."

I stabbed with my hand, the way the woman had, and the gang watched us walk away, toward the intersection forty or fifty paces away. It was brightly lit and there was a lot of traffic, and it all had the feel of a place that had recently become prosperous on tourism.

Gallin pointed across the road at the corner. "There's your bake shop."

I nodded. "And across the road from it is a big yellow building."

"The big yellow house. Cool. So she said to go down the street. To me, 'Go in down' means we go down the street, agreed?"

"Agreed. If there is only one hotel in the town, we'll soon find out."

It was a three or four-minute walk. The hotel was unmistakable. It was a slightly dilapidated, Spanish colonial house that had found a new use as the town's hotel. We went in through the gated courtyard, past a few scattered tables and into the bright, clean reception. There was a woman standing behind the desk, smiling at us with bright eyes.

Gallin drew breath but I got in first.

"Could you tell us, is this the only hotel in town?"

She nodded. "Only. Only one."

"We have arranged to meet my friends here. Jay and Marion. He is big, with a moustache." I mimicked big and ran my fingers down my upper lip to signify a moustache. The woman laughed like I was killing her. I went on, "She is small," I held my hand up shoulder height, "blonde."

She smiled at me with vacant eyes, like her brain had gone on holiday while I finished.

"Are they here? My friends?"

She was still vacant. "You police?"

The astonishment on my face was genuine, and

maybe that convinced her.

"No!"

"You friend problem with police?"

My frown of concern was a little more affected, but I think I pulled it off. "No! Not at all! Why?"

"Chinese meng rooking here for dem. I tell them gogo. I no wan no Chinese bastad meng. I tell gogo! Gogo!"

"What time?"

"Now. Ten minute."

I gave her my most reassuring smile. "I am sure it is nothing to be concerned about. Where are they now?"

She suddenly screamed like a parrot, screwed up her face, smacked the counter with the palm of her hand and said what sounded like, "*Aaaah, heshe nono gonna maky nookienookie bang bang, he nono, aaaah!*"

Gallin started to laugh and I asked, "Where?"

"Go swim, go eat, go make nookienookie bang bang." She shrugged.

"You don't know where?"

"Yeah. I don't know where."

"How many Chinese?"

"Four. You no make trouble for me."

"No." I laughed. "No trouble. Just friends."

"Chinese bastads."

"OK, thank you. Bye bye."

"Tally ho."

We went back out through the courtyard and onto the street. The building opposite was a vast, bare concrete wall with one lugubrious lamp on it. To left and right there were overgrown gardens with banana plants and palms casting mobile, spidery shadows in the amber light. I felt like I should stop, turn up my collar and light a

Lucky. Instead I said, "Four of them. We can be pretty sure that either she told him or he has figured that they have gone to the beach, and they are by now in one of the few restaurants."

Gallin nodded. "Most of these eateries are hole-in-the-wall, drag up a plastic chair and have a bowl of noodles affairs. If they are building up to nookienookie bang bang, they will have gone somewhere where they can at least share a table and have a bottle of wine."

"Something aimed at tourists."

"Zimo will have reasoned the same."

"So he will have spread his men across the seafront and they'll be checking out every restaurant on the beach."

She grunted. "That's not all that many. I go right, you go left, if we find Zimo or his men we kill them."

"Agreed, but, Gallin?"

She sighed. "What?"

"Think Ford Fiesta, not Corvette C8. Subtle. Quiet. Ninja..."

She arched an exquisite eyebrow and walked away down the street, to blend with the dark shadows in the amber streetlight. Somewhere visceral, deep inside me, Stan Getz played "Misty" on a smoky saxophone, just for her.

**

Somewhere visceral, deep inside him, Zimo felt about as close as he ever got to excited. This was always his favorite part of the hunt. He could practically smell his prey. He knew that they knew he was close. He knew they were scared and he could sense their fear as if by a sixth sense he were detecting and picking up their pheromones.

He had dispatched his men along the seafront and gradually, like a net, they were closing in, checking bar by bar, kiosk by kiosk. Restaurants were few and far between, but he knew that that was where he would find them. An American professor of law and an Oxford graduate would not eat at a kiosk. They were brought together by fear, they were being hunted, but right now they felt safe in this remote place. Their instinct would drive them to something familiar: waiters, candlelight...

His radio receiver crackled in his ear. It was Guangxi.

"Mr. Chew, sir, I think I have located them. They are on the terrace at the Asian Wok Restaurant, at the port, opposite the ferry terminal."

"Have they seen you?"

"No, but I need cover. There are some parked cars here."

"Good. Use one. I am coming."

He felt the warm glow of anticipation in his belly. He enjoyed his work. It was why he had chosen it when the MSS had offered him the opportunity, but he kept strict control over his feelings. He never killed purely for pleasure. That way madness lay. He only killed professionally, when he knew he had the support of the government behind him. But he never grew tired of that feeling, of that inexplicable moment which was beyond erotic, when his own life, his own being, invaded the life of another, and everything that was that other person was extinguished.

He smiled. He would take them in their room. Hoffstadder he would kill with a shot, suppressed, but the girl, so white, so pale, so pink, he would take her in an embrace, with a long, cold blade in her belly.

He arrived at the port walking at a leisurely pace with his hands in his pockets. Thirty or forty paces away he saw Guanxi trying to pacify an irate Filipino in Bermuda shorts and flip-flops. All of them wore Bermuda shorts and flip-flops. Guangxi had probably tried to get into the man's car and the man had seen him.

Zimo hastened his pace. He did not want Hoffstadder and the girl to become aware of the altercation. Guanxi had seen him approaching but had not reacted. He continued trying to placate the Filipino.

Zimo placed his left hand on the man's left shoulder, from behind, pressed the muzzle of his Glock into the man's ribs and said quietly in Tagalog, *"Papatayin kita."* Which translated roughly as, "I will kill you."

The man froze. Zimo laughed and patted him on the shoulder, smiling at him.

"No need to worry, my friend. I am just joking. We are all brothers and friends here. Now I tell you how we are going to solve this problem like brothers and friends. I am going to give you two thousand American dollars. In exchange you lend my friend your car for an hour or two. I explain why." He leaned in close and whispered in the man's ear. "His wife is in that restaurant, with another man. And he is watching her. But he must not be seen. You understand?"

The man was rigid, swallowing convulsively. He nodded a couple of times.

"Good, my friend. You are a good man. Now, here is what we are going to do. You give my friend the keys to your car. Then you and me, we go behind these palms to the ferry terminal and I give you the money."

The Filipino took out his keys and handed them to Guanxi, babbling as he did so.

"Please, take the car. I don't want it. Please, don't kill me. I have a wife, three children, please don't kill me."

Zimo laughed. He could feel his heart accelerated and his belly warm with adrenaline.

"Relax, I am not going to hurt you. I am just helping my friend expose his wife for what she is, a slut and a harlot. Come on, I will buy you a drink."

Guanxi climbed in the car and Zimo eased the man toward a kiosk near the entrance to the port. The man relaxed a little. Zimo laughed softly as he put away the Glock.

"Don't tell me you couldn't use a couple of thousand American dollars."

"Well, of course. I just didn't expect..."

He frowned. The pain was not sharp or intolerable. It was dull, but deeply penetrating. It slid deep inside him, and then slid out again. He became very tired, very sleepy and confused.

Zimo said, "What's the matter, my friend? Are you tired?"

He supported him with his last stumbling steps to the doorway of the ferry terminal. There was a bench there and he lowered him into a sitting, sleeping position. The benefit of the long, razor-sharp stiletto was that practically all the bleeding was internal, and there was very little pain. No shouting, no screaming, no messy bleeding. It was all over in a few seconds, and the body in all probability would not be noticed till the morning.

He returned to the car. Guangxi lowered the window. Zimo said:

"I am going to prepare things at the hotel. Tell me when they leave."

"Yes, sir."

Zimo walked away through the crowded port area, speaking into his miniature microphone to the rest of his team.

"Targets have been spotted at the port, opposite the ferry terminal, on the terrace of the Asian Wok Restaurant. Guanxi has eyes. Fujian, take up position two at the entrance to the port. Wu, you take position three, near the entrance to the hotel."

"Sir, Mr. Chew," Wu's voice crackled in his ear. "There is nowhere to hide by the hotel. What should I do?"

Zimo smiled. "You have seen these snakes sleep anywhere, on a wall, in the street. When they approach, make like you are sleeping in the street, then follow them in. We kill the man. The girl we take with us for interrogation. I will deal with her later."

"Yes, sir."

His earpiece crackled and went silent, and he hurried his way through the crowd, towering over the people around him.

CHAPTER NINETEEN

I watched from the lamppost across the street, drinking a beer from a bottle outside a bar-kiosk with a corrugated tin roof. I watched the Chinese guy and the Filipino get into an altercation, where the Chinese guy was trying very hard to placate the Filipino, who looked like, as Gallin might have put it, he was about to go all Muai Tai on his ass.

Then I watched Zimo appear, cool and relaxed in his sky-blue suit, and kill the Filipino. Beware calm men bearing stilettos. Finally I watched Zimo walk away, talking to himself like he was a schizophrenic trying to get his voices organized.

I didn't hesitate. I walked across the intersection, jostling through the people, trying to look like everybody else. Not making eye contact is a big part of that. The less eye contact you make, the less noticeable you become.

I drew up beside the car and knocked on the driver's window. He stared fixedly at the restaurant terrace, like if he ignored me I'd go away.

Wrong. I bent down and grinned through the glass. I knocked again and made gestures that meant nothing, pointing at my watch, putting my hand to my face with ear and thumb extended, like, "I'll call you," mouthing silently. He looked away and I knocked again, made the sign to roll down the window.

He did, and with a face as expressive as cold potato soup, he said, "You go away."

I leaned forward smiling and said, "Zimo told me to come and get you," as I drove two inches of Swiss Army knife blade through his jugular vein and his carotid artery.

I leaned on the door like I was talking to him while he jerked and kicked, and bled out internally. It was just five or six seconds. Then he sagged and I was able to pull the blade out. I wiped it on his jacket, opened the door a few inches and raised the window. Then slammed the door and mingled with the crowd. One down, three to go.

Up on the terrace of the Asian Wok I saw Hoffstadder sitting with the scruffy blonde. I moved back toward the entrance to the port and called Gallin.

"What?"

"I've missed you too, darling. I've just seen Uncle Leonard and Debbie."

"Where?"

"The Asian Wok on the port. There was some guy eyeballing them from the parking lot across the road."

"Some guy?"

"No, not him but a friend of his."

"Did you…"

I interrupted. "I severed his carotid artery and his aorta, and you know what? Nobody noticed."

"Bully for you. That leaves three. One will be headed for the port to join the guy you just iced. They'll want to tail them back to the hotel where Zimo and the third guy will be waiting. They'll nail them either in the street or in the hotel."

"My thoughts exactly. I'm going to take out this guy when he arrives. You go back to the hotel and take out the other guy and Zimo. I'll join you as soon as I can. Gallin?"

"What?"

"Please be very careful. This guy is extremely dangerous."

"Sure thing, Mom."

She hung up and I went to get a Coke from the kiosk. I took up my position by the lamppost and watched the crowd, waiting for the guy to arrive. He wasn't hard to spot. He was the only guy in a suit and he was walking fast toward where I was waiting for him. I pushed off the lamppost and dodged unsteadily through the crowd, calculating we would cross about level with the entrance to the bus terminal. I made like I was a bit pissed, kept my head down and steered a course that did not look like a collision course. I passed him about three feet away, spun on my heel and came up right beside him.

"You speak English?"

His face said he didn't know I existed. "You go away."

"Zimo Chew sent me. Listen to me."

He stopped and stared at me. I stepped in close and pressed the muzzle of the Maxim S9 against his belly while I whipped the earpiece out of his ear with my left hand and ripped the mic out of his shirt. I closed in a little closer and slipped my arm around his shoulders, urging him toward the dark, empty bus terminal.

"Let's talk in here."

"Talk?"

We stepped into the empty hall with the dark ticket windows, the Coke and candy machines and the benches. A couple of them were occupied by sleeping backpackers. I hustled him to one side where we could not be seen. I was still pointing the Maxim at his belly. I stepped in close with my right foot, went up on my toes and smashed my right elbow into his jaw. His eyes rolled up and I caught him with my arm around his neck as he went down. I heaved up and to the right and let the dead weight of his body do the rest. His vertebrae crunched and snapped and I lowered him onto an empty bench. Then I set off at a brisk walk toward the hotel.

Two down, two to go.

The road where the hotel was located was empty. It looked long and dark, with the lamp opposite the hotel casting long, very black shadows. A small breeze rustled the leaves of the palms and the banana trees in the front and back yards, but aside from that there was no sound to be heard.

I began to walk, scanning the inky shadows for any sign of Gallin. There was only the dull crunch of my shoes in the dark. Keeping to the shadows, with my hearing focused behind me, I came to the gate of the hotel. It stood slightly open onto the front yard. There were a couple of tables under an awning where I figured visitors ate breakfast in the morning. There were no lights in the windows upstairs, but the porch door was open and I could see light from reception.

I went inside. The lights seemed stark after the gloom outside. It was very quiet, and empty. I pulled the Maxim from under my arm and went behind the reception desk. There was a door to a small office. I pushed it open and saw the noisy receptionist sitting in a black vinyl swivel chair. Her eyes were very wide. Her mouth was very wide and her throat was also gaping very wide. The front of her blouse was saturated with blood which had sprayed onto the walls and the furniture.

The laughter was from a woman. It was high-pitched, a giggle. It was coming from the front yard and it was getting louder. It was answered by a deep murmur from a man. Then it transferred suddenly to reception. There was no pause. He kept talking, she laughed a couple of times and they made their way up the stairs. I peered through the crack in the door and was satisfied it was Marion James and Jay Hoffstadder.

I stepped out of the office, closed the door, slipped out of reception into the dark street and ran like I had all the hounds of hell biting at my ass.

***

Gallin had made her way back to the hotel. She had been careful not to run or draw attention to herself while she was on the crowded High Street, but as soon as she had dodged into the backstreet where the hotel was, seeing it empty and silent, she had broken into a sprint. It was about a hundred and fifty yards from the mouth of the alley to the hotel, and when she was slightly over halfway, she noticed a man lying curled up, just outside a gate to one of the front yards, maybe forty or fifty feet from the hotel. She slowed to a brisk walk and eased the Sig Sauer P365 XL from under her arm. The guy curled up by the fence snored and exuded a powerful smell of alcohol. She moved on past him and pushed through the gate into the hotel.

The lights were out upstairs, but the porch was

partially open and light was filtering out from reception. She moved inside. It was empty, still and quiet.

Her mind was thinking fast. She knew Hoffstadder and Marion James were still at the restaurant, but Zimo and his guy should be at the hotel by now. They weren't in reception. So were they up in the room?

She saw the door and moved behind the desk. Holding the P226 in her right hand she inched forward, turned the handle and gave the door a little shove. She wasn't sure what she expected to see, but it was not what she saw.

She saw the landlady with wide, terrified eyes staring at her. She was sitting in a black, vinyl swivel chair, facing the door. Behind her, Zimo was standing in his pale blue suit. His left hand was on her shoulder. His right hand held an antique British commando knife with the point resting lightly against the side of her neck. It took her a fraction of a second to process the scene. Zimo smiled and her finger tightened on the trigger. In that instant she got a powerful smell of booze; Zimo thrust the blade deep into the woman's neck and punched it forward.

Then there was a violent, crippling pain in her head.

* * *

I ran with a growing, dreadful certainty that things had gone badly wrong. Three hundred yards brought me panting to the Maharlika Highway, where it entered the town. I didn't pause. Every fraction of a second was vital. I dodged through the traffic, running diagonally across the road toward the park where we had landed. I vaulted the fence and powered across the grass. The ground was uneven and twice my foot twisted under me and I fell on my face. Each time I scrambled to my feet and kept running toward the chopper that was gleaming darkly near the trees.

When I got there I ripped open the door. As I had expected, Gallin was there, lying on the back seat. The amount of blood was appalling. Her face was covered in it. The front of her blouse and her jacket were saturated.

However much death you see, you never get used to it, but you become inured to it. You develop a callous on your emotions. But I had liked Gallin. In the short time I had known her, she had become special. I felt a hot rage in my head, I snarled, turned and ran back toward the hotel. My head was reeling, my brain was screaming the question at me—where were they? Had I crossed them? Marion and Hoffstadder were now in their room. I should have crossed Zimo and his boy returning from the chopper. I hadn't. So where were they?

And then other questions assailed me as I ran. And I began to think I was too late. I was much too late.

* * *

The door swung gently open onto the moonlit room. He was barely visible. It was just the pale glow of his smiling face. She felt the hot, sick well of terror in her belly, and her skin went cold. He stepped into the room and she saw he had a pistol with a long silencer screwed to the muzzle. He raised a long, thin finger to his lips and hunkered down in front of her. She saw another Chinese man in a suit step through the door behind him. Zimo spoke to her in a whisper.

"I am not going to kill you. I am very interested in you. I am going to kill him." He pointed toward Hoffstadder's sleeping form. "I don't need him. But I need you. I need you to explain so many things to me. So I am going to take you away with me. And then," he got closer, staring hard into her wide eyes, "we will form a very intense relationship. I will be like god in your life. I can cause you so much pain, more pain than you can imagine possible, but I can bring you peace, calm, salvation, even prosperity. All you need to do is obey me, and be my friend. Do you understand?"

Her mouth was pasty dry. She was trembling. "I don't know what you're talking about."

"I need to know everything that is in your mind. You belong to me now."

She stared at him, paralyzed by terror, then became aware of a movement by the door and looked up. The other Chinese was frowning, looking at an empty spot about three feet in front of him. He muttered "*Wŏde mā ya...*" which she knew meant, "Oh, my mother," reached for the foot of the bed to support himself but missed it and collapsed on the floor.

Zimo sprang to his feet. A figure moved fast through the doorway. Zimo staggered back. There seemed to be a man pounding him. Marion scrambled back on top of Hoffstadder, who cried out in inarticulate alarm.

Now the two figures seemed to be gripping each other, staggering back and forth, colliding with the door, knocking things from the furniture. There were grunts, suppressed shouts. Both men went down, then Zimo scrambled to his feet and made for the door. The other man grabbed his leg, got to his feet, tipped Zimo onto the floor and started kicking his inside thigh and stamping on his leg. Zimo cried out and kicked back, released his foot and scrambled out of view.

The other man got on one knee, pointed at her and Hoffstadder and said, "ODIN! Do *not* move. I am here to take you home!"

And he was gone.

She rose from the bed and went to the window. She saw Zimo, limping badly, stagger across the yard and out onto the dimly lit road, then make off running toward the Maharlika Highway at the entrance to the town. He seemed to blend into the shadows and Hoffstadder joined her at the window. Together they watched the other man burst from the porch into the front yard, rip the gate open and step onto the road. He stood, uncertain for a moment, looking right and left.

Marion and Hoffstadder spoke both at the same time.

"He went that way!"

"He was limping badly. He's hurt."

The man pointed up at them and snarled, "*Do not move! Stay there!*"

Then he made after Zimo at a run. Marion and Hoffstadder looked at each other for a moment. She said, "We have a dead body in the room. He's Chinese, or he was." She stared at the body a moment. "Now he's dead."

Hoffstadder stared at the body, then at her. "Why didn't you wake me?"

"It all happened so fast. And then that man appeared. Do you think he is really ODIN?"

"I have no idea. If these guys are Chinese, I guess he must be."

They turned and stared out of the window again.

CHAPTER TWENTY

I hurt everywhere. Zimo was a brute. Fighting him was like fighting a Komodo dragon. He was insanely fast and unnaturally strong and savage. I had caught him unawares and I knew I had hurt him badly. I had put a couple of straight leads into his jaw which would have put anyone else's lights out, and a couple of good hooks into his ribs. He hadn't liked that and he was on his way out, but I had damaged his leg, and he was not going very far.

He had hurt me as well. He was a dirty fighter and he had scratched and bitten me as well as pummeling me with his fists and his feet. But in that moment I didn't give a damn about that. I wanted Zimo, and I didn't care what I had to do to get him. A voice in my head told me to be careful. He was not a man you should underestimate, and he was probably most dangerous when he was badly hurt. But I couldn't make myself care. I kept seeing Gallin, covered in blood, and sheer rage drove me on.

As I ran, ignoring the pain in my lungs, I could see his twisted silhouette against the lights of the highway, shambling ahead of me in a broken, stumbling run. He was making for the chopper.

I redoubled my efforts, running on my toes for

extra, agonizing speed. I knew I could not keep it up, but I also knew I could not stop. He could not get away, and there was no way on Earth he was leaving with Gallin's body. Not while there was a breath of life in mine.

He had reached the main road and was crossing it diagonally as I had earlier, but holding up his hands to the traffic, making cars and bikes screech and stop. A couple of cars almost hit him. His tall, angular body shuffled and shambled across the blacktop, toward the cover of the park. I sprinted after him and, once again, vaulted the fence onto the green common.

He was still ahead of me, limping, dragging his right leg, occasionally letting out a cry of pain. I broke into a fast jog, closing the distance, fast and steady. I pulled the Maxim from under my arm. I wanted him alive for interrogation, but there was a wild anger inside me I was having trouble controlling.

"Stop! Zimo Chew! Stop now or I will shoot you!"

He didn't stop. He let out another cry of pain but kept going. I thought about shooting him in the leg. He was closing on the chopper.

I planted my feet and roared, "*Stop!*"

He stopped. He staggered forward one more step and leaned against the side of the helicopter. He half-turned and fell with his back against the bird. His right hand made a strange jerking motion and suddenly a fierce, burning pain bit into my right arm. My hand was paralyzed with pain. Zimo started to laugh. I looked down and saw a five-pointed shuriken sticking out of my shoulder.

He had yanked open the helicopter door. I reached with my left hand and tugged the jagged star out of my joint. The pain was indescribable. I dropped the star and tried to transfer the gun to my left hand. Zimo, limping and hopping, had emerged from the cockpit with a weapon in his hand, and was now trying to steady himself against the chopper to take aim. I raised the Maxim in my left hand and tried to line him up, but my hand was all over the place.

He fired, but the shot went wide and he staggered forward a couple of steps. I realized I was going to have to kill him. I aimed at his belly and he fired again. Again his shot went wide and he cursed savagely. The pain in his leg must have been excruciating. His whole body was trembling with the effort of staying erect. He raised his weapon. I aimed at his chest. There were two loud smacks, like firecrackers. Zimo Chew looked up at the sky and fell on his back, his pale, sky-blue suit turning black in the night. I had not fired.

Gallin was there, like a vision from a nightmare slasher movie, covered in gore, holding her Sig Sauer 365XL in her hands.

I frowned at her. "I thought you were dead."

"Why?" Her voice was borderline shrill.

"You were lying there," I gestured at the chopper, "covered in blood."

"*It's not my damned blood! It's that poor damned woman at the hotel's!* Next time take my pulse. What are you, a rookie? Where are Hoffstadder and Marion?"

"At the hotel."

"You left them *alone?*"

"Come on! Get off my back! I just saved your life!"

I knelt and rifled through Zimo's pockets.

"What the hell are you doing now? Looting?"

"He's here legally, Gallin, with the approval of the

government. He might have useful papers, documents."

"*Oy vey!*"

I took his wallet, his ID and his cell, turned and started back toward the hotel. I could hear her tramping behind me. "*You* saved *my* life! Ha!"

"Why do you think they had you in the chopper? They were going to interrogate you and kill you."

"Do you know how much my head hurts right now? Look at me!"

We eventually got back to the hotel and found Hoffstadder and Marion sitting huddled on the bed. They both gave small, involuntary gasps when they saw Gallin.

"It's not as bad as it looks. We need to get out of here fast. The cops will be showing up soon. Somebody is going to notice the body count before long. But I have to wash this blood off." She stared at me a moment and gestured dismissively. "And you! What's wrong with you? You get in a fight with a giant, paid assassin, you get stabbed in the arm, and you look like you're going out on a date."

As Gallin delivered this uncharitable observation, I noticed Marion was holding a gun on us. It wasn't shaking and though she looked worried, she was also calm.

"I am not going anywhere with you. Jay and I are going to get on the ferry tomorrow morning and you are not going to stop us."

Gallin seemed to lean forward at the waist and narrow her eyes at Marion. She shook her head, muttered something that sounded like, "*Ata tsochek alay?*" turned and slammed into the bathroom.

I pulled a hardback chair into the middle of the floor and straddled it. I was aware I was very tired, but also knew it would be a long time before I could rest. I smiled at Hoffstadder, who looked extremely worried, and then shifted the smile to Marion.

"He gives his harness bell a shake, to ask if there is some mistake. The only other sound's the sweep of easy wind and downy flake." I paused. Hoffstadder was frowning. So was Marion. I went on. "The woods are lovely, dark and deep, but I have a promise I must keep, and miles to go before I sleep, and miles to go before I sleep."

I let the silence sit there for a moment, then looked at Marion. In the bathroom, the shower started to hiss.

"I have two questions for you, Marion. First of all, do you truly think you will be on that ferry tomorrow, once the police start swarming in, with the Chinese authorities breathing down their necks? There are four dead Chinese MSS agents in this town, one dead Filipino and one dead Filipina."

"That nice woman? The landlady?"

"I'm afraid so. That is the first question. The second is this: even imagining that you somehow slip through the security clampdown that is coming in the next few hours, even assuming you somehow made it to Mindanao and on to Nayon ng Pangingisda, and then, what? To Darwin? Even if we imagine that you manage that extraordinary feat, and get back to London and Los Angeles, who do you think is going to meet you there, at the airport?"

"I don't know."

"Shall I tell you?" She didn't answer, so I tapped my chest. "Me. Because ODIN operates with jurisdiction in all the Five Eye nations, United States, Canada, Australia, New Zealand and the United Kingdom. So if you ever make it to Heathrow, I'll be there to meet you at international arrivals."

"How do I know you're telling the truth?"

I carefully reached into my jacket, pulled out my ID and tossed it to her.

She examined it a moment and handed it to Hoffstadder. She said, "It could be false."

I laughed. "It could be, but maybe you'd like to explain to me why I would go to all this trouble to get to this remote backwater and risk my life and my partner's, to eliminate Zimo Chew and his boys, and save yours, if I am not from ODIN."

I waited but she didn't answer. She just licked her lips.

"Right now, as of this moment, you have been rescued. We might just have time to get to the plane, or the chopper, and we might just have enough fuel to get to the American Embassy. But keep wasting time and you will get yourself and us caught by the same people who brought you Zimo Chew. So why don't you put the gun down, and let's get the hell out of here?"

She looked up at Hoffstadder. He nodded.

She handed me the gun. "OK."

They were pulling on their clothes when Gallin emerged from the bathroom toweling her hair. She was stark naked and said to Hoffstadder, "You got some jeans and a shirt I can borrow? And a belt. I'll need a belt."

He nodded and ten minutes later we filed out of the hotel and moved quickly along the road toward the highway and the common. When we got to the intersection there were a lot of people standing around watching, like they were waiting for something to happen. I figured they knew something we didn't, like one of them had called the cops, who were on their way from Bulan.

We vaulted the fence, ran across the green and within five minutes we were in Zimo's chopper, rising above Matnog, swinging east and north, back toward Manila, through the blackness of the night.

***

Next morning we sat over breakfast in a garden conservatory at the American Embassy in Manila. Paul was not with us—ODIN was grateful to the Company, but this was an ODIN case, not a CIA case. Gallin, on the other hand, was present. Perhaps the reasoning was that she had been involved in the investigation from the start, so there was little she could learn from this interview that she didn't know already. Or maybe it was simply that ODIN was happier to share with Mossad than with the CIA, because at least you could be sure what side Mossad was on. Whatever the reason, Gallin was present.

I sat, trying to ignore the dull ache in my patched-up right arm, and watched Marion James and Jay Hoffstadder tuck into pancakes, eggs and bacon, coffee and toast.

"What we are still not clear about," I said to both of them, but expecting Marion to answer, "is what Ed had done to provoke this reaction from the Chinese. I mean, he had been operating in Manila for several years." They both watched me, chewing, waiting for the cue to answer. I pointed at Hoffstadder. "I mean, he'd had you in the cell for a couple of years, right?"

He nodded with his mouth full. I went on.

"And you supplied a steady flow of useful information. The same was true of Carmona. He recruited Carmona about the same time as you."

Hoffstadder swallowed and drank coffee. "I met him a couple of times. Though Ed preferred that we didn't know about each other, I met Carmona because we worked together on a couple of jobs when Duterte was building up to his decision to cancel the Visiting Forces Agreement. On the whole he kept us apart, though."

I switched my attention to Marion.

"But you, Marion, you were the odd one out. You did not fit the profile of his typical recruit. You didn't operate at the social, academic or professional levels that his other recruits operated."

She raised her eyebrows. "Thanks," she said through a mouthful of eggs, bacon and toast. Then sipped her coffee. "No one else I met there had a first from Oxford."

"No offence intended at all. I've seen ample evidence of your brains. My point is that all his other recruits had access to intelligence—information—through diplomatic and academic connections. You, as I have discovered, were working as a translator."

"Yes, at the Chinese Embassy. And that's why he recruited me: partly because I graduated from Oxford with a first in Chinese and Oriental Philosophy, but partly also because he had learned, through his various grapevines—I assume he had contacts at Oxford—that I had an eidetic memory. That was a blessing for him, because it meant I could reproduce files and remove them from the embassy just by looking at them."

Gallin sat forward, elbows on knees. "OK, so here is something I am not one hundred percent clear on. You were dealing with documents that were in the original Chinese, that had to be translated to English?"

"And vice versa. I also did simultaneous interpreting, and could report back on what I had heard in meetings and discussions."

"So what was it you came across that got Ed so excited, and eventually got him killed?"

She sighed as she buttered a slice of toast and laid some bacon on it. "At first he wasn't sure. He was a brilliant man. He could hold enormous amounts of information in his mind at the same time, and see all the 3D connections and how it all fit together like a matrix." She took a bite. "I had reported to him on several meetings, letters and reports I had come across that related to transactions with IT companies. Some were in Britain, others were in Spain, Brazil—countries scattered all over the world. Mostly the transactions were for various software programs, usually cutting-edge firewalls and antivirus applications. And of course all the correspondence was in English."

I interrupted. "Was it unusual for the embassy to have that kind of dealings?"

"Well, yes, particularly as they had just invested huge sums of money in setting up a whole university faculty here in Manila, devoted to studying precisely that subject. Why would the embassy be buying random bits of software from all over the world, when their own government had just established that faculty? At first it struck him as odd, but gradually he began to realize it had a deeper significance."

Gallin snapped, "What significance?"

Marion gave a little nod and wiped a slice of bread across her plate, mopping up the egg.

"It was when I mentioned to him that I'd been translating an unusual number of studies into global economy models. But not just computer models of the global economy—" She gave a sheepish grin. "Sorry, I mean, these *were* models for analyzing the global economy, but they were also attempts to create predictive algorithms that could be used by major and national banks, ostensibly to maintain stability in international money markets."

"Why is that unusual?"

"Well, it's not, of itself. But in an embassy you'd expect to encounter one or two of those a year at most. The kind of volume I was seeing would have been normal somewhere like the London School of Economics, or a banking firm. I had to translate four in one month, and at an extremely high level of specialization. I had to call on the help of a mathematician and a bilingual economist."

"So what he suspected was that the Chinese were developing the virus to end all viruses. This is the country that specializes in cybernetic warfare, developing software that can map the worldwide web and simultaneously read and predict the movements of the entire global market. If they ever developed such a weapon..."

"They did."

"What?"

"I had been going over some English language documents with a Mr. Wang, the head of the MSS field office, when a young Chinese man was brought into the office. The young man was called Liu Bao, and he was informing Mr. Wang that 'the project' was complete. If it had not been for the work I had done with Ed, it would have meant nothing to me, but as they spoke I began to realize that this was the very virus Ed had been so worried about."

Gallin frowned. "They spoke about this in front of

you?"

"Of course. I was less than human to them. Bao had the virus on a pen drive. He gave it to Mr. Wang who put it on his desk, and then both of them left the room to go and talk to somebody. It was utterly incredible, but this is how arrogant they could be. So I didn't think twice. I made a copy on a pen drive of my own—I always carry several—and when Mr. Wang came back it was precisely where he had left it and I was reading the document."

"How did they find out a copy had been made, and that Ed had it?"

"I don't know. Ed must have had a leak somewhere."

I nodded and stared a moment at Gallin. Then I stood and walked out into the gardens at the back of the compound that overlooked the Bay of Manila. I pulled out my cell and called the Chief.

After voice recognition Lovelock put me through.

"What?"

I wondered absently if he and Gallin might be related.

"Sir, the reason Ed was killed, and the reason the MSS set out to eliminate anyone who might be associated with his Manila cell, was because he, Hampton, had discovered that the new university faculty the Chinese were building in Manila—"

"The Faculty of Viral Cybernetics."

"Yes. He had discovered that the faculty had a very particular function. It had been founded for a reason: to create a virus that would spread indiscriminately across the global web, seeping through firewalls and invisible to antivirus software. This virus would literally map the global economy, but instead of using topography, it would use algorithms. It would read, instantly and simultaneously, the dynamics at work in...," I shook my head, making an "on and on" motion round and round with my hand, "Amazon, Microsoft, Shell, Volkswagen, Surinam Rice, McDonald's, Bulmer's Cider, Martini, Oreos and every other publicly declared company you can think of, as well as reading a thousand other market indicators."

"Are you out of your mind? Have you started writing science fiction stories and smoking dope?"

"Sir, I am serious. We are talking about harnessing the power of every computer on the planet—trillions of gigabytes—to actually *run* this software. The World Wide Web *becomes* their computer. And they use that computer to analyze the entire global economy..."

"You're out of your mind."

"...and with all that information, those controlling the software could decide whether to use the market dynamics to their advantage at any given moment, whether to influence its movements in their favor, or whether to bring about localized or indeed global market collapse so that they could move in and buy up local companies, banks or indeed whole infrastructures."

He was quiet for a long moment. "Belt and Road policy on steroids."

"Exactly. And this virus exists on a pen drive in the Chinese Embassy in Manila."

"You have sound reasons for this nonsense?"

"Pretty sound. There is also a copy."

"Where? Who has it?"

"If I am not mistaken it is in the lavatory cistern of a restaurant called Starving Sam, where he hid it the night he was killed. We need to get that and we need to get Hampton's laptop back. In a hurry."

"Do whatever you need to do."

The first thing I did was dispatch a couple of operatives to Starving Sam's. The second thing I did was arrange a visit.

CHAPTER TWENTY-ONE

Zimo Chew's cell phone and wallet had yielded one thing of interest, and that was an address referred to a couple of times in his Telegram Messenger. From what Marion could make out by reading the messages, work that was started at the faculty was refined and perfected for specific use at the secret labs at this address.

It was in northern Manila by the Mesa Reservoir, on Katipunan Avenue. A preliminary investigation, in the form of asking around and checking Google, showed it to be a disused warehouse in a rundown industrial sector of the city. But when we got there the reality was a bit different.

From the outside the building looked much as you'd expect: a lot of corrugated steel, boarded windows and abandoned pallets. But the exterior wall and gate were new, and so were the security cameras.

We rolled past in my Toyota, turned into Santa Fe and parked behind a gray Chevy Express G3500, jumped out of the Toyota and clambered in the back of the van. There were twelve guys in there, plus the driver. They were in dirty work clothes and builder's helmets, and each one of them had a concealed M18 handgun and an

M27 IAR under his seat, because these were not workmen in the conventional sense. These were battle-seasoned Marines.

We rolled back along Santa Fe to the intersection with Katipunan Avenue, turned left and went at a steady pace as far as the dilapidated warehouse. There the driver stopped, put on his hazard lights, turned across the road, and reversed the Chevy right up to the gates. We all pulled on body armor.

One of the guys already had his balaclava pulled down over his face. He stepped out of the van with his M27 and took out both cameras, then he took out the lock on the gate and pushed it open. The van reversed in and he closed the gate again.

Then the whole compound was swarming with thirteen well-trained Marines. Five went round back. The other eight burst through the door, moving fast, taking positions. Here and there, there was the rattle of automatic fire. Then the shout, *"Clear!"* I ran up the stairs, Gallin just behind me. We came to a landing. Doors were opening and bewildered-looking Chinese men and women were stepping out of rooms. A tall, elderly man was standing in an office doorway. He had a weapon in his hand. I stormed toward him with my FK BRNO PSD 7.5 cal pointed at his head.

"Drop it! Drop the weapon now!" He dropped it. I grabbed him by his collar. "You run this place?"

He didn't say anything, but his eyes told me he was in charge. I hurled him along the passage, where he was taken up by a couple of Marines. I snarled, "This side up. Treat him with care. He's one of the packages we came for."

But then I saw the other guy. He was standing by

the desk. He was not much over twenty, scrawny and pale: a Chinese nerd, and just behind him was an open laptop. On the screen I recognized the ODIN logo.

I went in. Outside a couple of M27s clattered.

"*Clear!*"

"You speak English?"

"Yes."

"What's your name?"

"Liu Bao."

"Are you the engineer working on that?" I nodded toward the laptop.

He nodded. "Yes. Please don't kill me. I have a fiancée. I am not a soldier. I am just an IT guy."

"I'm not going to kill you, Bao. We just need to talk to you."

I went and grabbed the computer. Then I grabbed his arm and led him out to the landing. The place was buzzing with the last cries of "*Clear! Clear!*" and Marines were now grabbing and carrying away computer terminals and anything else that might be of IT interest.

Within five minutes we were all loaded up in the van again. The driver fired up the engine and the last two guys came running, hell-bent for leather, from the building. They jumped aboard yelling, "Go! Go! Go!" and we pulled out of the warehouse and back onto Kalipunan Avenue. One guy jumped down and pulled the gates closed, then jumped aboard again and slammed the door, and we cruised at a stately pace back to the Toyota.

There, as we transferred back to my hired car, the driver removed the fake, magnetic plates to reveal diplomatic ones, and we each went our separate ways. They to take their haul—including Wang and Bao—to a safe location, and Gallin and I back to the hotel to pack.

As we emerged from the industrial area onto Payatas Road, and moved along the shoreline of the reservoir, in the rearview mirror I could already see the column of black smoke billowing up into the air.

We drove in silence for a while. Then Gallin looked at me and said, "So that's it?"

"Almost."

"Almost?"

"There is still the question of how the Chinese began to suspect Ed was onto them."

"Yeah, I was wondering about that, but I thought you were keeping that between you and the Big Kahuna."

"No. But it is where this becomes delicate."

"Delicate."

"You wouldn't understand. I'll explain on the way to LA."

* * *

Forty-eight hours later, and seven thousand eight hundred and eighty-eight miles away, I parked my Mustang V8 rental outside number 1820 on Ocean Drive, in Los Angeles. I killed the engine and looked at Gallin. She had bags under her eyes from lack of sleep and body clock confusion. She said:

"You have bags under your eyes."

"You, on the other hand, look like a daisy, fresh kissed by dew."

"One day I'll make the mistake of believing you. Go."

We climbed out, went into the small, tiled yard, climbed the steps and rang on the bell.

The door was opened by a pretty Filipino woman in her early thirties. She looked comfortable and relaxed in blue jeans and a white, silk blouse.

"Hello?"

I said, "Are you Mrs. Mauie Marcos?"

"Yes, who are you, please?"

"Ma'am, this is Captain Aila Gallin, I am Alex Mason, we work for the Office of the Director of Immigration and Naturalization. Is your husband at home?"

"Yes."

"May we speak with him, please?"

"Of course." She stepped back and pulled the door open. "Nobody told us to expect..."

"We won't take up much of your time."

She led us into a comfortable living room, then disappeared up a short flight of heavy, dark wood steps through an arch. I heard her voice call, "Felix! Somebody to see you from Immigration!"

I smiled at Gallin and she rolled her eyes.

Two minutes later Felix Marcos, looking drawn and tired, entered the room behind his wife. We stood and exchanged elbow greetings, and Mauie Marcos said, "Can I make coffee for anyone? Herbal tea or fruit juice?"

I shook my head. "Actually, we would like to talk to you as well as your husband, and I hope this will only take a couple of minutes. Would you mind sitting with us?"

She glanced at her husband and they both sat.

Gallin smiled at Mauie, then engaged Felix Marcos's eyes.

"What we couldn't work out, Dr. Marcos, was how the Chinese got wind of the fact that Ed suspected what they were doing, and then copied the virus."

His jaw sagged slightly. Then he closed his eyes. "Office of the Director of Immigration and Nationalization—ODIN."

She ignored him and went on. "Whichever way we turned it, there seemed no clear way. And then it dawned on us. Every other member of the cell was either dead or on the run. But one person, and one person alone, had actually benefited and been transported *by the Chinese themselves*, to the USA. Or at least to the embassy."

His face flushed, his eyes became moist with tears. "I swear to you, I never betrayed a thing! I *hate* the Chinese! First thing I did when I got here was tell them, Chinese asked me to spy!"

I answered, "I have no doubts about your loyalty at all, Dr. Marcos. Evidence of it is the fact that you were given a nominal post only at the faculty. You were head of the faculty, but had no effective powers over staff or projects. Clearly they didn't trust you."

"But she is saying…"

I cut him short. "You are very much in love with your wife, aren't you, Dr. Marcos?"

I saw her cheeks flush red, and his drain to ashen gray.

"Yes."

"I think she loves you very much too. It may have been when she saw your career had run into the Great Wall of China, it may have been when she realized your American sympathies had got you sidelined by the new administration, I am not sure exactly when or exactly why, but at some point just after the new project started and she realized administration of the new faculty had been taken out of your hands, she sold her services to the Chinese."

He said, "No…"

But she was silent. I went on, "You were loyal to the Philippines, to your American allies and to ODIN, but you were also loyal and faithful to your wife, weren't you? You discussed your worries, your concerns, your colleagues and, if I know anything about people, you also discussed your hopes and dreams that ODIN would soon arrange for you to move to the States."

He buried his face in his hands. "No…!"

"But your wife was more cynical, more realistic, less naïve. She knew that as long as you were useful to ODIN where you were, they were not going to move you to the States. She knew you could be years waiting, and she knew that with every passing year you would become more isolated from academia, more powerless in your faculty, and of less value to anybody else. Then, when Ed got his copy of the virus, he needed to confide in you because only you had the specialized knowledge to tell him if it was genuine, or if it would work. So he told you about it, and you told your wife." I turned to Mauie. "Am I right?"

She nodded, once, then looked away from her husband. He stared at her and tears spilled down his cheeks.

"How could you? How could you do that to me?"

She turned back and screamed at him. "The Chinese were sucking you dry! Humiliating you! Treating you like *shit!* And all you could say was, 'The Americans will help us! The Americans will help us!' Help us? Like they helped Carmona? Like they helped Ed? You know who helped us in the end? You know who got us to America? *The Chinese!*"

He buried his face in his hands. "Mauie! Stop! Stop! It's not true!"

She turned to me and spat the words at me. "So now what? Prison? Execution? Murder?"

I offered her a lopsided smile. "You are a Chinese spy, Mrs. Marcos; you betrayed your husband and your allies. We would not execute you, though you could go on a very public trial and go to prison. But we don't want to do that, to you or your family. We'd like your husband to take up his post at the university and continue his career, and we would like you to continue spying for the Chinese, but under our careful supervision." Dr. Felix Marcos stared at me with wet eyes and wet cheeks. I shook my head. "I don't want any fights or divorces. I want a happy, stable family. She did what she did for you, Felix. Remember that. I want a happy, stable home for your kids. And you," I pointed at Mauie Marcos, "you work for me."

She sank back in her chair, staring into the middle distance. After a moment she looked at me. "Do I get paid?"

I smiled. "Yeah, you get to keep your life."

19th Street was a pedestrianized alley that led down to the white sand of the beach and the vast sweep of the Pacific Ocean under the Californian sky. We sat on the sand and let the sea wind batter our faces for a while with invisible salt and ozone.

"Well, it's been fun," I said, thinking that all the really cool chicks always move on. "What will you do now? Back to Israel, I guess, huh?"

She shrugged. "Even if I knew I probably couldn't tell you."

"No orders, then?"

She shook her head. "You?"

"I have a few days' sick leave." I flexed my right arm. "That shuriken hurt. And it ruined my suit. I'll have to go to London now to get another one." She looked at me like she wanted to hit me. I ignored her and changed the subject. "I was thinking of driving up to San Francisco. They have nice wines and good seafood up there."

"Huh…" She stared at the sea for a bit. The wind dragged strands of hair across her face. "That's nice."

"Not your scene, wine and seafood?"

"Yeah, well, I wouldn't say that. I can do wine and seafood. It's just, oysters open your appetite and beef closes it. Seafood makes you hungry. Meat satisfies."

"Feel like doing a little research?"

She shrugged one shoulder. "I guess. But I drive. You drive like a pussy."

I snorted. "Yeah, right. This is a stick shift, sister. A stick shift is a man's car."

She stood and dusted the sand from her ass. "Yeah? So how come you're driving it?"

I got to my feet and propelled her toward the Mustang. "That wasn't a clever answer when you were fifteen, and it still isn't. You can take it as far as Arroyo Grande. I take it the rest of the way."

"You're taking the *coast road?* So we get there next week now?"

And it was like that, all the way to Frisco.

Read on for a sneak peak of Ice Cold Spy (Alex Mason book 2), or buy your copy now:
davidarcherbooks.com/ice-cold-spy

Be the first to receive Alex Mason updates. Sign up here:
davidarcherbooks.com/alex-updates

EXCERPT OF ICE COLD SPY

Why was Dr. Robert Magnusson murdered? More to the point, why was he murdered five hundred miles from anywhere, in the frozen wilderness of Greenland?

And then there is the question of what he was doing seventy miles north of the UCLA base camp, where he should have been - and what were the instruments he had secretly set up and housed in the shack out there?

When Alex Mason is sent to Greenland to find answers to these questions, what he finds is something far more harrowing and far reaching than anyone could have expected. The investigation will take him, and Mossad Agent Aila Gallin, from DC to Nuuk, to London and the Bahamas – and to the very edge of perdition...

ICE COLD SPY
PROLOGUE

Bob Magnusson's great love was ice. The more the better. He had known since childhood that his spiritual home was Greenland, where the ice sheet —the size of Alaska, six times the size of Arizona and up to two miles thick—stretched for six hundred and sixty thousand square miles: white, pure and largely untouched by human madness. Others saw its infinite, frozen expanse and saw death. He saw the frozen vastness and saw home, safety, hope.

He had flown from Nuuk, the capital on the west coast, where he had his home and his office, nine hundred miles across the great frozen expanse to Ittoqqortoormiit, the gateway to the Northeast National Park. From there he had taken a King Air 360 four hundred miles north and slightly west into the interior, to the UCLA base camp, where he had most of his equipment set up. And from there, after greeting his team, he had taken a snowmobile fifty miles north to his sensor array, just three hundred and fifty miles south of the northernmost tip of Greenland. The sensor array and its data was something only he attended to.

He sped along under the pristine sky, ice-blue with not a cloud in sight. He slowed at the top of a hill and stopped, and, made cumbersome by his heavy, thermal clothes, climbed clumsily off the vehicle. It was probably only 49°F, but the chill factor of all that ice made it seem a lot colder. He stamped around a bit, clapping his hands, and stared at the broad, shallow valley ahead of him. He knew it well, and he knew that just at the far side, twenty minutes away, was the broad array of sensors. And just beyond the unmanned station where they were located were the moulins, vast, vertical ice-caves spreading and unpredictable, plunging a mile deep, sometimes up to thirty feet across at the mouth, but huge and cavernous beneath. He knew the area intimately, and he felt it posed no threat to him, but an inexperienced person might die within a few hours of a careless mistake.

He looked back the way he had come, and a different kind of cold twisted his belly. He felt his heart jolt and dread drained the blood from his face. On the horizon, barely visible in the glare of the ice, was a speck, moving fast toward him.

He clambered on his snowmobile again and accelerated away, down into the shallow valley, praying that its downward gradient would obscure him from view and render him invisible.

A sudden urgency told him he should call Silvia on the VHF radio-phone, but he dared not stop. In his mind he could see her in their apartment, lying on the sofa, reading the *National Geographic*. Her short, dark hair, her slim legs in Levi's, the big Aran sweater she had stolen from him. The image turned into an ache of desire and fear.

He rode on until soon he could see the blue hut,

raised on stilts, where the sensor monitors were housed. He knew that once he stopped there the snowmobile would be visible, and it would be clear that he was there too. He would then have no escape.

With trembling hands and unsteady legs he came to a halt, parked at the bottom of the steps, and ran with a laborious lack of speed up the stairs to the door. He rattled the handle, pushed in and moved quickly to the monitors.

The data he saw there momentarily made him forget his fear. What he had suspected was true. The nightmare he had dreaded was now a reality.

In a flash some part of his mind took him back to California, to Professor Ruud van Dreiver's office. Rudy was the head of the climatology department and had called Bob to meet Daniel "Danny" Bludd, CEO of the Green Tomorrows Corporation. Ruud had stressed to Bob that this meeting was important, and could be worth a lot of money to the department.

They had sat around Ruud's mango wood coffee table in beige calico armchairs and drunk black, Fairtrade coffee from brightly colored African Attitude cups, even though Ruud always had it with cream and white sugar. Danny Bludd had sipped his coffee once and set it down on the mango table, then leaned back in his chair.

"Let me lay it out for you as plainly as possible. We are, as you are, as we all are, worried about the impact of human activity on the climate and this planet's natural resources."

Ruud had nodded somewhat more than was absolutely necessary, and Bob had thought to himself that, if that was as plain as possible, he might need to lace his coffee with something stronger to get through the meeting. Bludd was talking again.

"According to my research, the Greenland ice cap is pretty important in the whole...," he waved his hand in a circular motion, "climate change issue."

Ruud nodded some more. "Your research is accurate."

"And there is a chance, a good chance, that under Greenland, because of the weight of all that ice—I mean we are talking trillions upon trillions of tons of ice, right? All pressing down, crushing all that organic matter into..."

He paused, realizing perhaps that he was sounding too enthusiastic, and Ruud came to his rescue.

"Aside from oil," he smiled, "natural gas."

Bludd pointed at him. "Exactly, natural gas. We believe, our research shows, that there are vast reserves. And the Greenland government assures us that there *are* in fact such reserves, of gas and oil...," he shrugged and made a face of skepticism, "but then they want us to invest there, so they would say that, right?

"Now, Greenland is not rich. Exploration alone, simple drilling, could bring industry, work and money to Greenland. So they are keen for that to happen. On the other hand, Denmark, who pretty much run the show as far as foreign policy is concerned, is playing cute. 'Maybe there is, maybe there isn't, we want to talk to a lot of people, we might develop it ourselves...' Because they want to get every penny they can out of those natural resources. So what we need is an independent assessment of whether there is oil and natural gas under all that ice. And we also need to know how hard it's going to be to get at it—I mean," he laughed, "we're talking about getting through over a mile of ice before we even start drilling! So how hard is that going to be?"

Bob had interrupted at that point, struggling not to be distracted by the blue sky and the sun gleaming on the leaves outside Ruud's office.

"So basically you want a survey of the ground beneath the ice, and a feasibility study on whether you can drill." He scratched his head. "Most of northeastern Greenland is a national park, so drilling there is going to be difficult and controversial on two counts: first it's a national park, and second, we are supposed to be moving away from fossil fuels. Greenland is melting *because* of fossil fuels."

Ruud cut in laughing, "But nothing that can't be overcome, I'm sure."

Bob ignored him and spread his hands. "That's something you'd have to lobby for in Greenland and Denmark, I imagine. But I have to tell you, I don't know how likely they are to go along with it. I mean, the Greenland ice cap is a kind of linchpin that holds the world's weather to certain patterns. It's also a cooling system. If you start digging oil wells, extracting oil and gas, it's difficult to know how that's going to affect the ice. It could have a major impact at a global level."

There was something unmistakably hostile in Bludd's eyes. Bob tried to ignore it and went on, "So it might be wise, while we're doing the feasibility study, if we did some projections of climate impact too."

"Yeah." Bludd had nodded. "Yeah, do that too." He had stared at the coffee on the mango table for a while, then spread his hands like he was trying to channel energy. "Look, I am being as clear as I know how. We need to secure contracts with Greenland and Denmark for the exploitation of that natural gas. And we need you to make it happen. Make it happen and there is *a lot* of money in it for you."

Bob had been about to protest, but Ruud had cut him short. "You can count on us. We're putting our best man on the job. Bob here has an impeccable reputation for integrity, so that is going to look good for the media, and it will reassure those people who may be concerned about the impact on climate that we are taking that seriously."

Looking through the window of the hut now, Bob saw the blurred spec of a figure entering the valley, speeding toward the station. He fumbled for the radio-phone beside the panel of monitors and called Silvia. It rang twice.

"Hello!"

"Honey, it's me, Bob."

"Hey, I miss you, baby."

"Me too, sugar. Look, I need you to listen very carefully, Silvie, I haven't much time."

"What's going on, baby?"

"I'm at the station, the sensor array monitor hut."

"OK, what's up?"

"There is a man approaching and I think he is going to try to kill me."

"*What?*" Her voice was shrill. "Honey, is this a joke? That is not funny!"

"Listen to me. I need you to get all my papers, clean out my account, and get the hell out of Greenland. Call Ittoqqortoormiit and see if they can send a rescue team. But you get out of here. Get out *now!*"

"*Baby!*"

He hung up. Through the window he could see the figure taking shape as it drew closer. He sat at the computer console which was connected to the sensors and started typing furiously, sending the data to Thor Olafson, his assistant, with the strict instructions, "Do not let Monet anywhere near this material. Submit it immediately to Dr. van Dreiver at UCLA." Thor would know what to do.

He heard the boots tramping up the steps and then the door opened. Cold, bright air swept in behind the giant who stood in the doorway. He pulled back his hood, removed his goggles and the mask that covered the lower part of his face.

Bob frowned. "What the hell are you doing here?"

The deep, baritone voice spoke quietly. "I can't let you do it. You know what the GT Corporation wants. It was made clear to you. You know what the university wants. There is no third way. I'm sorry."

"No!" Bob rushed forward, reaching out to grab the huge shoulders. "You don't understand. The consequences..."

The blade was long and thick, and razor sharp. It had to be to cut through the heavy clothes and penetrate into his liver. At first there was shock, then a strange sense of normality, like there should be a sensible, simple fix for the relatively small cut. Then, as the blade withdrew, a sudden and growing sense of weakness as the blood drained out, and time drained away with it.

He watched the big man turn and walk out of the door, without looking back. He heard the thud of heavy boots descending the stairs. He took a couple of unsteady steps to the chair by the monitor and picked up the telephone. It was answered instantly.

"*Bobby?*"

"Silvie, honey, I've been stabbed."

She was weeping. "*Oh, Bobby!*"

"It's in the liver, baby, so it's pretty bad." He could hear his voice beginning to slur. "You wanna hang up now and call Ittoqqortoormiit, and tell them it's urgent. And you, baby, you need to get out of Greenland, fast."

But she had already hung up. She was a good girl. She had your back. She was calling, and they'd send out the King Air 360 to get him. But he knew he wasn't going to make it that long.

He stood and hobbled to the door. Very carefully he descended the steps, feeling the warm blood trickling down his right leg. He walked away from the building a few feet, then sat down, looking north into the crystal-white ice, and the ice-blue sky. He remembered for a few moments the last modification the Green Tomorrows Corporation had made to his brief. He had had a sinking knowledge then that he was getting drawn into something he would not be able to get out of.

He had told Ruud it could not be. Even Ruud had been worried, and had promised he would talk to Bludd, but it had made no difference. Silvie and Thor had both agreed with Bob, but the relentless pressure of the corporation and the university had driven them on, with promises and assurance which, like the horizon, were always just out of reach.

He made a small pillow out of snow and lay down. He smiled as he felt the cool ice creeping in, chilling him, bringing him peace. He had been sitting with Ruud in his office, telling him, "The Green Tomorrows Corporation is owned by the NATOil Corporation, Rudy. It's a global giant, a giant that is anything but green. We are going to destroy our reputation and our credentials!"

Ruud had done what Ruud always did. He had flapped a hand at him and said, "Aah, relax, will ya? You worry too much! I already asked Danny about that. He said the Green Tomorrows Corporation was NATOil's first step toward establishing its green credentials. They *want* to change! They are going to start phasing out oil and non-renewable resources, replacing them with renewable ones. They, and we, are going to be spearheading that move. And you, Bob, will be the tip of that spear. This could make you, pal. The man who made the world a greener place. Just stay cool, will you? We have to go *through* the crap to get out of it, right?"

He lay smiling, allowing the cold and the ice to soothe him. California and UCLA seemed so far away. The battle to save the world belonged to others now. He was at peace, embraced in the bosom of that vast world of cool, cool ice and white, white snow. He closed his eyes, breathed softly, and went to sleep.

ICE COLD SPY
CHAPTER ONE

The phone rang in the dark.

I fumbled for it and uttered a noise something like, "Whaumngh?"

"Mason? You are unintelligible! You must enunciate clearly!"

I held the phone away from my face and squinted. It was dead center of the long dark night of the soul, three AM. It was also the Chief, the nefarious Nero. I put the phone back to my ear.

"It's the long dark night of the soul, sir..."

"Don't quote Fitzgerald at me at three in the morning. I will be there to collect you in twenty minutes. We will breakfast at the White House."

I skipped the hot part of the shower and stood under a stream of very cold water, gasping and grunting and repeating to myself, "Breakfast at the White House..."

Manny Pacquiao, my cat, was on the foot of the bed observing me with disgust as I toweled myself dry and got dressed. He had never forgiven me for having him castrated. I had never forgiven myself, for that matter, and he knew it and gloated.

"I don't often breakfast at the White House, Manny," I said, tightening my tie. I glanced at my watch and saw that I had five minutes in which to make coffee. "In fact, as far as I can recall, I have never actually had breakfast at the White House. This is a first."

He yawned and closed his eyes.

I took the stairs at a reckless three at a time, forwent coffee, grabbed my coat from the closet and stepped out onto predawn Adams Street. It was cold. The birds were still in bed and the light from the streetlamps cast inky shadows and evoked saxophones and dames with long legs and husky voices; and that made me want to go back to bed.

Two headlamps glowed at the corner of North Capitol and a black Caddy pulled up in front of my gate, with the Chief's huge head glowing like a moon in the back window. I pulled open the door and he shifted to make room for me. I climbed in and we took off as I closed the door. A smoked-glass partition segregated us from the driver. The Chief, whom some called Nero because he was allegedly a pyromaniac, scowled at me through the folds of his face.

"Did you have time for coffee?"

"No."

He grunted and looked away. "We'll have breakfast at the White House."

"You said that. Now is when you tell me *why* we will have breakfast at the White House."

"We are going to have a meeting with Stephen Adamopolous, Presidential Advisor on Sustainable Energy, regarding the van Dreiver Report requested by the Presidential Commission on Sustainable Energy."

"At four in the morning."

"I should have thought that was obvious." He remained silent, staring out at the empty streets, with his ghostly reflection staring in at him. The steady flow of amber lamps washed him with light and shadow. Suddenly he expostulated furiously, "I mean, Alex, if we were going to have breakfast at nine, like any civilized person, *we would not be driving to the White House at half-past three!*"

I smiled. Nero was so mad he was ready to set fire to the District of Columbia. He detested breaking his routine, and if he ever had to, you could count on his being as cheerful as a hornet with a hornet up its ass at least until dinnertime.

"I take it this is not a social call, and that Adamopolous has some reason for dragging us out of bed at this time of the morning to discuss the van Dreiver Report."

He grunted and sulked like a kid offered a lollipop instead of a double chocolate waffle cone.

"They have lost a scientist in Greenland. They should have three but they have only two."

"What's that got to do with us? He probably fell into one of those holes…"

"A moulin."

"Uh-huh, or a crevasse."

We entered Logan Circle and began the long curve to exit on Vermont, headed south.

"I have no doubt Mr. Adamopolous will enlighten us. Clearly he is not satisfied that he fell into a moulin or a crevasse. It seems there may be foul play involved. His girlfriend appears to have decamped, taking all his money and all his papers."

"Papers relating to the Presidential Committee on Sustainable Energy."

"Evidently. And the van Dreiver Report."

I groaned. "Climate change at four AM, before breakfast."

"Precisely."

We turned out of H Street onto Jackson Place and crossed Pennsylvania Avenue, where the gates to West Executive Avenue were opened to give us access. We pulled up outside the West Wing, where a long, white awning extended over the sidewalk. Two men in dark blue suits ran to the car and opened the doors for us, then led the way inside.

Everything in the White House is shiny. The parquet floors, the marble floors, the antique furniture that sits on those floors, the walls, the eighteenth-century lamps and clocks, the brass on the doors, everything, every bit of it shines, as though polished by the constant, daily brush with temporal power.

We were led along parquet corridors, over crimson carpets, past paintings and busts of men, and the occasional woman, who had wielded great temporal power in earlier times, and from there down a short, oddly arched passage to a heavy, white door with a brass handle. One of our two guides departed and the other knocked on the door, then pushed it open and allowed us in.

The room was roughly twenty foot square, painted cream and lined with books. The furniture all looked eighteenth century, with spindly legs and latticed sides, and floral cushions. There was a small, mahogany desk with a green leather blotter, and a couple of settees at either end of the room. In the middle of the floor a folding, mahogany table had been placed and set for four with white linen napkins and just about anything you might want for breakfast.

There was a fire in the grate, and a short man who seemed to be wearing his older brother's bargain basement suit was standing in front of it, watching us with his hands behind his back. When the door had closed behind us he stepped forward, holding out one of those hands.

"Mr...."

The Chief took his hand and cut him short. "No names, please! Well," he added as an afterthought, "You two may exchange names," he waved his two hands at us dismissively and hurried over to the table, removing his coat. "I am averse to the excessive use of my name. You know who I am. That is enough."

Adamopolous and I shook. I offered him a smile and said, "He's an eccentric genius."

"Right, Well, it's good of you to come. And my apologies for the hour. It is a matter of some urgency. Please, sit, I had the kitchen rustle up some breakfast."

The Chief was already sitting, pouring himself coffee. I sat opposite him and Adamopolous sat between us. I helped myself to bacon and eggs while he spoke.

"So here's the thing, we're running late because we only got to hear about this a few hours ago. This comes to us from Nuuk, in Greenland, via UCLA and the Danish police, and in a pretty garbled state."

The Chief was spooning jam onto a slice of toast and chewing at the same time. He said, "Perhaps you had better start from the beginning, Mr. Adamopolous."

Adamopolous nodded. "Yeah, it's been a long day. So, about a year ago, at the end of last August, the president established a Commission to look into the reserves of oil and natural gas under Greenland. Professor Ruud van Dreiver, head of the Climatology Department at the University of California, was appointed head of the Commission. He in turn appointed Dr. Bob Magnusson to head up the team of scientists in Greenland to carry out the necessary research and tests."

The Chief interrupted. "Obviously you secured all the necessary permissions from Greenland and Denmark."

Adamopolous nodded. "Obviously. Greenland was very receptive, but Copenhagen was more cagy. It's a tricky relationship. Greenland is an autonomous nation within the Kingdom of Denmark. Greenland is a very poor nation sitting on vast mineral wealth, and the ownership of that mineral wealth is a moot point: Greenland? Denmark? Both jointly? Greenland has home rule, but does not conduct independent foreign policy, and that would include ceding mining rights."

The Chief said, "Greenland is keen to have someone tell them exactly what they are sitting on, while Denmark is cautious about America muscling in on a potential source of vast wealth."

"Right, so anyhow, we got the green light and Bob and his team shipped out there. Now, here is where it started to get a little complicated. The Green Tomorrows Corporation..."

"Daniel Bludd, CEO," the Chief interjected, and drained his coffee cup, then sat back and sighed, "an effective captain of dubious green credentials."

"Indeed, Daniel Bludd is the CEO of Green Tomorrows. He is an old friend of the head of the Commission, and of the president's, and he wished to donate funding for the research that would eventually lead to the report.

That is irregular..."

"It reeks of corruption."

"Well, it certainly invites scrutiny from those who do not love us; however, the head of the Commission—"

"Ruud van Dreiver—"

"Indeed, Ruud van Dreiver, approved the donation by the Green Tomorrows, just so long as it was clearly a donation and nothing more. So the donation was made and Green Tomorrows became what we might call an interested party in the report. After which, and this is strictly between us three, Bludd began to exert influence so that the report should expand to include issues of interest to Green Tomorrows."

"Such as?"

"Such as particular details about oil deposits as well as gas, such as various different feasibility studies on gaining access to oil and gas through the ice, such as—and this was *very* controversial—creating artificial moulins so that drilling equipment could be inserted. We are talking about a mile of ice or more before you get to the soil, and then that soil might be frozen. Bludd was clearly trying to use the report in order to prepare a proposal for the Greenland and Danish governments, to exploit those minerals."

The Chief said, "Whereas the original purpose of the Commission was...?"

"Simply to know what lay under Greenland, but without the feasibility report. I think the president was more interested in keeping an eye on it, in case any predators like China or Russia came along seeking to mine it. Don't forget, Russia is just a thousand miles away, across the Arctic. And these days China seems to be just about everywhere."

I spoke for the first time.

"So what you're saying is that Bludd was trying to turn it from a situation report into a feasibility report preparatory to a plan of action."

"Yes, that's it. Now, this was embarrassing because, from a strictly ethical point of view, Bludd and Green Tomorrows should not have been a part of the study at all, but it seems van Dreiver was unwilling to act, and he simply looked the other way. Honestly I suspect his thinking was, better Green Tomorrows makes the bid than Beijing or Moscow. At least he could control Green Tomorrows, right?"

"OK, so what happened?"

"Bob, the lead scientist, was a man of great integrity. That was one of the reasons van Dreiver chose him for the study. So he began to protest, rather vociferously, at the influence Bludd was beginning to exert over the direction of the study, and its ultimate purpose. He complained to the university, he complained to van Dreiver in person and he complained to the Presidential Commission officially as a body. It was causing a lot of embarrassment and the fear was that some of his memos and emails might be leaked."

"But they weren't."

"No, it was worse than that. He was murdered."

The Chief had his cup halfway to his mouth. He stopped, sighed and put it down again.

"Details."

"Sketchy so far."

Adamopolous hadn't touched his coffee until now. Now he picked up the cup, sipped it, made a face and put it down again. He thought for a moment, then started to speak.

"Wednesday morning, very early, Bob flew out from Nuuk, across Greenland to Ittoqqortoormiit. Ittoqqortoormiit is a small town on the eastern side of the island, which serves as a last base before tourists and scientists make excursions into the national park. Here, apparently, he picked up a King Air 360 that flew him to the UCLA base camp, and from there it seems he took a snowmobile to what he referred to as the sensor array. It was a set of instruments he had set up about eighty miles north of the base camp. He had not shared the purpose of these instruments with anyone on the team, or the data he was receiving from them. He claimed it was confidential."

He paused and sighed. The Chief had become immobile, watching him. Adamopolous spread his hands and shrugged. "We have to assume that he arrived at this location at about four PM. The weather was good, visibility was good and there were no high winds. At shortly after four we know he made a call to his girlfriend. It was brief, less than a minute. And we know that about fifteen minutes after that he called her again. Obviously we have no information as to what they spoke about.

"However, we do know that very shortly after the second call, an anonymous woman telephoned the police at Ittoqqortoormiit and told them Dr. Robert Magnusson was in mortal danger, and gave them the correct coordinates to go and find him. It took them over an hour to get there, and by the time they did they found him lying in the snow outside a wooden shack kind of affair, raised on stilts, where he had all his equipment set up. He had been stabbed in the liver with a large hunting knife."

I asked, "What about his girlfriend?"

"So far it seems she's vanished without a trace, and she seems to have taken all his research with her: computer records, files, hard drives—everything—it has just gone."

The Chief spoke suddenly. "So what precisely do you want from ODIN?"

"We want his research, above all. We want to get hold of his research before anybody else does." He gave a dry laugh. "If they don't have it already."

"Are you saying you think Daniel Bludd may have killed Bob Magnusson because he wasn't cooperating, and is now after his papers?"

Adamopolous licked his lips. "I am not saying that, no. But I am saying that any investigator would have to consider that as one of many possibilities."

"Understood."

"We also want to know who killed Bob. Aside from the fact that he was a good man who did not deserve to die like that, we can't have people running around killing agents of the president. And he *was* acting as an agent of the president, so he was entitled to the president's protection. We should have seen the risk, and we didn't. I feel bad about that."

I said: "So you want Bob's research recovered and you want his killer brought to justice."

"Yes. That's pretty much what we want."

"You realize," said the Chief carefully, "that this investigation could cause a great deal of embarrassment to friends of the government, and of the president."

"Yeah." He nodded. "I'm going to be advising him to distance himself from those friends."

"So be it."

He stood. I stood too.

"Thanks for breakfast."

I helped the Chief on with his coat. He said, absently, "We'll be in touch. I assume the car is waiting."

We made our way out again along the shiny, parquet and marble corridors and out to the waiting Caddy. There, dawn was thinking about breaking and the birds were going crazy about the idea. To the driver he said, "Adams Street."

To me he said, "You go home and make whatever arrangements you need for your cat. I'll have documents and instructions sent to you before lunch."

I sighed and figured I'd have a nap on the plane.

ICE COLD SPY
CHAPTER TWO

The flight was a little short of six hours. There are no flights direct from DC to Nuuk, so I had to fly first to Reykjavik in Iceland, then change to an Air Greenland airbus and fly back across the Atlantic to Nuuk.

Nuuk Airport is small and made of corrugated steel. It is strangely reminiscent of a dilapidated New England church crossed with the kind of space station you might have seen in a sci-fi movie from the '60s. The terminal was a short walk across the tarmac, the line for passport control was short and everybody seemed to know each other, and baggage reclaim took about four minutes. So twenty minutes after landing I was carrying my bag to a Ford Ranger parked out front.

Nuuk is the biggest city in Greenland, but it's actually a small town. It has about fifteen thousand inhabitants and covers an area two miles long by one and a half miles across. I guess it's smaller than most ranches in Wyoming, and the area it covers is sparsely populated. That suits me. In my book, being big and densely populated is nothing to brag about.

It took me about seven minutes to cover the four miles from the airport to my hotel, on the other side of town. It could have taken a lot longer if I had stopped and got out to look at the views every time I wanted to. I have seen a lot of unusual places on Earth, but few were as stunning or as downright odd as the average view you see at every street corner in Nuuk. Most of the houses are clapboard and painted striking colors. And each one is unique. You get the feeling real humans live there, and the hive-mind has not taken root yet.

My hotel was the Sømandshjemmet, which translates as the Seaman's Home, located on a street that gloried in the name Aqqusinersuaq. Why anyone would feel the need to put three Qs in a single name, and two of those together, beats me, but that's the way they roll in Greenland. I checked in at the desk and was helped to my room by probably the friendliest staff on the planet. They were two women, one a six-foot-three blonde and the other a five-foot brunette. Neither of them stopped smiling, or talking to me in Danish, until they left the room, laughing, making cautioning sounds in Norse and wagging their fingers at me.

I had brought only hand baggage—I didn't plan to be there all that long. I unpacked, found my file and sat reading it for a while by the window, in the strange, burnished silver light that hangs over the Arctic from March till October.

Bob's closest associates, aside from his girlfriend, Silvia, had been Dr. Thor Olafson and Dr. Bernard Monet. Both were his assistants, though according to Stephen Adamopolous, Bob never really warmed to Monet. Both Monet and Olafsen were based in Nuuk, and both were nearby. I decided to go talk to them.

I had a shower, changed my clothes, flipped a coin and decided to talk to Dr. Bernard Monet first.

It was a five-minute drive among randomly scattered, colorfully painted clapboard houses with gabled roofs that looked like Viking halls and gave you the impression things hadn't changed much since Erik the Red settled here.

I came to Jesus Christ Square, which was really a circle, turned left into Aqqusinersuaq and after half a mile took a left into Noorlemut.

Number 3954 was an apartment block with four upper stories plus a ground floor. It had lots of blue, yellow and orange squares, oblongs and circles on it that made it look like a bad Cubist painting by an architect who wished he was Picasso but worked for IKEA instead. I parked out front and climbed out of the cab into a breeze that had turned suddenly icy after the sun had dipped toward the horizon.

Dr. Bernard Monet had his apartment on the fifth floor. I stepped out of the cramped elevator, crossed the small, dark landing and leaned on his bell. The man who opened the door was of above average height and build, with short dark hair and large brown eyes. He had a dark gray sweater on and managed to be completely unremarkable. I made a pleasant face.

"Dr. Bernard Monet?"

"Sure…" The accent was hybrid and might have been French Canadian.

"My name is Alex Mason, I work for the United States Office of the Director of Intelligence." Actually I work for ODIN, the Office of the Democratic Intelligence Network, but I like to mix it up a bit. I showed him my badge. He glanced at it and gave me an ironic smile.

"Must be a tough job. How can I help you?"

"I was hoping we could talk about Dr. Bob Magnusson."

He frowned at me a moment, then stepped back to let me in.

"Sure, come in, we'll go in the living room. My wife is cooking dinner in the kitchen." I looked at my watch and saw it was seven PM. He gave a small laugh. "Don't worry. This eternal light takes some getting used to. Then in the winter it is always dark."

The living room was bright and sparsely furnished. He gestured me to a cream sofa and sat in a cream-leather-and-pine chair a Swede would have thought was cool. Through the window I could see chunks of ice the size of city blocks sitting in the bay. He waited.

I said: "From my window I just see houses."

He didn't smile. He blinked in a way that suggested he was wise and said, "Every window has a different view. It is the emptiness inside that makes the window useful. What would you like to know about Bob?"

"That's a good question, Dr. Monet. I don't honestly know. He was murdered. What is your take on that?"

He had his feet on a very white sheepskin rug. He stared at it for a moment with his elbows on his knees, and sighed.

"My take? I am not sure I have a take, Mr. Mason. You may be surprised to learn that Greenland has a very high murder rate. Everybody loves the Danes, because they are so civilized and polite!" He laughed, but only for a moment and without humor. "But the Inuit do not see them like that. They seem them as an occupying, privileged force. There is a lot of racial tension between Danes and Inuit, and people get killed."

I studied his face for a moment. He held my eye.

"Dr. Bob Magnusson was not a Dane. He was an American."

"Of Danish extraction. If your name is Magnusson, the Inuit don't care where you were born. You are a Dane."

"He was murdered in Northeast Greenland National Park, five hundred miles from the nearest town, in the middle of a frozen wasteland."

"But only eighty miles from the UCLA base camp."

"OK, so how many people were at the base camp?"

"Four at any one time."

"And were there any Inuit researchers there who might have hated Dr. Magnusson for being a Dane?"

"I don't know who was on the roster for that day." He shrugged reluctantly. "But none of them was Inuit."

I frowned again. "You don't know who was on? I thought you were his assistant."

"I was. Me and Thor. But I had a couple of days off and I do not know who was on duty at the camp." He suddenly sat back and spread his hands in a helpless gesture. "I am sorry! I have no theory for why or how Bob was killed."

I nodded like I understood.

"What happened to all his research? He must have had files, papers, removable drives, a computer..."

He shrugged again. "As far as I know all of that was kept at his house. He shared with us what he wanted us to know, which was not so much. In fact it was increasingly little."

"He was secretive?"

"A bit."

What happened to his girlfriend?"

He gave a short, humorless laugh. "Silvia? I am waiting for you to tell me. She disappeared." He made a very French gesture with his fingers, opening them like a small explosion, and said, "*Puff!*"

"How was your relationship with Dr. Magnusson?"

"Good." He made a Gallic face, shrugging and pulling down the corners of his mouth. "We worked well together. Of course his friend was Thor, you know how it is with Scandinavians, they stick together. So him and Thor were close friends, but we were good. OK. No problem."

"What was your opinion of the research?"

His face creased into an ironic smile and his gaze shifted to the icebergs in the bay.

"You know? When you move from graduate student to postgraduate, and you are working for your PhD, you move also from naïve idealist to pragmatist. Is industry causing global warming? No climate change, *global warming!* The answer is very simple. It is another question: Who is paying for the research? The research is funded by the United Nations with money from Third World countries who want to level the playing field? Then industry causes global warming. The research is funded by Shell or BP? Then we call it climate change and we say it is part of a natural process."

I shook my head. "You seem to be about ten years behind the times, Dr. Monet. The last IPCC report was more than unequivocal."

He snorted. "Nothing has changed but the language and the masks. Climate change is happening, of course! Global warming is happening, *of course!* So the vested interests put on their green suits and talk about renewable energy, *but there is no renewable energy!* Because *renewable energy must be made using non-renewable fossil fuels!"*

I went to speak but he interrupted me. "How do you make a solar cell? Do you know? All so-called *green* technologies are depending on fossil fuels. Every single step of the production of solar photovoltaic power systems—solar energy—requires the use of fossil fuels," he counted them off on his fingers, "for carbon reductants, for smelting silicon from ore, for providing heat and power for the manufacturing process, for the transport of materials across nations and continents, for construction and installation. The *only* truly renewable materials consumed in solar photovoltaic power systems production, you know what they are?" He waited. I shook my head. "Trees, torn down and obtained from the burning of vast areas of tropical rainforest, mainly in the Amazon, for creating charcoal—carbon—which is needed for extracting silicon. Now add to this the mineral resources and fossil fuels necessary for constructing factories, processing equipment and maintenance of the solar energy infrastructure! And at the end of this process, you know how long a solar panel last? Maybe twenty years. You know how long a solar battery lasts? Five, maybe ten years maximum. You think in five, ten, fifteen year this cell and this battery have balanced out all the CO2 that was generated to manufacture them?"

"Probably not."

"Let me tell you, Mr. Mason, a silicon smelter, a polysilicon refinery, a crystal grower, all require nonstop energy input twenty-four hour a day, three hundred and sixty-five days of the year. And this power, where is it coming from? It is coming from coal, oil or gas. Solar energy, wind energy, cannot replace fossil fuels for *eight billion people!* The world, the global, consumer society, is totally *dependent* on fossil fuels!"

"OK, I get it, but my question was: What was your opinion of the research you were conducting?"

"You know who funds it?"

"Sure, the Commission on Sustainable..."

He flapped his hand at me like he was batting away a ball. "Pah!" he said. "The Commission puts in some little money from the taxpayer, the university puts in some money from its funds, but seventy or eighty percent of the money is coming from Green Tomorrows."

I was surprised but hid it by shrugging. "Who have an interest in developing green energy."

He laughed. "And so they are looking for oil and gas? They are looking for oil and gas because they have an interest in green, renewable energy? I want a banana so I go to my fridge looking for a burger?" He laughed. "And they want to know can they make artificial moulins to get drilling equipment down through the ice to get at the oil and the gas. This is legitimate research for a company dedicated to green, renewable energy?"

"So you did not approve of this research?"

He looked at me like he'd just found me stuck to the sole of his shoe.

"No, I did not approve of this research."

"How about Bob and Thor?"

He spread his hands and shrugged, like he was rendered helpless by my stupidity. "I do not understand what is your question. What is my opinion of Bob and Thor? Or what was their opinion of the research?"

"How about both?" I smiled pleasantly at him while I imagined throwing him out of the window. "Let's start with their opinion of the research."

"We all agreed that Green Tomorrows, and their parent company NATOil, had an agenda with this report. They were seeking to make a deal with the Greenland government, and maybe also with Denmark if Denmark was willing. But if Denmark was not willing, I think they would be happy to foment separatist feelings and fund the independence movement, if that will help them secure the sole rights to Greenland gas and oil. But we all were resigned. If we want to keep our jobs, pay the rent and eat, then we must accept the job and do the research."

"Green Tomorrows' parent company, the NATOil Corporation."

"One of the so-called Big Eight."

I was quiet a moment, thinking. "Bob knew this, obviously."

"Obviously. It was Thor who discovered the fact. Bob confronted Rudy, Ruud van Dreiver, who commissioned Bob to make the report. They had a meeting with Daniel Bludd, the CEO of Green Tomorrows. Bludd was all, 'Oh we are fighting to make the transition, we want to give you so much money so you can help us to break free of fossil fuels...,' but is all bullshit. If you want to break free, why you are looking for ways to drill through the fucking ice, man?" He waved his hands in the air, saying, "Transition, transition... But there is no transition! Who are you fucking kidding, man? You want to make cars, and TVs and cell phones and fashion sneakers and houses and planes and airports and food and so on and so on for *eight thousand millions of peoples*—with windmills? With solar panels? Come on!"

"OK." I nodded. "Then, I have to ask you the obvious question. Had Bob decided to challenge van Dreiver and Bludd? Was he threatening to go public, expose them...?"

He was laughing and shaking his head before I had finished. "Bob? No, man. That was not Bob's style. Bob was all about the compromise. We can all work together and find an answer. Bob was the one who used to say, 'The cure for climate change would cause more harm, suffering and hunger than a managed transition to sustainable energy.' And that was his goal."

"Was he wrong?"

He gave a small, exasperated snort. "It depends what you expect to do with sustainable energy. Yeah, you can run Greenland, *maybe* Iceland, on sustainable energy, when you are keeping population in the thousands or hundreds of thousands. But keep the world like it is today, with eight billions of people? You gotta be kidding me."

"So let me be clear about this, Dr. Monet. Bob was not in conflict with the university or the corporation?"

"No, no way, not Bob. Bob was never in conflict with nobody. He was a diplomat, even an appeaser."

I watched him a moment and he watched me back. In the end I said, "So if I understand you correctly, you are telling me his relationship with his employers was good and they had no reason to eliminate him."

"I don't know if that is what I am telling you. I am just telling you that as far as I know, they were happy with him, and he was trying to make everybody happy."

"He didn't manage to make you happy, clearly."

He shrugged and pulled down the corners of his mouth.

"He didn't make me happy or unhappy. I am an existentialist, Mr. Mason." He gave a small laugh. "Let me ask you: Do you realize that in the next hundred years more than eight thousand millions of people will die?"

I frowned. "Why is that?"

He raised his eyebrows, shrugged and spread his hands in that Gallic expression that says, *It's obvious!* "It is obvious! Because nobody lives for one 'undred years! So in one 'undred years, all of us who are alive today, will be dead! *Voila!* So, when you adopt this perspective, you do not get so upset. *Carpe diem!*"

I grunted. "So you can't offer me any guidance on who might have wanted to kill Dr. Magnusson."

"No," he shook his head, "and I do not believe anybody *wanted* to kill Bob. Greenlanders, like Icelanders, they are crazy people. Bob had a very attractive girlfriend, maybe somebody was jealous. The ice, the cold, no day in winter, no night in summer, it makes people crazy." He gave another Gallic shrug. "What is important is that the research goes on. The research must continue."

I looked out at the massive icebergs sitting in the bay, at the strange silver light, and wondered if Dr. Bob Magnusson had been killed in a moment of crazy hot blood, or ice-cold pragmatism.

– END OF EXCERPT –

To see all purchasing options, please visit:
www.davidarcherbooks.com/ice-cold-spy
www.blakebanner.com/ice-cold-spy

ALSO BY DAVID ARCHER & BLAKE BANNER

To see what else we have to offer, please visit our respective websites.

www.davidarcherbooks.com

www.blakerbanner.com

Thank you once again for reading our work!

Made in United States
North Haven, CT
08 December 2022